Sign up for our newsletter to hear
about new and upcoming releases.

www.ylva-publishing.com

AFTER Happily Ever After

EDITED BY ASTRID OHLETZ
AND ALEX K. THORNE

Table of Contents

Foreword

Interlude *by Lola Keeley* 7

Dress-Tease *by Jae* 25

The Cat Emergency *by Chris Zett* 36

Love Is Not Nothing *by Lee Winter* 52

Water into Wine *by Roslyn Sinclair* 79

All Wrapped Up *by G Benson* 88

No Going Back *by Cheyenne Blue* 109

What Happens at Game Night... *by Alex K. Thorne* 130

Two Hearts—One Mind *by RJ Nolan* 146

The Brutal Lie *by Lee Winter* 163

Partners *by Jae* 186

Other Books from Ylva Publishing

About the Authors

Foreword

So many amazing lesbian books leave readers breathless and wondering what happened to the couple after their happily-ever-after ending. Did they stay together? Are they still happy? What are these passionate lovers, fighters, executives, and explorers up to now?

Well, what if their stories didn't have to end? What if nine Ylva authors sat down and wrote eleven couples' happily-ever-after stories that allow you to take a peek into their lives now?

That is what this anthology is about—giving you what you're looking for. These charming, funny, and entertaining short stories can each be read as standalone pieces to whisk you into new and different worlds…or immerse you in universes you already know and love and can't wait to revisit.

We had a lot of fun editing this anthology. Now it's up to you to enjoy it!

Astrid and Alex

Interlude

by Lola Keeley

"No, no, no!"

Anna's eyes snapped open, only to find strands of hair stuck to her face again. Pursing her lips, she blew cool air over her skin and dislodged the ticklish hairs that were irritating her. Sweat trickled down the back of her neck, which seemed like an excuse to push away from where her head was resting against Gabriel's broad, muscular chest. In doing so, she came down from being en pointe and turned to face her fate.

"What?" She shouted into the darkness of the auditorium, something she would never have dared to do even a year ago when first dancing as a principal. "What was wrong that time?"

"Just…no." Irina's voice brooked no argument, even as her criticism lacked detail.

Anna could still hear the Ukrainian inflection to her words, although a full season of leading the company had softened Irina's accent. No more sulking in corners as she'd been prone to do while she was still dancing. Still, at moments like these, waiting for feedback on a performance, Anna missed Victoria most of all. In that echoing silence, the company would have been treated to a full three-minute rant on their incompetence. The insults would have been vicious, the language colorful. Instead, the assembled thirty or so dancers now stood in expectant silence.

Then, finally—footsteps. Irina marched down the center aisle in her high-heeled boots, until she emerged, fully visible in the stage lighting, far from its full performance strength. "No," she repeated. "Odette does not die here. Why do you lean on Gabriel like you were still shot in the duck hunt, hmm?"

Gabriel spoke up for them both, rubbing his hand through his close-cropped afro. "Irina, we know that this is the way it was done in Russia, but—"

"You all want the depressing ending? In this climate, this world, you all think people pay to get more depressed? Your Swan Lake is a bummer. This way? Our audience go out cheering. Nobody likes applause anymore?"

"I was playing Odette as alive but exhausted by the battle," Anna replied, resisting the urge to cross her arms. She knew plenty about standing up to determined women; she'd fallen in love with one of the most determined after all. "But I can do it differently if—"

"Three days from now we open this tour in Berlin!"

Irina didn't have to remind them. They'd been working their asses off for a month. Anna had her own reasons to be more excited than most about their European tour, but she hadn't allowed herself to get carried away. The performance had to come first, otherwise the whole trip would be ruined.

Irina wasn't done with her remonstrations either. "If you embarrass me in Europe, I will take your return ticket and tear it up. At the moment you are all so bad that I think in Berlin they will rebuild the wall. Now one more time, and please, everyone: be less awful."

Anna trudged off to the wings for the reset, hoping there would at least be time to check for any new messages from Victoria.

Victoria hesitated as she approached the theater, staring up at the grand old building with unashamed appreciation. It was still light despite the 8pm curtain, and swarms of tourists continued to trickle toward Bebelplatz and its underground monument to historic book burnings, their shorts and backpacks at odds with the finery of the opening night ballet crowd.

Huge banners hung from the streetlights, strips of vinyl rippling in the gentle breeze. While the Metropolitan Ballet branding was muted by American standards, no doubt restrained by their guest status, there was still no missing their presence to dance Swan Lake. Though it had never been her favorite ballet, Victoria still drank in every splash and flourish of the production's design. Familiar faces with artfully stony expressions beamed down at Victoria from every direction.

And there, with pride of place, was Anna.

Had she been in company Victoria might have hidden it better, but being alone gave her the luxury of fully reacting to the sight. She was far from the only one; every patron who entered stopped short at the sight of the woman Victoria loved, pictured in all her glory.

Not for Irina's company—and oh, how strange that still sounded, even in Victoria's head—the traditional feathers and flounces for Odette's costume. For the woman trapped in the body of a swan, most productions went overboard with tulle and feathers. Not so for this portrait, which had Anna's lithe frame, all five-foot-eight of her, scarcely covered in strips of white leather held together with just the suggestion of mesh over bare skin. It seemed like forever since Anna had last sent a photo with her messages, and seeing her for the first time since setting foot in Germany was a little overwhelming. After so long apart, now they were barely separated by the walls of the Opera House. Victoria took one last lingering look, realized her mouth had gone dry, and strode across the square to take up her invitation for the evening ahead.

As soon as she entered the throng of people in search of a few hours of culture, Victoria accepted a glass of champagne. She turned away from the growing crowd at the bars that populate the *Lindenoper*'s stunning foyer, a sea of white marble and Greek-style columns reaching toward the evening sky.

Things had been revamped considerably since her own appearances in Berlin. In the ensuing decade and change, the major opera and ballet companies had merged into one association, sharing their beautiful theaters and opera houses. Even after spending a year in Paris, leading its crown jewel of a ballet company, Victoria hadn't quite learned to relax on the matter of public funding for the arts. It certainly hadn't reduced the number of donors and philanthropists she had to charm on a monthly basis.

One of whom had invited her here tonight, including a first-class plane ticket, which Victoria had been powerless to refuse. Perhaps had it been the local company, Berlin's Staatsballett, she could have made her excuses. But when it had been a rare touring stop for the Metropolitan Ballet? Wild horses couldn't have dragged her in any other direction. She'd been on the verge of asking Anna for a ticket and booking her own flight when the generous offer had fallen in her lap.

"Victoria! Darling!" Her benefactor had found her more quickly than Victoria expected.

She gave him a rare, genuine smile as he approached, arms wide to embrace her. Handsome and polished, he looked every bit the European gentleman in his white tie and tails. Pushing eighty, he had his wife at his side, decked out in her pearls and finery.

"Hello, Herr Hamman. This is quite an event."

"Now, now, you call me Rudi. Sponsoring tonight is just part of my new plan. Bring the best of the world to me, and I don't have to travel so much. I have grandchildren here now. Can't be jetting off to New York or Moscow to see every new production."

Victoria sipped at her drink, the bubbles having already dissipated. "As long as you still come to visit me in Paris sometimes. Bring the grandchildren when they're old enough."

"Of course, of course. May I introduce my wife? She was a great fan of your dancing, Victoria, and she's very keen to meet the woman who's been causing such a storm in Paris."

Victoria nodded, her smile tight. A storm would be one word for it. Almost quitting three times, constant berating in the French press, and a company on the brink of mutiny most weeks—that qualified as turbulent. Victoria hadn't expected to miss New York, to miss those familiar modern hallways of the Metropolitan, but there had been times when they seemed the only refuge from the gilded cage of the Paris Opera ballet.

The conversation with rich old people flowed as most of them did, Victoria turning on the charm and soaking up their praises. Answering obscure questions to let them show off their knowledge and attendance at some of the finest performances, to flaunt their access and involvement. It was no great strain, and it eased away the last nervous minutes before the theater bells summoned them to their seats.

Grateful to be on the center aisle, Victoria lingered a moment before taking her seat. Her hosts were chattering quietly over the program that Mrs. Hamman held in her lap. Victoria felt the curious glances coming her way, knowing she was still a familiar face with all the coverage in the European press that had dogged her first season in Paris. A tap on her shoulder interrupted the rising nerves that had the champagne churning in her stomach.

"Vicky. You came all this way to cheer for me?"

Victoria turned to find Irina looming over her, dressed to kill in a navy-blue pantsuit, dark silky lapels offsetting the distinct lack of anything worn beneath the jacket. Diamonds trailing in a tasteful cascade from the bottom of her throat, shimmering raindrops that caught the light from every angle.

"Wouldn't miss it," Victoria replied without any particular confirmation. "You're watching from the house?"

"We can't all prowl the wings like a caged tiger. Did you tell her you're here?"

Victoria considered feigning ignorance for a moment, but she was painfully aware of how much time Anna had spent with her new artistic director, and the matching flash of a diamond on Irina's ring finger confirmed that she had made things official with Anna's sister, Jess. Life in New York had certainly been continuing apace without Victoria, and the thought gave her a fresh pang of homesickness. "No. No first-night distractions. She'll see me when the lights come up; that's enough."

"Hmm, just a few nights here, and then we're off to Beijing," Irina said, almost letting a smile break across her stern features. "Biggest tour in ten years, you heard?"

"Of course. I never was a great fan of touring."

"It is good to see you. You should look out for your wedding invitation. Jess will want her best woman to have a date, yes? And call me sometime. I would like to compare notes."

"I think you're starting," Victoria answered, and they grasped each other by the forearms, exchanging two air kisses near each cheek. Sure enough, the lights went down, and Victoria slipped into her seat with a smile for the Hammans. She'd already declined their offer of a late supper and an invitation to stay at their grand apartment in the center of the city. A hotel room granted far more freedom, and with luck, Victoria would have a guest to make the queen-sized bed a little less lonely.

Tchaikovsky's first mournful notes were as familiar to Victoria as her own heartbeat, but she'd barely taken in the conductor with her slicked-back red hair that skimmed the collar of her tuxedo jacket when the heavy damask curtains rose. Interesting. Irina had gone with the additional prologue of discovering how dear Odette became a swan in the first place. Most productions still opened on the waltz, a huge party scene for Prince Siegfried.

Then the spotlight fell on Anna, a vision in white. Any care about the plot or the staging dissolved at the sight of her. It took considerable resolve for Victoria to remain in her seat. Every sinew was straining to reach out somehow, to touch Anna at her most untouchable.

Her technique was flawless, but Victoria expected no less. The audience seemed enraptured by the vision of sweetness, bordering on innocence. Victoria smirked at her very private knowledge of how Anna could be anything but. The simple white silk of her dress hid lines and curves, but there was no disguising those long legs or those toned arms that could lift as readily as any male dancer thanks to Victoria's careful training.

Despite her jaded views, despite her hyperfocus on Anna herself instead of the character, Victoria still found herself stifling a gasp as the evil Rothbart transformed the innocent into a swan, cursing her to be found that way by the prince in the second act. With a series of pirouettes and some almost invisible stagecraft, the dress seemed to disintegrate in mid-air, revealing the risqué slashes of leather from the posters. Another spin and the simple braids of Anna's blonde hair were twisted up in an elaborate headdress that gave the faint impression of feathers.

Their swan.

As the scene gave way to the raucous waltzes of the first act, Victoria settled back in her seat, the last of the tension finally easing from her shoulders. She would watch the rest of the ballet through fresh eyes and hope for a happy reunion as soon as the curtain fell for the final time.

Anna reveled in her early solo, knowing it framed the story firmly around her. While the principal female dancer carried most of the story, playing both Odette and Odile, it was easy for a handsome prince to become the focus.

She'd gotten in the habit of not scouring the house for familiar faces back in New York. Other than when her family was in attendance, or some old friends who'd come in from out of town, she didn't need the nerves of spotting someone she knew. The stage lights left her only able to see a few rows back anyway, just as far as the house seats. That was why Anna didn't give the faces a second glance for those first two minutes, concentrating on the feel of the stage beneath her feet and waiting for Elliot to come in as Rothbart and cast his wicked spell on her.

As her fellow swans came to join her in transformation, hiding some of the tricks that let her change so quickly right on stage, Anna felt a prickle at the back of her neck. A pleasant sort of shiver, really, like seeing her apartment for the first time when coming back from a trip. Sinking to the floor to finish her sequence, she risked a proper look out at the audience, holding her chin high and proud.

Victoria.

For weeks they'd been skirting around the topic of Anna's coming to Berlin, of how relatively close it was to Victoria's new home in Paris. Vague, noncommittal comments about "seeing how her diary looked," or, "if everything is calmer by then," had made Anna feel guilty about making demands on Victoria when she'd been dealing with a rebellious company and incredibly demanding bosses, including the French public who funded the ballet partly with their taxes. Everyone had an opinion, and although Anna had come out to support Victoria's first mounted production, their time together in the ensuing months had been frustrating and too fleeting by half.

Irina sat out in the house during the show, so Anna had no one to query when she came offstage, one of her few breaks from being out there under Victoria's watchful eye. Anna only wished she'd been able to look longer, really wallow in the sheer presence of her. What was she wearing? Was her hair longer than the last time Anna had seen her in person? When they video-called for hours at a time, it tended to be near one of their bedtimes, with hair pinned up and the day's stresses washed away. The sudden nearness made every detail she'd been missing hit Anna like a truck. She grabbed at a handy support beam and gathered herself, sucking in air to tamp down the sobs that had come out of nowhere.

There was an act break to get ready for. Anna could have her feelings at a more opportune moment. God knew Victoria would expect absolutely nothing less. Skipping through the wings to the quick-change spot, Anna was sure her body felt lighter, each step a bit steadier. Working under Irina had been a difficult but rewarding year, stretching Anna's mental and physical capacity at times. But nothing would ever match the way it felt to dance for the most particular audience of one.

Tonight, she would dance only for Victoria. At that thought, Anna could barely wait to step back out on the stage.

Victoria hadn't suffered through curtain calls in years. Even when dragged on to take her own bows as director, she would slip away while the company took the remaining applause. She'd lived for it as a dancer, soaking up every second in the knowledge that those nights would one day be gone. Companies got applause, but primas got the raucous cheers. Anna had certainly received plenty of those tonight as an Odette who lived and triumphed. Some of those shouts had come from Victoria herself, letting her pride and excitement take voice without a single damn given for who might witness it. Besides, who knew the old cynic Irina would choose the happy ending to drag halfway around the world?

Her position gave Victoria a chance to congratulate Irina first, but when they shared a brief hug, Irina whispered "I put you on her guest list." Security hadn't always been tight around the Metropolitan buildings, but it made sense they'd control access more in unfamiliar locations. The news that she had a free run to Anna's door should have set Victoria running, but the milling crowds held her up no matter how quickly her damaged knee decided to let her move.

It seemed an eternity to push through the sea of bodies, and despairing at the slow trickle exiting the theater, Victoria resorted to her most demanding mode and found the front of house manager to demand a quicker route backstage. Luckily, as a ballet fan himself he recognized her right away. Johann chattered to her in slightly broken English as he led her down a hidden corridor, one which opened up into the wings, stage left.

"Danke," she bid him, following the noise of the company straight toward their dressing rooms. The place had the palpable energy of a giant elastic band just snapped; raised voices and slamming doors and blasts of music all competed as the dancers let off so much steam. The responsibility of performance became entwined with their muscles, and Victoria nodded in acknowledgment to a few of them as they raced around, smacking chests or bumping fists or dangling from the fixtures and fittings. There were shouts of recognition, but most of the company were too weary to stroll up and hug her the way Irina did. A few years of Victoria's toughest teaching had that effect on people.

"Aren't you a long way from home?" David asked, appearing from one of the dressing rooms with a clutch of tutus in one hand. "It's damn good to see you, Victoria."

As her second-in-command, Victoria had been closer to David than anyone else, at least until Anna showed up two years ago and turned her world upside down, and inside out for good measure.

"You've kept my company up to standard then?" Victoria replied, pulling him into a brief hug. She felt people stopping mid-step to watch the spectacle. Dancers did love any opportunity to gossip amongst themselves. "Irina seems to rely on you as much as I did."

"We're getting there," David said, his smile a little tight.

Victoria felt less than generous about someone reserving their gushing praises for her replacement but enjoyed it all the same.

"No question who you're here to see. She tries not to talk about you too much, but that girl is pining. I thought she was going to plead with the pilot to reroute the plane to Charles de Gaulle on the way here, you know."

"Oh, shush." Victoria batted at his arm with her purse, still more pleased than she had any intention of showing to anyone. "But since I'm busted, perhaps you can direct me the rest of the way?"

"Follow this corridor right around. Prima's dressing room is closest to the stage, just on that side of it."

Victoria did exactly that, taking her leave with a little wave and racing around the curving corridor at a pace that made her wish she'd skipped the heels and not been so vain as to leave her cane back in her hotel room. Some lessons she'd proven spectacularly slow at learning, but it didn't matter as the adrenaline of seeing Anna again took over.

Where once she would have barged in to put the fear of God in her newly promoted principal, this time Victoria raised her knuckles to the wooden door and gave the prima her due deference by knocking and waiting. The wait felt like a few small eternities, all crashing into each other as Victoria slowly combusted out there in the hallway. Then finally, finally the universe took pity on her, and the small mercy of the door handle's being turned was given to Victoria's impatient soul.

"You came!" Anna's words were almost lost to the squeal that rose out of her, unbidden. Fresh from the shower, dressed in just a tiny silk kimono, she launched herself at Victoria until she was pressed back against the opposite wall.

The white-painted brickwork scratched at her jacket, but Victoria could barely feel it. She had her arms full of Anna, which meant she could do the one thing she hadn't been able to in months.

She kissed her.

Anna was sure her knees buckled the moment Victoria's lips touched hers. Whether just from the kiss or over two hours of dancing was hard to tell. Either way, it felt beyond fantastic to be caught and held up and kissed so damn thoroughly that it seemed as if the kiss might never end.

"Get a room!" came the shout from somewhere on the balconies above, where the ensemble mostly had their dressing rooms higher up the open staircase.

Anna paused in her effort to reclaim every inch of Victoria's mouth just long enough to flip them off, drawing scandalized howls of laughter. Then it felt prudent to take their advice, so she guided Victoria carefully back across the threshold of her dressing room, slamming the door firmly behind them.

"It is so, so good to see you," Anna said, unable to let go of Victoria for even a moment.

Together they sort of folded themselves down onto the leather sofa that dominated one corner of the room. Victoria kissed her again, stopping just long enough to pluck a pair of unworn ballet slippers from between them and toss them on the floor. Anna looked around at that, noticing the chaos of the space. The immaculate nature of Victoria's dressing rooms had been legend at the Metropolitan, and Anna panicked at the thought she might somehow be letting down the good name of its prima ballerinas.

"I wanted to tell you I was in tonight, but the surprise was too delicious," Victoria replied, running her thumb over Anna's bottom lip as her palm rested on Anna's jaw. "I told myself if I wanted to be truly mysterious I'd slip in and slip out without coming to see you after the show, but we both know I'm nowhere near that strong when it comes to you."

"Strong enough," Anna argued. It wasn't like Victoria to just blurt out a weakness like that, even in this advanced stage of their complicated relationship. "Strong enough to insist we not see other people while we have to be apart, even though you could no doubt have your pick in Paris."

Victoria's eyes flashed a little darker at that, their green irises seeming to almost disappear in the low light. Only the dressing table bulbs were on, leaving this side of the room half in shadow. "If this is your way of telling me you've met someone back in New York…"

"No! God, Victoria. We only spoke the other day. You know I'm not even looking."

"Not even to have a date to your sister's wedding? Irina told me you wanted someone on your arm."

Anna felt like smacking her forehead against the wall for a moment. "I want you on my arm. Did you not... Okay, first of all, Irina is always trying to make you mad. Also, I know she's sending you an invite, so the only person I want to go with is you."

"Anna, that might not—"

"No, not tonight," Anna interrupted, holding up her hand to stem the tide of any argument Victoria might have, a technique stolen from the woman herself. "Listen, it's been a long day and a lot of long days before that, including a really long flight. And lately we've had to say no to a lot of things. A lot of opportunities to be together have just passed us by. That's the deal; we both knew what we were getting into when you got your dream job in Paris, but that doesn't mean it's been easy."

Victoria nodded. The fact that she was letting Anna ramble on was the kindest gesture she could make at that point. She smoothed the black silk of her blazer, making it tug at the neckline of the black gown she wore beneath it. Anna bit her bottom lip for a second, refusing to be distracted at the thought of exposing more skin, of having Victoria naked right there on the couch.

"So let's not talk about plans and complications tonight. I have a hotel room, or I'm guessing you have one where the rest of the company won't be staying, and we can just have a few hours without the world getting in our way."

"I'm beginning to think you've missed me," Victoria replied. "But I agree with your plan. No planning. No more buts and maybes and checking the calendar. Get dressed enough to get out of here, and then we're going right down the street to my hotel."

"I have missed you." Anna stood up with some reluctance, feeling the loss of Victoria's body against hers like a sudden chill. "Did you miss me?"

"What do you think?" Victoria asked, before grabbing Anna's favorite jeans and throwing them at her. "Come on, once we're out of here I can show you just how much."

They practically skipped down the street after running the gauntlet of dancers and assistants and lingering ballet fans who wanted a glimpse of the new prima without many noticing the former one at her side. Victoria forced herself to enjoy the anonymity, though it stung a little each time until a few of the real aficionados gasped, *Victoria Ford*, right before they made it clear of the theater. A little balm for a healthy ego.

In a mood like this, Victoria hardly felt the pain in her knee. Sometimes a good burst of adrenaline was as effective as any dose of low-grade opiates or a steroid injection. Unfortunately, as with those, she would pay for her hubris when the thrill wore off.

They darted across her hotel lobby like uninvited guests trying to sneak past the watchful concierge, even though Victoria had the keycard to her suite pressed into her palm. Another expanse of white marble, much like the opera house they'd just fled from. Getting the elevator to themselves was too much temptation to ignore, and by the time the doors pinged open on the top floor, Victoria's jacket was bunched up in Anna's hand, the other having already found its way beneath the hem of her dress.

"Do try not to get us arrested," Victoria warned, letting Anna practically carry her along the corridor with just a nod in the right direction. Only at the suite door did Anna relent with her open-mouthed kisses down the column of Victoria's neck, hands retreating just long enough to set Victoria fully on the ground. Her turn to actually open the door was far from a pirouette, but much to her mortification, Victoria found her hands trembling as she aimed the plastic card at the waiting slot.

Anna wrapped her arms around Victoria, grounding her with a simple embrace. "Take your time," Anna said, her voice a murmur disappearing against Victoria's collarbone. "Or don't," she amended as Victoria unlocked the door and kicked it open with her stronger leg, dragging Anna into the suite along with her.

They didn't pause to take in the decor, not the spiral staircase in one corner leading to the second bedroom, nor the artwork above the bed that mimicked the heavy red curtains of a theater. This private space was no stage, and Victoria had spent far too much of the day in a state of anticipation. It was officially time to enjoy having Anna in her arms without interruptions or obligations elsewhere.

Anna knew that Victoria probably had an elaborate plan for their night together because that bossy, brilliant brain of hers rarely took so much as an hour off. But Anna had been alone in New York for months, a relentless slideshow of fantasies parading through her head whenever she hadn't been too exhausted to daydream.

Besides, what kind of prima couldn't take charge of the scene on command? Their clothes were long gone, and Anna had Victoria just where she wanted her: flat on her back, soft curls streaming across the crisp white sheets. Her hair had gotten longer, and there was a tiny hint of silver at her temples, blending in with the blonde.

"You really are a work of art," Anna said, her voice too quiet for the huge room at first. "Do you know how often I've pictured being with you, just like this?"

"How often?" Victoria asked. "Can't possibly have been as often as I caught myself thinking about having you back in my studio every day, watching you bend and flex for me."

Anna closed her eyes for a moment, picturing exactly that. The frisson of excitement had been missing from every rehearsal and costume fitting without Victoria there to invade Anna's personal space, to touch in ways just short of inappropriate as long as they had an audience. "I've kept up the work on my lifting, just in case," Anna wasn't sure where the bragging was coming from, but it felt important to tell Victoria that much. "And you know what it's like after a night like tonight, an audience like that. I've got a lot to burn off right here."

She flexed her arms as she leaned down to claim another kiss, letting her lips wander down to graze each of Victoria's hardened nipples in turn. Anna's reward was a throaty moan that seemed to ripple right through them both, a first warning not to tease for too long.

"You want more," Anna said, trailing the fingers of her dominant left hand down over Victoria's flat stomach, her blunt nails making the skin pale in three faint stripes. There was no question in the way Victoria's hips tilted up to meet her touch. "You want me inside you, don't you?"

Anna didn't wait for the obvious response, just followed the arch of Victoria's body and let her fingertips slide through the slick heat between Victoria's legs. Teasing her clit with just a glancing touch, it was enough to draw a keening sound from Victoria's lips. She hadn't seemed so desperate for Anna's touch since their first

19

time together, or at least it felt that way in the feverish relief of being in the same room, of being able to touch and taste and tease again at last.

A few ragged moments passed with Anna pressing just a single finger past Victoria's entrance.

"No…teasing…" Victoria finally said through gritted teeth. "I swear to God, Anna, I can't…"

"I've got you," Anna replied, slipping a second finger inside and pressing her fingertips against Victoria's g-spot, knowing that hooked motion drove her crazy. Sure enough, Victoria's response was a brief slap of her hands against the mattress, balling the sheets in her fists as Anna picked up the pace. "I'm not going to make you wait tonight, darling. Clearly you need me too much for that."

Victoria did try to glare, but it was undermined completely by Anna's third finger and the shuddering gasp as their bodies moved against each other as if they'd never have another chance. Anna banished the thought. No last times, no worrying about the future. Not when she could rub the side of her thumb just to the left of Victoria's clit, knowing how that particular spot was her undoing. And it worked, with Victoria almost tearing the sheet as she arched her back up into her climax, clutching at the sheet like it was the only thing anchoring her to a solid surface.

"Don't," Victoria said as Anna flexed her fingers to slide them out. "Good, so good, but…"

"More?" Anna finished for her. She loved Victoria most like this, insatiable and lacking in her usual eloquence. Only Anna got to see this half-undone side of her. Victoria Ford didn't *need* anything from anyone, wouldn't lower herself to ask and certainly never to beg, but in the quiet of a hotel room or an apartment with Anna, the usual rules did not apply. She dipped forward again to kiss Victoria deeply, enjoying how she hadn't quite caught her breath yet, the press of their lips punctuated by wispy moans.

It helped that Victoria was soaked; Anna couldn't remember her hand getting quite this wet before. That made it easy to squeeze her fingers together, making room for her pinky to be the fourth. Victoria clamped around them with a noise from her lips that landed somewhere between relief and a plea for more. Propped on her forearm, watching Victoria's face, Anna felt as if she could do this all night. Every thrust of her arm made all the extra gym hours and lifts seem worth it, especially when Victoria relinquished her grip on the sheets and tangled one hand in Anna's hair instead.

"Did you bring anything?" Anna asked, the air between them thick with sex and the wet sounds her hand was making. "I mean, if you want my whole hand, shouldn't we…"

"Won't need it," Victoria answered, her eyelids flickering as she forced herself to make eye contact with Anna. "Not now, trust me."

It was true that Anna could move her fingers freely in and out, even as Victoria rocked her hips to bear down on each thrust. She was close to coming again, muscles already tensing around Anna's fingers, and soaking her hand, and the sheet. It really wasn't much work to tuck her thumb in the next time Anna withdrew her fingers, not quite all the way, and push back in with her whole hand, slowing it way down and moving only in the tiniest increments. The way Victoria kept tugging on Anna's hair urged her on, and after a moment of resistance when Anna almost pulled away, suddenly Victoria welcomed all her fingers inside, crying out in pleasure.

"Gorgeous," Anna whispered, twisting her wrist a few inches right and then back to the left. "Oh sweetheart, you needed this. Didn't you?"

Victoria could only nod in response, as Anna placed wandering touches across Victoria's body, playing it with virtuoso ease. Stroking, scratching, and pinching in each sensitive spot, Anna filed away every reaction as though filming it. These sounds and pictures would be her comfort and her pleasure when she was back in New York. Anna didn't dare miss a second.

She could feel Victoria's pulse thundering around her hand, and with careful, shallow thrusts Anna was able to work her up to yet another peak. Victoria was fully writhing beneath her at that point, their bodies touching at random points that seemed to set off new sparks. Victoria was clutching at Anna's shoulders when she climaxed this time, the grip tight enough that Anna thought it might break the skin. That didn't matter, not in the face of a low and steady throb of an orgasm that seemed to reduce the world to nothing beyond the feel of each other.

They were both breathless, panting as Anna collapsed on top of Victoria, careful of her injured knee as always. With the most gentle of movements, Anna worked her hand free, marveling at the miniature flood that had splashed across the sheets.

"I am going to…" Victoria lost her train of thought quickly, nuzzling her face against Anna's neck and letting her turn them onto their sides. "When I can function again, Anna…"

"I have every faith," Anna said, thrilled at having satisfied Victoria so thoroughly. To then have Victoria return that pleasure felt almost too lucky, but she certainly wouldn't be refusing the chance. "But right now I just want to look at you like this. This is the most beautiful I've ever seen you, I swear."

Victoria had a hand over her eyes as she recovered, lifting it just enough to squint suspiciously at Anna.

Maybe she'd been too used to everyone saying she looked her best on stage. Maybe she just didn't see what Anna did, but the statement was absolutely true. Gathering herself, Victoria shimmied toward the headboard, lying on her back once more.

"I might need a little more recovery on the acrobatic side of things, but there's nothing to stop you coming up here. You must be so on edge, hmm?"

Anna nodded, biting her bottom lip. She crossed the short distance between them on her hands and knees, hair falling around her shoulders and across her face. "Sure you're up to it?"

"I had a couple of orgasms, Anna. I didn't run the New York City Marathon. Unless you're not interested in exactly what I can do to you with my mouth while you're straddling me...?"

Anna moved more quickly then, grabbing for the headboard and getting in position. Victoria's questing fingers were already exploring her thighs, charting invisible lines and patterns, in constant motion.

"I really have missed you," Victoria said, and then her mouth was too busy for more sentiment. Anna let her head drop backwards and rode out the oncoming storm.

Victoria woke in a tangle of sheets that seemed to both trap her and simultaneously not cover anything at all. The faint weight of a hand resting on her lower back seemed to have her pinned to the mattress, but with some stiffness and no small amount of pain, she managed to extricate herself and make it to the bathroom without waking Anna.

Conscious that they should be making the most of every moment spent in actual proximity, Victoria still let her sleep on. It was simple enough to shower and dress, discreetly order room service, and be tucked up on the sofa with the morning's digital edition of *Le Monde* by the time Anna stirred and joined the land of the living.

"Hey," she said, springing from the bed without a single visible ache or pain. She leaned over the couch to kiss Victoria good morning. "Can we—"

"Breakfast is imminent, I figured you'd need to reload," Victoria said. Although most dancers lived on the minimum protein they could get away with, Anna had maintained her healthy appetite. After the considerable exertions on stage and on the bed, she'd be ready for at least two servings of breakfast, which Victoria would be providing alongside her own coffee and eggs. "You have time to freshen up."

"You showered without me?" Anna was definitely pouting.

Victoria gave her ass a playful squeeze as she turned toward the bathroom. "We can make up for that later. You have another show tonight, can't overdo it."

Anna scoffed with the invincibility of someone who still had good years of dancing ahead of her.

Victoria swallowed a pang of something that tasted a lot like jealousy. It had been a while.

"After the show tonight," Anna began to ask, but Victoria had her own invitation already in her purse.

"You'd like a date for the gala. I was planning to stay another night, now that you mention it."

That earned her another kiss before Anna skipped off to the shower, serenading Victoria off-key with a song utterly distorted by the echoes from the tiled walls. Still, the noise was welcome. It made the space feel alive in a way Victoria's Parisian apartment had yet to experience.

When they finally settled into breakfast, the busboy having taken his time to check out Victoria in her short silk robe, Anna was full of her usual enthusiasm.

"We don't have to make it a thing, like we can go separately tonight. But just knowing you'll be there, that we can sneak off to a corner with our drinks instead of making small talk with donors and politicians..."

"Mmm," Victoria agreed, sipping at her coffee. "And fuck separately. I want you on my arm tonight, Anna. I intend to show you off while I can."

As recommitting to their long-distance mutual pining went, it was pretty suave on Victoria's part. Unfortunately, every pleasure lately had a sting in the tail.

"I'd love that," Anna replied. "But there's a catch, right?"

"I won't be able to make the wedding," Victoria said, ripping the Band-Aid right off. "I checked my diary this morning, and yet again the French press has another hatchet job out on me, on the new season that isn't even public yet. I'll have to be there, have to see it through. This will be the year they realize they can't live without me, you'll see."

"Of course they will," Anna said, plucking at a strawberry with an apparent lack of appetite. "Living without you is pretty fucking hard, you know?"

Victoria absorbed the snap and burn of Anna's equivalent of an angry outburst. "It's not forever," was all she could offer. "Once I'm established, and if you have another season of reviews like that… maybe then we can pick and choose where we get to be. But for right now…"

"We have Berlin. And a whole day and night together before I'm off to China, and you go back to making Paris fall in love with you." Trust Anna to rebound the quickest of the two of them. "How could they not?"

"We'll make it count," Victoria promised, reaching across the small table to take Anna's hand. "You know you're worth all these complications, don't you?" It was as much romance as she had in her at the moment, but Anna seemed to draw strength from it.

"You're always worth it, too," she said, popping the strawberry in her mouth with a smile. "Now let's see how comfortable that sofa is."

Victoria let Anna scoop her right out of the dining chair and onto the plush leather. Maybe a brief interlude really could be enough for now.

If you enjoyed this short story, check out *The Music and the Mirror* by Lola Keely, the novel in which Victoria and Anna met and fell in love.

Dress-Tease

by Jae

Lauren loved lazy afternoons in the cottage above Topanga Canyon. Holed up in Grace's loft bedroom, she could pretend that they were the only people in the world and that Grace wouldn't have to fly to England on Monday to start shooting her new movie.

Crickets chirped outside, and a light breeze stirred through the open skylight, bringing with it the citrus scent of the shrub that bordered the backyard.

Up here, they weren't a publicist-turned-screenwriter and a world-famous actress who had outed herself on national TV a week ago; they were just Lauren and Grace. Nothing else mattered when they were here—no movies, no paparazzi, no script deadlines, just the two of them.

Too bad they had to leave their sanctuary in about an hour to meet Grace's hair-and-makeup artist and then head to the premiere of Nick's new action film. This was one of the few times Lauren wished Grace hadn't stayed friends with her ex-husband.

Sighing, she sat on the edge of the bed, put on her wristwatch, and secured the cuffs of her white satin blouse.

Downstairs, the bathroom door opened, and the tapping of Grace's bare feet across the hardwood floor drifted up. "Are you okay?" Grace called.

"Yeah, why wouldn't I be?"

"You're coughing. You've been doing that a lot lately," Grace said, a hint of worry in her voice. "You're not getting sick, are you?"

Lauren shook her head, even though Grace couldn't see it. "No. You know me. It's just my little quirk when I'm tired. Certain activities have kept me up most of the night—and I'm not talking about my writing."

The ladder creaked as Grace climbed up to the loft. "Are you complaining?"

"No. Never," Lauren said and realized that her voice had dropped a register. She didn't regret a minute she'd spent making love with Grace, even if it meant she'd fall asleep during the showing of Nick's movie. Sometimes, she had a hard time believing that Grace returned her feelings.

The first thing that appeared over the edge of the loft was Grace's long hair, piled on top of her head and held there by a large claw clip; then the rest of her followed—covered by a towel that was knotted above her full breasts. A single blonde strand had escaped from the clip and caressed the nape of her slender neck.

Lauren, who'd been about to stand up from the bed, sank back onto the mattress. Even after four months together, the sight of Grace's half-naked body made her weak in the knees. Her gaze followed Grace as she strode past the bed and went to the closet built into one side of the loft.

Grace rummaged through her wardrobe and selected a powder-blue silk dress—Lauren's favorite. She held it out for Lauren to see. "Do you think this will do?"

"Will do?" Lauren echoed. "It'll blow their socks off."

"Let's hope so. I need to look good today."

"You always do." Lauren took in the shapely behind that peeked out from beneath the towel.

"Maybe." Grace sighed. "But it's different now that the press knows about us. Every paparazzo in Hollywood will take about a million photos of Grace Durand and her lesbian lover."

Lauren swallowed around the lump lodged in her throat. As a former publicist, she had a lot of experience with the press, but so far, she had always been behind the camera, not in front of it. "I think we should—"

Grace let her towel drop to the floor and stood in front of the closet completely naked. Sunlight streamed in through the skylight, making her skin—flushed with the heat from her recent shower—seem to glow.

Lauren forgot what she'd been about to say as she stared at Grace. Her gaze tracked a single drop of water that ran down the long lines of Grace's neck. *God, does she have any idea how beautiful she is?*

When Lauren fell silent, Grace glanced over her shoulder and arched an eyebrow at her. "You think we should do what?"

Go back to bed and forget about the premiere and the paparazzi. "Uh, never mind."

Grace stretched with feline sensuality and walked over to the dresser in the corner of the loft.

Nearly hypnotized, Lauren watched the soft sway of her hips.

Once Grace reached the dresser, she bent a little and opened one of the drawers, directing Lauren's attention to her firm ass. Then she turned, her breasts swaying enticingly, and slipped a pair of dark red panties up first one long leg, then the other. The smooth silk slid over her skin with a seductive slowness.

Lauren's mouth went dry. She leaned forward on the bed so she could take in every sensual detail.

Grace swiveled back to the drawer and bent over it. When she straightened and turned, she held a strapless bra and slung it around her back with practiced ease. Her fingers moved slowly to the front clasp and closed it; then she cupped her own breasts, settling them into the cups.

Heat swept through Lauren's body. She had thought that nothing could be more erotic than watching Grace take off her clothes, but this reverse striptease was making her breath catch and her heart beat triple-time.

The rustle of silk teased her senses as Grace lifted the off-the-shoulder dress over her head and let it slide down her body with excruciating slowness. Somehow, she managed not to get it tangled in the hair clip. The dress settled around her curves, cradling her like the hands of a lover, and Grace smoothed her palms over her hips. Every movement seemed to linger for a second longer than strictly necessary.

Was Grace playing with her, putting on a show to tease her? Lauren wasn't sure. Grace's expression was innocent and self-absorbed, as if she was completely unaware of Lauren's rapt attention, but then again, she wasn't a three-time Golden Globe winner for nothing.

The fabric stretched over her ample chest as Grace reached up. She took out the hair clip and set it on the dresser. Her long, blonde tresses cascaded onto her bare shoulders. Grace looked up and met Lauren's gaze. Her full lips curled into a knowing smile, and there was a twinkle in her ocean-blue eyes.

She knew exactly what she was doing. *Tease.*

"Ready?" Grace asked.

The low, intimate tone of her voice sent a shiver through Lauren. "Oh, yeah."

Grace quirked a smile. "I meant, are you ready to go?"

Nothing was further from Lauren's mind than leaving the cottage and having to share Grace with hundreds of fans and paparazzi. "It's not your premiere. We could stay home."

"You know we can't," Grace said, regret obvious in her voice. "The media will make up all kinds of stories about Nick and me having a falling-out over my newfound sexual orientation if I don't show up at his premiere. Zip me up?" She walked over to Lauren, a swing in her step, and presented her back.

Lauren regarded the zipper through narrowed eyes. Why would she cover up this beautiful body when all she wanted was to see more of it, to caress, kiss, and worship every part of it? She got up from the bed and stepped closer—close enough to feel the heat of Grace's body against her own, even through her clothes. "There's a problem."

Grace craned her neck and peered over her shoulder. "What problem? Is there a stain on the dress?"

"No. But you did this all wrong."

"Wrong?"

"Yeah." Lauren moved even closer, her chest now brushing against Grace's half-bare back, separated just by the thin material of Lauren's blouse. "You didn't do this in the correct order. See, this is how it's done." She reached out and trailed her fingertips over Grace's hips, allowing herself to enjoy the smooth silk and the heat she could feel beneath it for a moment before sliding the dress down. With her lips, she followed its path and placed a string of soft kisses along Grace's spine.

Grace clutched the dress to her chest before it could drop to the floor. "We don't have time for this," she said in a halfhearted protest. "We need to get going."

"You need to take the dress off to make it down the ladder anyway." Lauren kissed Grace's shoulder blade and then lightly licked it. "I'm just helping."

"Helping?" Grace laughed. "Your kind of help will make us late."

Lauren shrugged. She moved the soft hair aside, pressed her lips against the nape of Grace's neck, and swirled her tongue over the warm skin. A contented hum escaped her as she breathed in the peach aroma of Grace's shampoo and the even more appealing scent that was all her.

Goose bumps broke out all over Grace's body.

Delighted, Lauren traced them with her lips and tongue. She coasted her fingertips down Grace's sensitive sides until the dress, which was now pooling around Grace's hips, stopped her. "God, Grace, I want to touch you all over." She nipped one shoulder with her teeth. "But if you really think we should get going…"

The dress landed in a heap on the floor. "We have to make this quick," Grace said, her voice rough.

"No problem. I can do quick." After Grace's little dress-tease, she was more than ready.

Grace tried to turn and step out of the pool of fabric around her ankles, but Lauren stopped her by wrapping both arms around her from behind. "Oh no. Stay just like this. I'm directing this scene."

"You're a screenwriter, not a director." Grace again tried to turn around.

Lauren trapped her against her own body. "Up here, I get to be whatever I want. Today, I want to be a director."

A visible shudder went through Grace.

Lauren grinned, knowing how hot Grace found it when she took control.

"A rather hands-on director, I hope," Grace said.

"Oh yeah. Very hands-on." Lauren splayed both hands over Grace's hips, enjoying the feel of the sensuous curves beneath her palms, and pulled her even closer until their bodies were pressed against each other all along their lengths, Grace's bare back against her breasts. For a moment, she wished she were naked and could feel every inch of Grace's skin sliding against her own, but she knew if she undressed now, they'd never make it to the premiere, so she focused on Grace. Lightly, she scraped her teeth up the side of her neck, lingering for a moment to kiss the pounding pulse under her lips and to taste her skin.

A breathy moan escaped Grace. She turned her head, and Lauren caught a glimpse of her pupils that were dilated with desire.

Knowing how much Grace wanted her instantly made her wet. She leaned forward and brushed her lips over the edge of Grace's ear, enjoying the shiver that went through Grace. When Grace turned her head even more, she flicked her tongue out and teased her with little licks along the corner of her mouth. Still holding Grace tight against her chest with one hand, she trailed her fingertips up Grace's belly and circled her bra-clad breasts.

"Don't tease."

"Oh, you mean the way you did earlier?" Lauren slid one finger beneath the bra and let the pad of her fingertip brush back and forth just beneath Grace's nipple, without fully touching it.

Grace groaned. "I have no idea what you mean. I was just getting dressed."

"Sure." Finally taking pity, Lauren opened the front closure of the strapless bra and pulled the material free from where it was trapped between their bodies. She caressed the incredibly soft skin of Grace's areola, which pebbled beneath her touch, and then took one of the hard points between thumb and index finger and gently rolled it back and forth.

With a moan, Grace threw her head back against Lauren's shoulder, exposing even more of her delectable neck to Lauren's mouth.

Pushing several strands of blonde hair out of the way, Lauren leaned down and placed a string of open-mouthed kisses along Grace's neck. She released her hip and trailed the other hand up Grace's body to cup the neglected breast too.

"God." Grace jerked against her, her firm ass pressing against Lauren's crotch.

Heat coiled in Lauren's belly. She clenched her thighs together and forced herself to focus on Grace. Alternately, she massaged her breasts and teased her nipples. She sucked on the skin of Grace's neck, stopping just short of marking her since she knew the dress wouldn't cover any hickeys.

"I thought you wanted to make this"—Grace gasped when Lauren lightly pinched one nipple—"quick."

Lauren gave the soft skin one last soothing lick and then took her mouth off Grace's neck. She skimmed one hand down Grace's body and cupped her through the silk of her panties. The fabric was damp against her fingers. "Oh, don't worry. I don't think this will take long at all."

A trembling breath rushed from Grace's chest. "I don't think so either." She covered Lauren's hand with her own and pressed her more firmly against herself.

"Oh, no." Lauren pulled Grace's hand away. "I'm the director, remember?"

"Yeah, but all the good ones give the actors some space to improvise." Grace rubbed herself against Lauren, the contrast of her naked skin against Lauren's fully dressed body a powerful turn-on.

Lauren playfully bit her shoulder, making Grace gasp. "Not this time. We have to get this right in just one take."

"How about some action, then?"

"You mean something like this?" She took her hand away and smoothed it down Grace's leg before trailing her fingertips up the inside of her thigh. Using only one finger, she dipped under the elastic band of her panties.

Grace groaned her approval and instantly widened her stance to give her access.

Tightly leashing her sense of urgency, Lauren directed her so they were both facing the mirrored closet door and marveled at the way they looked together, with her taller body framing Grace's from behind. "Look," she whispered into Grace's ear. "Look at us."

When Grace raised her head, their gazes met in the mirror.

Maintaining eye contact, Lauren trailed her index finger through the trimmed curls that were already damp with desire and felt Grace tremble against her. When she brushed the swollen sex, Grace let out a gasp and shifted her hips.

The movement made the pad of Lauren's finger slide over Grace's clit.

Both of them groaned.

Quickly, Lauren withdrew her hand.

"No! What are you—?"

Lauren shushed her by lightly pressing her finger—the one she'd just used to touch Grace—against her lips.

Grace flicked out her tongue and tasted herself on Lauren's finger before sucking the digit into her mouth.

A shudder went through Lauren. Only when Grace finally released her finger did her brain start to work again. "As sexy as they are, your panties have to go."

Grace immediately reached down to take them off, but again, Lauren stopped her.

"Let me." She knelt behind Grace and slid the panties down, letting her hands trail over the smooth skin of her legs. On the way back up, she kissed a path along Grace's thighs, hips, and spine. Each touch set her nerves tingling, and from Grace's much-too-fast breathing, she knew it had the same effect on her. Lauren took in Grace's now completely naked body in the mirror. A rosy flush dusted her face and neck.

For a moment, Lauren cupped Grace's world-famous ass in both palms and massaged gently before sliding her hands around, trailing one up to caress her breast and the other down to stroke the sensitive area where Grace's thigh met her torso. It thrilled her to watch the path of her hands in the mirror, to watch Grace's eyes glaze over with passion—a view she knew she'd remember through the lonely nights while Grace was in London.

"Lauren. Please." Grace reached back and clutched Lauren with both hands.

No more teasing. Lauren slid her hand down.

Grace's breathing hitched before Lauren even touched her.

Their gazes still locked on each other in the mirror, Lauren brushed one finger over the folds of Grace's sex, keeping the contact light at first, then started drawing slow circles around her clit.

Grace arched, seeking more contact, and rocked in time with each of Lauren's movements. Heat radiated from her, filtering through Lauren's blouse and sending her own body temperature skyrocketing.

God, how Lauren loved the way Grace reacted to her touch. She brushed her lips over the line of Grace's jaw and closed her teeth over her earlobe, dragging a low moan from Grace.

"Inside." Grace bucked her hips. "Now."

Lauren gave her earlobe one last nip before whispering into her ear, "I'm the director, remember?" She rolled her fingers across Grace's clitoris with a little more pressure.

Grace let out a groan that was part pleasure, part frustration. "Please."

On the one hand, Lauren wanted to draw out every moment with Grace and make them both forget that she'd be leaving soon. On the other hand, she also wanted to give her whatever she needed, so she eased one finger inside.

With a loud moan, Grace rolled her head back against Lauren's shoulder. Her eyes in the mirror grew heavy-lidded. Her hands restlessly roamed Lauren's hips and the outside of her thighs. "Bed," she got out, her voice sounding raw. "I can't stand."

"Oh, yes, you can. I'll hold you up." One arm wrapped around Grace from behind, Lauren began a slow, steady rhythm. The scent of Grace's arousal drifted up, sending a rush of desire through Lauren. "God." She bit her lip. "So wet."

The little sounds Grace made spurred her on, so she slid a second finger inside while she kept watching her reflection in the mirror.

Grace's groan of pleasure resonated through Lauren, and her nails dug into her hips.

"Feel good?" she whispered into Grace's ear, intentionally bathing the rim of her ear with her hot breath.

All Grace managed was a nod. Her hips moved faster against Lauren's fingers, urging them deeper.

Lauren's pulse tripped. She sped up her movements, eager to push Grace even higher. If she twisted her fingers a certain way...

"Yes!" A raw cry escaped Grace. "There! Right...there."

A rush of liquid heat coated Lauren's fingers. Still angling her wrist, she used the heel of her hand to press against Grace's clit. The muscles in her arm started to burn, but she ignored it.

Grace twisted her head around and sought out Lauren's lips for a breathless kiss. Soon, she wrenched her mouth away, though, and sharply drew in air. Her breath came in short gulps as she rocked faster against Lauren.

When her legs started to shake, Lauren pulled her more firmly against her own body and steadied her. Grace's hungry little sounds of need sent bolts of desire through her.

She could sense that Grace was close. Just as she was about to send her over the edge, a need of a different kind gripped Lauren. As hot as watching her in the mirror was, she wanted to be face-to-face when Grace came, wanted to see pleasure wash across her beautiful features firsthand, without having to rely on the reflection. "Wait. God, please, wait. I want to see you face-to-face."

Exhaling sharply, Grace nodded.

Lauren pulled her around and immediately pressed kisses to Grace's flushed chest and neck. She backed her up to lean against the closet and then started to thrust again.

Grace's eyes drifted closed.

"Don't close your eyes," Lauren said in a throaty whisper. "Look at me. Look at me, Grace."

With obvious effort, the incredibly blue eyes she loved fluttered open. Grace clutched two handfuls of Lauren's blouse and surged against her.

They kissed again, this time with a much better angle, before Lauren tilted her head back to watch. She moved her fingers faster and flicked her thumb over Grace's clit.

The first contractions of Grace's muscles fluttered around her fingers. Grace's grip on her blouse tightened. "Oh. Lauren! I..." Her mouth, swollen from their kisses, fell open, and she came with a long, low groan.

Lauren gentled her touch but kept up her rhythm, guiding Grace through her orgasm and drawing every bit of pleasure from her that she possibly could. She watched in awe as Grace's eyes grew hazy and the flush on her face deepened.

Finally, Grace's knees buckled and she collapsed against Lauren, who tightened her one-armed grip and held her close.

Small quakes continued to run through Grace.

When the quivering around her fingers stopped, Lauren eased her hand away and wrapped her right arm around Grace too.

"God." Grace panted and burrowed her head against Lauren's neck. Heat came off her in waves. "That was…" She shook her head as if unable to find the right word and then lifted her face to kiss Lauren instead.

Lauren hummed into the kiss. She felt nearly intoxicated from directing Grace's pleasure that way. "Yeah," she whispered when their mouths drew apart, "it was. You are incredible."

"Me?" Grace laughed. "You were the director of this scene. I'm just sorry we don't have time for a reverse shot." She played with the top button on Lauren's blouse.

Lauren covered her hand with her own, stilling it against her heart, which was beating just as rapidly as Grace's. "That's okay," she murmured. "I plan on doing a couple more takes later."

"Oh, yeah?"

"Yeah. Just to make sure we get the perfect shot, you know? That's what directors do, isn't it?"

Grace nodded. "Unless…"

Lauren arched an eyebrow. "Unless…?"

"Unless the actors take over the scene. It's been known to happen." Grace leaned up on her tiptoes, slung her arms more firmly around Lauren's shoulders, and kissed her, teasing her with hot, slow circles of her tongue before withdrawing. "I need another shower. And you," she playfully slapped Lauren's ass, "need to get changed. Your blouse has more wrinkles than a ninety-year-old."

Lauren looked down at herself. Grace was right. The blouse was wrinkled in several places where Grace had clutched at her in the throes of passion. "Well, if I'm getting undressed, I might as well join you in the shower."

"Oh, no. We're already late as it is, and if you join me, it'll turn into the longest shower in the history of mankind." Grace pushed her back with both hands flat against Lauren's chest, but her palms lingered longer than necessary. "Later," she promised, heat in her eyes.

"Later," Lauren repeated.

One last look, then Grace turned and strode to the edge of the loft without bothering to pick up her towel first, confident in her nakedness.

Lauren followed her with her gaze, drinking her in.

When Grace reached the ladder, she turned and climbed down the first few rungs but then stopped with just her head visible. Her full lips curled up into a soft smile. "I love you."

The words still made Lauren's heart stutter. She wanted to rush to the ladder and pull Grace back up and into her arms, but she forced herself to stay where she was. "I love you too."

When Grace climbed down, Lauren listened to her footsteps on the wood floor for a moment and then let herself sink onto the bed in her wrinkled blouse. She rubbed her face with both hands and groaned when she caught a whiff of Grace's scent.

"Lauren," Grace shouted from the bathroom. "I forgot my dress. Would you mind bringing it down?"

"On my way," she called and then picked up the dress. She inspected the silk for wrinkles and stains. It looked none the worse for wear. Grinning, she placed it over her shoulder, climbed down the ladder, and headed toward the cottage's small bathroom. God, she loved afternoons in the cottage—especially since she would now get to witness another dress-tease from Grace.

If you enjoyed this short story, you might want to read Jae's *Damage Control*, the novel in which Grace and Lauren met.

The Cat Emergency

by Chris Zett

"I hate Christmas!" Liz sank onto the couch in the staff lounge and massaged her temples. "And the day after Christmas even more. Why does everyone need to come to the emergency department today?"

"Nah, you're just cranky because we missed lunch." With two mugs of coffee in one hand, a yogurt in the other, and a medical journal balanced on top, Diana sat down next to her. She placed both mugs on the table and nudged one over to Liz.

"Mm, maybe. Thanks for the coffee." Liz unwrapped her sad excuse for a lunch and studied the greens in her sandwich. Not wilted, so that was a plus. But the cheese looked awfully boring. "Or maybe the people are up to more and more crazy stuff over the holidays each year. Mixing too much food, alcohol, and emotions is a recipe for trouble."

"Oh yeah. I took Emily to the family Christmas dinner for the first time. All my nieces and nephews were on a sugar high." Diana laughed. "What did you do?"

"Work." Liz poured a package of sugar in her coffee and stirred longer than necessary. She couldn't remember the last Christmas dinner she'd had with either of her parents. But even if Diana had become more her friend than her resident in the last few months, she wasn't about to discuss her family at work.

"Ouch. Two days in a row." Diana opened her yogurt and took a big spoonful with a happy sigh.

Three days. But who was counting? Just as Liz was about to bite into her sandwich, the door swung open.

Tony strode in. It was never a good sign when the head nurse wore a frown that suggested he'd stepped in a pile of poo. "Sorry to disturb you on your break, Liz. But I've got a patient for you. Cat bite."

"Really?" There must be more to it than Tony was saying. Cat bite sounded more like a job for a resident than an attending. She glanced at Diana next to her.

Before Liz could say anything else, Diana put down her spoon and sat up straighter. "I can do it."

"Nah, Diana, I think it would be better if Liz took this." Tony winked at Liz. "We might need your special magic."

Liz knew all too well what it meant. The patient was a kid, more often than not with difficult parents. "Okay. Five minutes?"

"Take ten. I'll put your name down on the board. Room eight." Almost at the door, he paused. "You have no new allergies, right?"

"No?" Where was he going with this? Could this day get any weirder?

Instead of answering, he winked again and closed the door behind him.

Curiosity hadn't let her finish her sandwich. Or take ten minutes. Liz's inability to relax and wait would be the end of her one day.

Curiosity killed the cat. Liz could almost hear her mom's exasperated tone and chuckled.

She entered room eight without a glance at the chart. She'd find out soon enough. "Hi, I'm Dr. Clarkson. What can I do for you?"

So far, the family huddled around the exam table seemed pretty standard. Angry Dad hid his concern behind a frown, and Weepy Mom hugged her son with one arm and clutched a wadded tissue with the other. The boy was a chubby nine, maybe ten-year-old in that stage of the accident where he didn't know if he should cry or play the stoic hero. A bright red towel was wrapped around his right forearm and hid any clue about the seriousness of the wound. Why hadn't a nurse cleaned it yet?

"When is the doctor coming? We only want the best for Billy, not another nurse." Angry Dad took a step forward and towered over her.

Liz suppressed a sigh. If she got a dollar for every time she'd heard that one, she'd be able to retire by now. She didn't mind being called a nurse because of the professional implication, but she detested the underlying misogyny that all women were automatically nurses. "I'm Dr. Clarkson, an attending ER physician." She smiled at Angry Dad, nodded at Weepy Mom, then focused on the boy. "Hi, Billy. What happened to you?"

He pressed the towel-clad arm closer to his middle and looked down.

Weepy Mom was about to answer, as expected, but Liz beat her to it.

She crouched down until she was at eye level with the kid. "Your outfit looks cool. Did you get it for Christmas?"

"Yeah." He sat straighter. "It's real hunting wear, just like Dad's. With pockets everywhere."

"Pockets are great. I could use some at work." Liz patted her scrub pants to show she had none. "Only the towel doesn't match. Let's take it off. Do you want to do it?"

Shaking his head, he held out the arm to her.

Liz put on gloves and unwrapped the towel. Dark brown spots stained the last layer that stuck to the skin. "Hold on a second." She wheeled a stool and the instrument table Tony had prepared to Billy and sat down. "Lay your arm on the table, here. I'll soak the towel so that it comes off easier." She could have called a nurse to do it, just to teach Angry Dad a lesson, but she was over playing power games like this.

"So tell me, what are you hunting? Bugs? Worms?" She kept her tone light and teasing, and it produced the desired effect.

Billy's face lit up, and he didn't watch her work. "No! I hunt deer! And wolves and bears. I already killed seven bears this year. But no tiger."

"Seven bears?" Liz played along with his joke. At least she hoped the kid was joking. Where would you even find seven bears?

"On the internet." Not-so-angry-anymore Dad ruffled his son's hair. "But one day I'll take you on a real hunt. You've got great aim."

Liz carefully examined the wound while the boy was distracted by his father's praise. A few shallow scratches flanked a wound that looked like a small cat bite. It wasn't so deep that it needed surgical cleaning or stitches, but deep enough to be still open. "Okay, Billy, the wound doesn't look so bad. If your parents agree, I'll give you a shot to numb it, then clean it, and you'll be as good as new. You'll need to take antibiotics for a week, just as a precaution."

Both parents nodded as Liz made eye contact with them.

Slipping off her gloves, Liz went over to the counter and opened Billy's file on the computer. "Anything in his medical history? Prior illnesses? Allergies?"

"No, nothing, he's always been healthy." Pride filled the mother's voice. "We never had to take him to see a doctor before."

Ding! A warning light the size of a lighthouse went on in Liz's mind. "When was his last tetanus shot?"

"Tetanus?" The shrill tone confirmed Liz's fears. "We didn't poison him with any vaccines."

Oh, fun. Liz wanted to groan, but her professionalism won out. "Okay." She finished her notes, then checked if everything she needed was on the table. It was. Tony had been meticulous as always.

"So, Billy, how did this happen?" Liz hoped that the boy would concentrate on his story instead of the work she needed to do.

"I hunted a tiger. I chased it through the jungle and caught it in the net." He started to gesture with both arms.

Liz caught the injured one and secured it on the table. "I'll just ice the wound a bit with this spray, then I'll numb it with a shot. A tiger, hm?"

"Yeah." Billy nodded. "I wanted to tie it up to carry it back to the base, but the stupid cat didn't want to play with me and scratched and bit me."

"Wait." Liz almost slipped with the needle but caught herself just in time. "Did you catch a real cat with a net? Not on the internet?"

"Yeah. Stupid cat." With his free arm, he hit something behind his mother's back. Plastic rattled.

A loud hiss answered him, and he drew back.

"Billy, no." His mother shook her head, but his father just chuckled.

"Did you bring the cat here?" Liz looked up. This couldn't be happening. Why hadn't Tony warned her? Had he forgotten about the Great Cat Incident of 2015?

"We thought you could have a look at her if she's sick. Maybe she has rabies or tetanus or whatever." Weepy Mom stepped to the side and revealed a small pet carrier.

And there she was. A cat cowered at the far side of the door. In the shadows, she looked young and frightened.

"I'm not a vet, but rabies is not that common. You don't get tetanus from sick animals, but from traces in the dirt. Is she an outdoor cat? Has she been bitten recently?"

"No, not as far as we know. We only got her from the mall the day before Christmas, and they said she's never been outside. And that she was great with kids. All lies." Angry Dad frowned at the cat. "And we'll bring her right back to that shop when we're finished here. Or to the shelter if they won't take her. Nothing but trouble."

"We thought she'd motivate Billy to take a break from his computer, but we didn't want him to get hurt." She pressed her tissue to her eyes. "Please, take a look at her and make sure that she doesn't have anything poisonous."

"Let me finish here, and I'll take a look." Liz didn't correct the use of the word poisonous. She needed to stay on the good side of the family if she wanted to convince them to let Billy get the tetanus shot he really needed.

Carefully, Liz rinsed the wound. When she was sure it was clean, she closed it with a couple of steri-strips and wrapped a clean bandage around the arm.

"Okay, let me have a look at her. What's her name?"

"Tiger." Weepy Mom pushed the pet carrier in Liz direction as if it was a container of toxic waste.

Of course. Tiger. "Hey, cutie." Liz stretched out her hand in the direction of the door. When Tiger didn't flinch or hiss, she opened it.

Tiger was aptly named, only the coloring was wrong. Dark gray stripes adorned her light gray coat, and amber eyes stared at the woman who had opened her prison. She took a few steps forward and studied Liz's hand. With a decisive "meow" she pounced out of the carrier and first brushed her whiskers against Liz, then her whole head.

Liz risked a light touch on the cat's neck. The fur was soft and warm beneath her fingertips, and she suppressed a sigh. She missed having a cat.

Tiger leaned into her touch and let Liz scratch her for a few seconds until she decided she'd had enough. The cat jumped onto Liz's lap and curled herself into a tight ball, licking her front paw.

"As I said, I'm not a vet, but this isn't the behavior of an animal with rabies." Liz gestured at Tiger purring on her lap. "You don't need to worry about that. Tetanus is a different problem. Once the disease has infected someone, we don't have a cure.

40

We can only give the anti-serum, provide intensive care, and hope for the best. The survival rate—"

The door swung open. "Liz, do you need any help?" Tony stopped as if he'd run into a wall. "You let the cat out? Don't you remember…?"

Tiger jumped up, and before anyone could stop her, she slipped between Tony and the door, out into the hall.

Oops. Liz looked at Tony; his expression of shock mirrored her own panic. Now they'd done it again.

Liz sprinted out, closely followed by Tony. But they were too late.

The hall was empty.

Tony clutched her arm. "You go left; I go right. We've got four hours until the evening shift arrives."

"But…" Liz looked back at the room and her patient. If she took too long, she might miss the window of worry that allowed her to talk about vaccinations. "You go and get the others to help you. I'll be with you as soon as I can."

Ingrown toenail or chronic constipation? Diana studied the electronic intake board in the hope that something else would pop up.

Emergency medicine wasn't always about saving lives, but toenails? The only real emergency this morning had been a young woman with acute heart failure, but this patient was now safe in the hands of the cardiology department. And probably stable, as she'd just seen Jess, the attending cardiologist on call, leave the house.

"Diana, fast, I need you." Tony ran around the corner.

Oh-uh. In her first week as a student, she'd learned that running was a big no-no at the hospital. Adrenaline rushed through her. Something big was going on. "What can I do?"

"Code cat! We need to find her." Tony gesticulated with both arms in the direction he had come from.

Did he just say…? No… "Code red?" That was the official code for resuscitation, but Tony wouldn't be so out of sorts for that.

"No. Listen." He grabbed her with both arms. His eyes were wide. "Cat! We've got a cat on the loose. Go find her!"

"Okay." She didn't get his panic, but looking for a stray cat promised more fun than toenails.

Tony stepped around her to the nurses' station and grabbed the intercom. "Code cat. Everyone, code cat. Report to Tony." He rubbed one hand over his face. As if he just noticed Diana still standing there, he swiveled around and glared at her. "This is not a drill. We have a cat emergency. Go, go, go!"

Before this situation got any weirder, Diana headed in the direction he'd come from.

Where would I go if I were a cat?

Somewhere quiet. And probably somewhere that didn't smell of disinfectant. They'd had a cat when she was a kid, and she'd never liked the smell of her dad when he'd come home from work at his family practice.

Diana walked toward the back entrance, but the door to the garden was closed, as was the stairwell. She'd stood next to the closed door to the waiting room for the last ten minutes, and no one had gone in or out. So the cat should still be in the emergency department.

Maybe in one of the offices? She walked to the hall in the back of the ED, but neither the offices nor the locker rooms had open doors.

What would I like if I were a cat?

Food and a comfortable place to rest.

Diana's favorite part of the ED, apart from her partner's office, was the staff lounge. She'd spent countless hours on the comfortable couches, rehashing cases with her colleagues, having lunch or dinner, or taking a nap. She hurried to the other side of the ED.

Bingo. The door wasn't fully closed, and a cat might have slipped inside. Diana entered and closed the door behind her.

At first glance, the room was empty. But something wasn't quite right. Pieces of green were scattered around the floor.

Diana picked one up. Salad. And wasn't that a bit of bread? She followed the path of the breadcrumbs to the couch that was farthest from the door. It was empty, so Diana kneeled on the floor to look under it.

There she was. A cute tabby cat munched on the rest of Liz's sandwich. Or rather toyed with it. She seemed as unenthusiastic as Liz had been.

Diana sat back on her heels. Should she call Tony? Or attempt to catch the cat herself? The animal didn't look threatening at all, and if Diana couldn't save any lives today, she could at least be another sort of hero.

What would motivate the cat to move out from under the couch? Just grabbing and dragging her wouldn't work. Diana knew from experience that cats could be even more stubborn than her ex. But they were curious and playful too.

Diana moved a few feet away and sat cross-legged on the floor. She had no toy or string to entice the cat, but maybe something else would do. With her fingertips, she tapped a rhythm on the linoleum floor. Slow at first, so as not to startle her feline audience, then faster. She added a nonsense song, mostly words like *kitty* and *come here.*

After a couple of minutes, toes scratched over the floor as the cat crept closer.

Ignoring her, Diana kept on with the music, until the cat came over.

Purring, she brushed against one knee, then crossed to the other and back again.

When Diana stopped singing, the cat meowed in protest but didn't run. She stretched out her hand to pet her.

With another long-drawn meow, the cat settled on Diana's lap.

"What should I do with you now?" Diana fished her phone from her pocket and dialed Tony's number.

He answered almost immediately.

"I got her. In the staff lounge."

"Don't move. I'm on my way." Steps slapped on the floor as if he was running, then he disconnected.

"Mm, kitty, that was weird. Even for Tony. Why are you so special? Can't be your cuteness."

The cat only purred in answer. As if to emphasize her cuteness, she snuggled closer and licked her tail.

The door to the staff lounge opened and closed in quick succession. "Where are you?"

"Over here, behind the couch." Diana let her hand hover over the cat to stop her from escaping, but she didn't even blink.

Tony tiptoed to her and set a small cat carrier next to Diana.

The cat hissed and tried to get up.

Diana quickly restrained her. "I don't think she likes that thing very much."

"But it's all we've got. Put her in." Tony opened the door.

"I don't know." Diana's protective instincts urged her to cuddle the cat, not lock her away. "Whose cat is it anyway? And what's her name?"

"A patient's. Tiger." Tony gestured at the carrier. "We need to hurry up. Not one word to Emily!"

"Tony! I can't keep secrets from her." Diana had learned her lesson about keeping secrets—it never worked, especially not in a hospital. She cuddled Tiger closer. "And you just announced over the intercom that we lost a cat."

"Oh." Tony paled. "I didn't think... I'll talk to everyone once we get her back in the cage."

"Good luck." Diana doubted it would work, but it was his time to waste. "Okay, Tiger. We'll get you into your temporary home, and then you can go back to your family."

Diana lifted the cat toward the carrier.

Tiger wriggled in her grip, hissing and trying to scratch Diana.

The door opened, and someone entered the staff lounge. "Achoo!" Someone sneezed loudly.

Diana's grip slipped for only a second.

It was enough. Tiger used her chance to break free. Before either Diana or Tony could react, she ran toward the door and freedom.

"Achoo! Achoo! Achoo!"

"Hi, Alexis." Tony greeted the newcomer without even looking up.

"Tony?" Dr. Alexis Pine's growl was almost as annoyed as the cat's hiss had been. "Don't tell me—achoo—don't tell me we've got another Catpocalypse on our hands!"

Tony jumped up, still holding the open cat carrier. "No! This is nothing like the Great Cat Incident. We only lost one cat today, and we almost had her until you startled us."

"What are you talking about? Catpocalypse? Cat Incident?" Diana was grateful that Tony split the blame between them for losing Tiger, but she had no idea why everyone made such a fuss about it.

Tony looked guilty, an expression she'd never before seen on the usually upbeat nurse.

Dr. Pine ran a hand through her short hair and used her other to wipe tears from her eyes. "Ask Emily."

"No! Don't ask her." Tony closed the cat carrier and placed it behind his back. "Short version: A few years ago, a couple of cats got loose in the ED, created chaos, and our highly allergic surgeon here slipped with her needle and sneezed all over the wound. The patient sued the hospital. Emily took it personally because she'd been in charge of the ED that night for the first time."

Diana couldn't help herself. She laughed until her eyes were as teary as Dr. Pine's. "Really?"

Twin glares cut through her mirth. Why couldn't the others see the humor in the situation?

"Okay, okay." Diana raised her hands. "I'll go search, and I won't breathe a word to Emily. She'll find out soon enough anyway. Do you need anything, Dr. Pine?"

"No, I'll be fine. I'll stick to the surgical floor and take some antihistamine. Let's hope we won't have any surgical emergencies tonight."

Tony groaned. "Don't say it. Don't even think it. Let's just pray that your residents can handle whatever you lured here."

"Achoo!"

"Are you sure you don't want to wait until we find Tiger?" Liz handed the discharge papers and the new vaccination record card to Weepy Mom, who wouldn't meet her gaze.

"You lost her. She's not our problem anymore. You keep her or bring her to the pound or whatever. We're done with cats." Angry Dad crossed his arms in front of his chest and glared at his wife. "I told you we should have gotten a dog."

"Dogs are smelly." Billy played with the superhero Band-Aid on his left deltoid muscle. "Can I get ice cream now? And a burger?"

"Of course." Weepy Mom hugged her son with one arm and steered him toward the exit.

There was nothing Liz could do to stop them from leaving. Maybe it was better that way. Even if they found Tiger right now, she wouldn't be treated fairly by that family.

If only she could adopt the cat herself, but her roommate's allergy prevented her from taking the cat home even for a day. Alexis would kill her.

Liz glanced at the electronic whiteboard. Still relatively empty and no real emergencies. Good. More time for her to find Tiger.

No one was at the nurses' station, presumably because everyone was searching for the fugitive. Before Liz could call Tony for an update, Courtney jogged around the corner.

If anyone else ran in the emergency department, Liz would immediately be alarmed. But the pace was typical for the overeager resident.

"Oh, Liz, great, you're here." Courtney skidded to a stop, narrowly avoiding a crash. "All the nurses are gone somewhere. How do I get a psych consult?"

"You call psych." Liz pointed to the laminated list of telephone numbers on the wall. Other residents in their third year knew that. But Liz was never sure if Courtney really hadn't learned the working process of the ED by now or if she played dumb for a reason. But that was a question for another day. The more important question was why Courtney was looking for a consult. "Aren't you with a woman with a respiratory infection?"

"Yeah, probably just a cold. But the old woman seems a little bit crazy. I don't know if it's her age or fever or something else."

"Why don't you try to use a more medical and less offensive term than crazy?" Sometimes Liz wanted to shake Courtney.

"Um, yeah, sorry. She's hallucinating. She insisted a cat is hiding under the supply cart." Courtney snorted. "A cat. Here."

Today was definitely a shake-Courtney-day. "Did you look under the cart?"

"No. Why should I?" Reaching for the phone, Courtney rolled her eyes. "I thought we shouldn't encourage hallucinations."

"Didn't you listen to the announcement and call Tony? We lost a cat, and she's hiding somewhere in the ED. So forget about the consult and help me catch Tiger." Liz stalked in the direction Courtney had come from. "What room?"

"Ten." Courtney hurried after her. "Tiger? I thought you said cat."

But when they arrived at room ten, the sight of the open doorway wasn't encouraging.

The patient, an elderly woman clad in a flannel nightgown and thick robe, sat on the gurney, and her short legs dangled half a foot off the floor. Her wrinkles deepened in her flushed face as she smiled at Courtney. "There you are again; I was about to look for you. The cat left." She pointed out of the door, then brought her hand to her mouth to cover it as she coughed.

Even from the doorway, Liz could see and hear that she suffered from more than a cold. "Courtney, check her for pneumonia and assess her for sepsis. Get her on antibiotics and find a bed. Call from here, if you need anything; don't leave until a nurse gets here." Liz pointed to the phone on the wall.

Calling Tony, Liz headed in the direction the patient had indicated. "I've got a lead, but please let some of the nurses return to work. Courtney needs some help in room ten."

"You mean a babysitter." Tony grunted. "Where are you?"

"Between room ten, where the cat was just spotted by a patient, and the back entrance."

"Almost there."

Liz walked slowly, checking under every piece of equipment. She had never consciously noticed all the medical paraphernalia clogging the hallway. Not only was it a paradise for a hiding cat but a fire hazard as well.

Tony came around the corner, carrying the cat carrier. The uncharacteristic worry lines made him look much older than his twenty-nine years. "Emily will kill us all."

"I don't think so. She has a much better sense of humor than you all give her credit for." Diana followed closely behind Tony. Her hazel eyes twinkled with amusement. "Have you found her?"

Liz wasn't so sure about Emily, but Diana had the advantage of knowing her partner best. "Not yet. She can't be far. Maybe she's hiding somewhere."

Placing the carrier on an old gurney with only three wheels, Tony nodded curtly. "This is a dead end as long as no one opens the back door."

"We really should clean up our emergency escape route once this is over." Liz pointed to the gurney.

"Once what is over?" Dr. Emily Barnes, senior attending and the last person Liz wanted to face right now, stood in the open doorway of the back entrance.

As if they'd trained for that emergency, everyone sprang into action. Everyone but Liz.

Tony flung himself between the cat carrier and Emily as if he was a secret service agent shielding his charge from view.

Diana hurried to Emily, hugged her in an impressive move that spun Emily around, and kissed her soundly. Behind Emily's back, she made shooing motions with her hand.

Clutching the carrier to his chest, Tony fled the scene.

Only Liz was rooted to the spot. The drama unfolded around her like an action scene in a movie, and she was as helpless as if she was sitting in the movie audience.

Tiger used this exact moment to jump down from her hiding place—a bunch of IV stands covered by a sheet—onto Liz's shoulder and down to the floor. She ran toward Diana and Emily.

Liz's stomach clenched. The collision seemed inevitable.

At the last millisecond, Tiger veered to the side. Brushing Emily's leg, she hastened out of the door.

The door swung closed, shutting Tiger out of the emergency department. Now she wasn't Liz's responsibility anymore. She should be relieved. She should go and tell Tony.

Instead, the only thing she could think of was that Tiger would be alone out there in the cold and dark December night. Plus, the small park wasn't enclosed, and she could end up on the road.

Ignoring the still kissing couple, Liz hastened to the back door.

Icy dampness enveloped Jess as if it would rain any minute and pricked her cheeks with tiny needles. She shouldn't linger outside, but she needed a minute to compose herself before she drove home. And what better place to find some positive thoughts than the bench in the garden behind the hospital where she had given birth to her daughter. That summer day seemed like a lifetime ago, but it had been only six months. Six months of fear and anger and finally joy and happiness.

Today had brought back all the worst emotions. She'd had to give a young mother the same diagnosis that had rocked her world: peripartum cardiomyopathy. As a cardiologist, Jess knew the odds were likely that she'd encounter more women like herself, who suffered from acute heart failure after their pregnancy. But she hadn't been prepared for the emotional impact.

Her patient's eyes had held the same panic Jess remembered all too well. Her hand had gripped Jess's arm as she begged her to tell her it wasn't true. *And what about my daughter?*

Jess rubbed her arm. The indentations of her patient's nails were probably still visible. She didn't check; it didn't matter. She was fine, and she would do everything in her power to ensure that her patient would be fine too.

Something warm and soft streaked across her feet. Warm, soft, and furry.

"Eeek!" Jess pulled up her legs on the bench, as far away from the ground as possible. Rats? Here, on the hospital grounds? Her heart raced as it had all those months ago, as if it would burst from her chest any minute.

Even though some light from the hospital's windows filtered through the trees, most of the ground was cast in shadows. It was too dark to recognize anything but a moving shape.

Oh, fuck. That was some really big rat.

She pulled her phone from her coat and fumbled until she activated the light.

Eyes reflected in the darkness. "Meow." An annoyed cat jumped away from the light, onto the bench.

Jess let out a shaky breath, shut off the light, and stretched out her hand. Only a cat.

Carefully, the cat crept closer and sniffed Jess's hand. After a moment, it nudged its head in her hand as if to tell Jess to pet it.

"Where did you come from?" Jess ruffled the fur at the cat's neck. It didn't look like a stray. The fur gleamed in healthy shades of gray and black, and it seemed well-fed.

The soft fur and responsive body calmed Jess's racing heart better than any medication could. When the cat jumped on Jess's lap, she opened her coat to share the warmth with her new friend. "No collar. Is someone missing you?"

"Tiger?" Someone plowed through the trees.

"Mm, I guess that's a yes." If it were up to her, Jess wouldn't mind spending another hour with her new friend. Or longer, much longer. Who'd have thought that cuddling a cat would be so calming?

"Where are you, Tiger?"

That sounded like Liz's voice. Why was an emergency doctor looking for a cat?

"Over here, on the bench," Jess called back.

"You're answering to Tiger now, Jess?" Laughing, Liz emerged from the darkness of the trees. "Is that something your girlfriend calls you?"

"Ha ha." At the mention of her partner, Jess's mood lifted. Instead of moping on the park bench, she should get home as fast as possible to cuddle with Lena and their daughter. "I guess you're looking for this tiger?" She opened her coat to reveal the cat.

"Oh, thank God." Liz sank on the bench next to her. "You found her."

"More like she found me. Is she yours?"

"No, a patient's. But she's my responsibility now." Liz carefully reached out and, when Tiger didn't protest, petted her on the back. "She ran away, and the family left before we could catch her. They don't want her anymore; she was a not-so-well-received Christmas present."

"Poor Tiger. What are you going to do with her now, take her home?" Jess stifled the urge to clutch Tiger to her chest. She had known her for all of five minutes, and it wasn't her place to be jealous.

"Can't. My roommate is allergic." Liz sighed. "That reminds me, I need to shower before I go home or Alexis will kill me."

"Oh, right, the Great Cat Incident." Jess had been working at another hospital across town at the time, but the story had made the rounds through all the hospitals in Seattle.

"Don't remind me." Liz groaned. "Maybe Tony or someone else can take her until we find her a permanent home. I don't want to take her to the shelter; it'll be crowded after Christmas."

"So, no one has a claim on her?" An idea formed in Jess's mind and filled her with anticipation like the first budding green after a long winter. "Could I take her?"

"Um, sure. But don't you have to call your girlfriend first?"

"Fiancée." Jess grinned. "I asked her to marry me on Christmas."

"How wonderful." Liz hugged her with one arm. "Does Lena like cats? Are you sure about it?"

"Like is not strong enough. Lena told me, all she ever wanted was a family: a wife, kids, and a cat." The more Jess thought about the idea, the more she loved it. Yes, she had regretted her enthusiasm for her own ideas more than once in the past, but there wasn't even a trace of doubt in her mind. Lena would love Tiger as much as she did already. But she had learned her lesson. Communication was more important than her beliefs. "I'm sure. She'll fit right in with our small family. But I'll call Lena and ask her before I leave."

"Congratulations. You just became a mother again on the park bench." Liz winked. "I'm looking forward to the next time."

If you enjoyed *The Cat Emergency*, you should check out Chris Zett's *Irregular Heartbeat*, the novel in which Diana and Emily fell in love in the emergency department, or *Heart Failure*, the novel where Jess met Lena, and they healed each other's hearts.

Love Is Not Nothing

by Lee Winter

Part One: Masks

Requiem

Natalya Tsvetnenko entered the Wellness-Oase in Spittelberggasse and pushed her sunglasses onto her forehead. Soothing nature sounds filled her ears as she glanced around the foyer. This was one of the most luxurious massage salons in Vienna and, during the past three years Natalya had lived in this city, it had been invaluable for easing the side effects of excessive cello practice and playing with the Vienna Philharmonic Orchestra.

That some of her aches came from injuries sustained in her former career was neither here nor there. Explaining her old war wounds had actually resulted from encounters with underworld assassins was not exactly high on her agenda. Nonetheless, Wellness-Oase's highly trained massage therapists were the model of discretion. And Natalya paid well to have their deep-tissue, full-body, elite athlete's massage that did wonders for her sore points.

She was greeted at the counter by Lotte, an angular, distinguished woman in the white waffle-weave kimono robe and Japanese clog sandals all her staff wore. Lotte raised her hand with an elegant swish. *"Christiane erwartet Sie bereits in ihrem üblichen Zimmer, Fräulein Tsvetnenko."*

So Natalya had Christiane this week, who was waiting in Natalya's usual room. She picked apart German easily these days. Natalya nodded to Lotte and followed her instructions, pleased to have her preferred room, far from the others, which added to her sense of privacy.

She padded softly down the off-white, carpeted hallway, finding room twelve by the usual potted plant on a stand outside it. A sad little *Alocasia sanderiana*.

Natalya leaned forward to inspect it and came away disheartened. Underwatered. Her lips thinned. She would point this oversight out to Christiane. It was always disappointing when the details were overlooked.

Stepping into the cream-coloured room, she smelled vanilla incense and something else with a touch of spice to it. Pleasant enough. In one corner was a crock pot of hot rocks slowly warming. For the next client, most likely, as Natalya had little interest in the latest new-age fads.

Her gaze drifted higher, to the peace symbol mobile dangling from the ceiling, then trailed to the framed prints of bamboo forests and a small bronze Buddha statue on the windowsill under the timber horizontal blinds. She wondered whether Christiane realized the Buddha was about as Japanese as her faux kimono robe was.

The masseuse in question turned at Natalya's arrival and offered a polite greeting, then pointed to the table. Her gelled-back, blonde hair was pulled into a perfect bun that shone under the warm lighting.

"Machen Sie sich bitte frei, Fräulein Tsvetnenko. Ich bin in fünf Minuten wieder da."

Natalya translated that to "Please get ready, I'll be back in five minutes".

She shed her clothes, folding her black linen pants, leather jacket, crisp white shirt, and undergarments into an exacting pile, before lining up her polished, black ankle boots together under the chair in the corner.

Naked, she arranged herself on the table, placing a towel over her rear to signal her readiness. Natalya had no modesty concerns, especially when it meant Christiane's expert hands could fully access the pressure points and aches in her backside and lower back from too many hours spent sitting.

Natalya had never suffered from modesty anyway. When she examined herself each morning, mapping her scars, she saw power, control, discipline, and beauty in her muscled flanks, strong shoulders and glossy, straight, black hair. And, sometimes, she also saw delicate hands slipping around her waist and clutching her tightly against an equally naked body, still warm from the shower.

Natalya's lips twitched at the pleasing memory.

It was hard to believe it had been three years since she'd settled here, after a year of touring all over Europe. Four years away from her former life in Australia. A life that was nothing as she'd imagined it would be when, as a teenager, she'd first sought sponsors to allow her to take up a cello scholarship here in Vienna.

The sponsors, associates of her stepmother, Lola, had turned out to be a Melbourne underworld crime family which had sought its pound of flesh, training her as their deadliest of tools. No one would expect a female, especially one so young, and a musical prodigy at that, to be a crime gang's secret assassin. This was what had made her so devastatingly effective, far exceeding expectations.

She'd agreed to only five years. A fair exchange for the investment in her studies. But none of the associates in the crime family had understood why, when her indentured term to them had finished, she'd kept doing their lethal work, freelance. Especially since she still filled the souls of patrons with her music each night.

What those men with empty eyes failed to understand was that each career had its addictions and contained a thrill for Natalya not easily dismissed. Both made her feel like a god who held beating hearts and quivering minds in her hands. The mistake was in ever seeing her as two different people. Assassin or cellist. Requiem or Natalya.

She had always been both. For her it was so simple—the dominant strengths required to face any given situation leapt to the fore, with an attitude to match. No different from choosing different shoes for a change of event. You put them away again when unneeded.

Such philosophical meanderings were usually left in the past these days. Natalya was forty-five and a world away from Victoria's seedy underbelly. Nowadays she only ever stirred the human soul instead of destroying it. She'd made her choice. She had few regrets. It was the price she'd paid to have a little mouse in her life. She'd paid it willingly, once she'd understood.

Natalya closed her eyes, wondering what Alison was doing. She'd said something about going to a farmer's market close to their apartment in Neubau before lunch. She was doing cooking lessons, between taking some violin masterclasses and teaching English as a second language to refugees in a Public Learning Centre in the nearby Fifteenth District. Her enthusiasm for each of these activities was unabated.

It had been unnerving at first, being with someone so different from Natalya. Meshing her existence had been difficult with one so filled with life, love, and empathy, and especially with emotions brimming so close to the surface. Many a time Natalya had questioned her sanity at allowing anyone inside. Not to mention the chaotic way Alison never once lined up her shoes, or always threw her clothes over the back of a chair when a perfectly good hanger was available.

But Alison would smile at her appalled expression and tease her until she decided to overlook the disarray. It turned out the woman had been like the mouse she'd dubbed her four years ago—she'd curled up, small and soft, close to Natalya's heart, and stubbornly refused to move.

What defense did a world-class assassin have against that?

The massage room's door opened and clicked shut. Natalya felt her back cool as the towel was slid down to her thighs. The slippery noise of massage oil being rubbed into hands filled the air before she felt Christiane's fingers on her back.

The masseuse began slowly, mapping Natalya's contours. As she progressed, Christiane became far more forceful than usual, and twice Natalya swallowed a grunt. She hadn't realised the woman had it in her.

The sound of wet, slapped flesh, and the heat of hands near her neck took Natalya back. It reminded her of the first kill she'd witnessed as a sixteen-year-old. It was an execution for one of the crime family's own, a man caught in the act of betrayal. She could still feel Lola's open hand at the back of her neck, the press of her warm skin against the collar of her school uniform, forcing her to watch.

"Orientation", her stepmother had called it. For what was to come, after Natalya returned from Vienna, once her scholarship was complete and her duties to the crime family began. It was grooming. Ensuring she understood what she was in for.

Natalya had forgotten most of the faces in those lessons. But what she did remember from that first time was the man's eyes. Bleak, black, and terrified, they had made her want to crawl into a hole and hide.

And she also remembered *her* perfume. Sensual, exotic, and arousing.

Natalya's verdict was not unique, judging by the furtive, lust-filled looks the men gave Lola when she wasn't watching.

The accompaniment to the scene was the satisfied grunts of those standing witness when the battered betrayer took his last breath. Their way of saying it was done. Over. The grunts were a ritual to disguise the horror. Natalya understood more than most the need for ritual. Her entire life was ritualistic, from the way she stretched each day, to the way she straightened her possessions, turned on her MP3 player, and held her bow.

After the chilling deed was done, no one had met her eyes. Not even Lola. Natalya had been sent to do her homework.

The wet slap of flesh—pleasure and pain—it all sounded the same. Natalya had learned that lesson often over the years.

Christiane's blows became harder, stronger. Punishing. Like…hatred. Wariness curled through Natalya, her eyes sliding open as she processed the unexpected sensations.

A lone, oiled finger slid up the scar next to her spine and dug in viciously. She gritted her teeth at the pain and stared at the woman's feet. White socks covered them, bisected by the black silk of the sandals.

"The plant outside needs watering," Natalya said softly in German. "It is in terrible condition."

Christiane merely hummed evenly and gave no reply. As if she didn't understand her words. Those telltale toes in the white socks, however, briefly clenched.

Natalya shifted her hands up to sit flat under her chin, lifting her face just a few inches out of the headrest.

"What part of Melbourne are you from?" she said in English, taking a guess. She used her friendliest tone. Her hands slowly edged apart, feeling the roughness of the white towel beneath her fingertips, as she mentally mapped the edges of the massage table.

"Prah…" The word, begun reflexively as a thoughtless reply to small talk, stopped halfway through "Prahran", a distinctively Melbourne suburb.

The masseuse's toes clenched just as the hands on Natalya's back froze. Natalya's narrowed eyes flew open at the confirmation, the knowledge of imminent danger filling her with an electricity she'd not felt in three years, eleven months, twelve days. The numbers came to her without conscious calculation. She knew them each day the moment she woke. The days since she'd hunted as Requiem.

She felt her alter ego slapped from her slumber, unleashed, burning, alive—like molten metal coursing through her veins. In her mind, she could hear the thrumming, primal drum beat of Two Steps From Hell's *Protectors of Earth* shaking her.

Alertness and adrenaline ripped through her with the familiarity of an old friend. She had not felt this sensation since the night she'd ended a corrupt, killer cop—a man she'd choked and drowned in pig swill. Even almost four years on, she could still taste the twisted jubilation mingled with ice-cold rage over what he'd done to the woman Requiem had claimed as hers. Over what he'd done to Alison's family.

Without warning, Requiem flung herself from the table, smashing the masseuse to the floor with her bent elbow and snatching up the towel she'd been lying on.

She stood above the groggy woman, bouncing on her heels while she spun the towel into a twisted rope and tested the ends threateningly. Requiem studied the crumpled form on the floor—small, lean, and most definitely not the Austrian woman she knew.

"Unless Christiane's had a lot of work done in the past twenty minutes, you aren't her," Requiem said, voice cold. "Who are you?"

The woman offered her a mutinous look but didn't answer.

Requiem kicked her solidly in the ribs. "Speak up."

The intruder was a short, wiry-looking Asian woman, with brooding, dark eyes, and an appraising stare. She didn't seem alarmed by Natalya's reaction. Rather, she appeared to have been expecting it.

"Where's Christiane?" Requiem demanded.

"Linen cupboard. She'll have a bad headache when she wakes up." The woman's voice and eyes openly taunted Requiem.

"Who are you?" she repeated, menace mixed with danger.

Silence.

Requiem's leg swept out and smacked the side of the woman's nose, snapping her head to the right with the momentum. A satisfying spurt of blood spattered across her white kimono robe.

Still she didn't speak. The woman ran lazy eyes over Requiem's nude form with a hint of appreciation before focusing higher, meeting her furious gaze. Finally her amused lips parted. "I am someone confirming a theory." She wiped her nose and examined the blood on her fingertips. "I see you've lost none of your edge."

"I have no idea what you're talking about." Requiem's tone became low and dark. She tightened the ends of the twisted towel, snapping it straight and relaxing it. Anyone with any self-preservation instincts would have scuttled back.

Her prey did not. Instead she tilted her head back, studying Requiem. "A woman making a garroting cable out of a towel wants me to believe she knows nothing about killing?" came the sceptical response. "That she's not Australia's most infamous assassin, Requiem? A woman who police can't find for years? Not that they're looking too hard. I mean, I found you."

"I'm a cellist," Requiem said with a sneer. She bent down and viciously flicked the woman's bloodied nose. "Vienna." *Flick.* "Philharmonic." *Flick.* "Orchestra." *Flick.* She gave her a withering look. "Anyone around here could tell you that."

"I don't think so." The woman's laugh was light, sounding genuine despite the blood soaking her swelling nose.

Requiem studied her in confusion. Her face had to be hurting like hell, yet she was still smiling.

"Well, you're not *just* that, are you?" the woman continued. "I know you killed dozens of underworld scum before you ran off here."

"Last chance." Requiem yanked the towel in her hands so taut that her sculpted biceps, honed by two-hour workouts every day, stood out in sharp relief. Her voice became terrifyingly soft. "Now—Who. Are. You?"

The smile widened. "A recruiter."

Requiem threw the towel to the floor and squatted in front of her. She wrenched the upper half of the woman's kimono apart with force. Beneath the garment she wore a simple white bra, and Requiem rapidly inspected her for surveillance wires, running her fingers under the bra and around to her back. She felt lower, patting down her groin, thighs, and calves. Finding nothing, she slid her fingers up into the woman's long black hair, pausing behind her ears. Still nothing.

In annoyance, Requiem pushed her away so hard that the woman fell back in a sprawl. Then she pounced.

"Now, let's start again," she said coldly, bracketing the woman's knees with her thighs. "Who the hell are you, and why are you here, invading my space?"

Rather than answer, a slow gaze raked Requiem's body. Something familiar about the way she studied her niggled at Requiem. When the woman finally spoke, her voice was breathless.

"Invading *your* space? Says the naked assassin with her cunt in my lap?" An elegant finger traced across Requiem's muscled stomach, swirling across a small scar above her hip. She arched an eyebrow.

Requiem glanced down at her nude state, then at the finger. "Distracted, are we?"

They both watched the finger drop a little lower, edging towards her neatly trimmed dark hair, and Requiem hissed in a breath of surprise. It had been so long since she'd played with her prey. And even longer still since one of them had the temerity to toy with her back. She'd forgotten how heady it could be.

Arousal shot through her when the dancing digit slid a little lower—merely a fingertip, a fingernail, away from her clit. A prickling sensation shot down Requiem's spine, a warning as sharp as a knife's blade, and Requiem wrenched the hand away and jumped to her feet. She picked up her clothes and said with a growl, "Fine. You have your space. Now talk."

Even with distance from the woman, Requiem's heart thudded in awareness, her body tightly strung. The base, raw emotions were almost overwhelming. This was what she used to do. *This* was the real game. The absolute power. Her body ached to feel it again. Requiem's mounting excitement in her lower gut told her just how close that wandering finger had come. How close the woman would have been to discovering the effect she'd had on Requiem. And that would not do.

The woman sat up casually and leaned back on one arm, a picture of relaxation. Like one of those perfect specimens on the cover of a yoga DVD, all poised class and easy beauty. "I am someone who needs your unique skills, and who understands that you're available and most likely ready for a change."

"Not interested." Requiem slipped on her bra and slid her black boy shorts up her legs.

The woman teasingly began to fiddle with her own robe, widening it. "You haven't even heard my pitch."

"Still not interested." Requiem pulled her pants up with sharp, snapping actions, and almost groaned when the seam hit her groin and shot a bolt of arousal through her. She reached for her shirt, casting her intruder a withering glare. "No pitch can win me over."

"Really? You've been based, or should I say, tied down, in Vienna for three years, I believe. You must be bored by now. Are your little concerts enough? Do you still feel the thrill in your blood, the need to hunt? What if I said the targets were exceptionally vicious and you'd be doing society a favour? These men are the worst of the worst. The challenge of just getting to them would be exciting. Can you honestly tell me what you do now is satisfying enough? Or have they tamed you, Requiem?"

As she spoke, the woman shifted to allow a view of her smooth, flawless legs, all the way up to her white panties. Requiem frowned as she gazed at the ample skin on display. Her heartbeat lifted again, but this time it was not just arousal heightening her senses.

No scars. *At all.* No wounds, nicks, or cuts.

Who the hell was this woman who seemed to have underworld connections and yet skin this flawless?

"You're just an amateur," she said with a dismissive glance. "Playing with fire. What do you know about satisfying me? How could you know? Who have you been talking to?"

"There are stories—more like legends, now—that float around Melbourne, of a female assassin, lethal and sleek as a panther. A predator who hunted, fucked any woman who crossed her, and loved the darkness. Lived it, breathed it. Killed in it."

"Sounds like a tall tale to me."

"Is that so? Shall we test that?" The woman shrugged her robe off her shoulders, dropping it to the floor, fully revealing her sheer white bra. Dark, plump nipples were clearly outlined, erect, straining beneath the silk. "Your needs would be fully catered to, of course. They would be part of the remuneration package. And if I don't meet your requirements, well, we have other women who'd greatly enjoy taking my place."

Requiem studied her, fighting her arousal. She could all too easily imagine having the woman spread before her, crying out for a release that Requiem would take enormous delight in denying her. She *should* be denied—for her presumption in thinking she set the terms. For presuming she could have any place at Requiem's table.

"You think I *need* that?" Requiem reached for her boots to hide the tremble in her fingers at the intoxicating thought. The scent of arousal was in the air, and she was only too well aware it was her own. She hardened her voice in irritation at her own weakness. "How little you know me."

The woman laughed. "You're only human, Requiem. So, back to my offer: Kills, thrills, and unmarked bills. And a pretty perk or two. No one would ever know. Discretion would be absolute in all matters." Her fingers dropped to her own breast and slid across the hard nipple, then slipped her breast out from her bra. It was as smooth, plump, and as perfect and alluring as the rest of her. Her eyes dared Requiem to be interested. Dared her to be tempted. *Dared. Her.*

So presumptuous.

But she was right about one thing—she had been restless lately. She'd never acted on it, but neither had an offer been so tempting. It would be so easy. It wasn't as though Alison would ever know. Requiem could take this job and, while she was at it, take this smug, alluring creature, and make her understand the terrible error she had made in trying to play her. Requiem's smile felt more like a snarl.

It wouldn't even be cheating—it wasn't sexual in the least. It was all about power. It was *always* about power. She was Requiem, damn it. *Requiem.* Once Australia's most feared assassin. She shouldn't have to check herself like some little housewife. Wildness burned inside her, like an animal straining to be let off its leash. Of late, her pulse often quickened at the thought of being out there, being *all* that Requiem was. The darkness was still there. You couldn't turn that off with a pretty penthouse apartment, a classy job, and a sweet woman.

Alison's face floated into mind, fresh-faced, eager, loyal. Loving.

Her lips thinned.

The other woman seemed to sense her hesitation and swayed closer. "It's been three years, Requiem," she said, her voice low and sultry. "Three years of being tied down, playing the meek cellist. And let's not forget you're now being trailed around by that little groupie. You must be tired of both by now."

Requiem froze at the mention of her lover, her breathing compressing into a faint sliver of exhalation. Alarm and rage coursed through her in equal measure.

Had this creature worked out who Alison really was? Who she'd been in Melbourne?

She frowned. They'd known her by a different first name professionally back home. A name she hadn't been interested in reclaiming when she moved here. So how could she have been recognised a world away?

Requiem thought furiously. Since settling into Vienna, Alison had changed her clothing style to sleeker, darker European fashions, and her hair had gone from a messy, brunette ponytail to an auburn pixie cut. Alison's own sister hadn't recognised her at first at the airport during their last reunion. So was it even possible for Alison to have been identified here?

No one alive in the underworld even knew of the connection between them. If this woman had managed to figure out Alison's identity, then that would be it—Requiem would end her. Immediately. Because no one threatened her mouse, or those whom Alison loved.

No one.

Decided, Requiem glanced at the three exits she'd assessed earlier, as she did every time she entered a room: the window, the air vent, the door. She calculated her options. How it could be done efficiently. How it could be done with minimal mess.

"What's her name?" the woman was saying casually, as though she hadn't just signed her own death warrant. "I've seen her. She looks adorable. Where on earth did you find her? The library? At the stage door, clutching an autograph book?" She laughed.

Requiem's nostrils flared. It was the only reaction that betrayed her enormous relief. *She didn't know. She didn't have a damned clue. Alison was safe.* Her heart reduced its manic thudding to a less furious juddering roll of a timpani drum.

"She's sweet, yes, anyone could see that, but where is the challenge?" The women smirked, heedless to the danger that had been coating the air like ash moments before. "You need letting off the domestic leash. *You* were never meant to be a pet."

She stepped right inside Requiem's space, fingers brushing her jaw, and it took every ounce of effort not to crush her for her insult to Alison. Requiem's entire focus and being went into revealing nothing at all of her emotional state.

"So what's it going to be?" the woman asked, sounding bored. "Shall we make a deal? Meet my boss? You're not the only one on my list, you know. Yes, you're at the top, obviously, but I can headhunt someone else. So are you willing? Do you wish to…fill my slot?"

Requiem gave her a stony look, the woman's charm having evaporated the moment she'd dared speak a word about Alison. She could not believe she had weakened briefly in the face of temptation. It wasn't worth it. She *knew* that. The rush that came from a power fuck was just that—hormones, highs, and control, all in a sticky mess. Ultimately meaningless.

For Alison, though, the sexual act was a different thing, entirely one of love. She saw it framed in softness, tenderness, and care. For Alison, it was never about release or power. For her, it was about sweetness, lightness, and surrendering to someone. And while Requiem did none of these things...Alison *did*. She would never brush off sex with someone else as nothing. This deal with the devil would not be nothing to her.

The woman was watching Requiem carefully. She was so close Requiem could feel her breath, smell the faint musk of her arousal. The woman arched herself forward, pressing her breasts into Requiem. Sweetening the deal, she probably thought.

Natalya leaned forward and ran her finger over the erect, bared nipple. It was soft, warm, and oh-so-inviting. Just like old times. Old times that did not have Alison in them. Requiem tapped the nipple pointedly. "I think not," she said with a cool glance and stepped back.

Because it came down to one thing: the mere thought of the crushing disappointment in Alison's eyes if she ever found out Requiem had screwed someone else, even just to teach the cocky creature a lesson, would crush the air from Requiem's lungs.

She could see Alison packing her bags and leaving, because she surely would, given she was that sort of woman. Alison was soft but substantial. Sweet but fierce. She had her pride and Requiem admired her for it, especially after a life of Alison being taught that her needs were nothing and that she was inconsequential. She'd spent most of her adult life believing that her sum worth was that of a nursemaid to her emotionally abusive, narcissistic mother.

When she had broken free, a piece of fire had entered her eyes and never left. It satisfied Requiem beyond words to see it. Women *should* know their worth. Alison knew hers. And her conditions had always been clear in agreeing to throw away her safe, respectable life and follow an unpredictable, dangerous, ex-assassin to Europe. Alison's terms had been simple—they were equals and they now belonged to each other.

The image of Alison's faith and affection flickering and dying...the look of betrayal...it would be like a dagger's stab. If anyone else had inflicted pain like that on Alison, Requiem would have torn them apart. The thought that her own darkness had allowed her to push aside the consequences even for a heartbeat filled her with dismay.

Requiem's voice was cold when she spoke. "Get dressed. You have no idea how to meet my needs. I have no interest in what you offer."

The surprise on the other woman's face was almost comical. "I don't understand. I offered you what you want." Confusion, doubt, and a hint of wariness entered her eyes. "This is what Requiem wants. *This.*"

Requiem reached down and handed her back her white robe. A protest formed on her lips, then fell, unsaid, as she looked deeper into Requiem's eyes.

The woman pulled the robe on with jerky movements. The confidence of minutes before was evaporating and, as she slid her hand around one ear to curl her hair into place, the familiarity of the gesture hit Natalya in a blinding flash.

"It's Mi Na, isn't it?" she said in surprise, and she ran her eyes over her curiously. "Nabi's sister? You were the one at boarding school while Nabi followed me around like a shadow, watching me as I learned the business. So you took over? In *all* her pursuits?" Her eyebrow lift was deliberately condescending.

How had this slip of a girl thought she could ever be as good as her assassin sister? Requiem studied her unmarked skin and bright eyes. No. There was no way she was an assassin. So what was she?

"Fuck you," Mi Na said flatly, and the intonation was exactly the same as Nabi's had once been when Requiem had shown her in vivid, naked detail the futility of trying to kill her. Worse, of trying to best her.

Mi Na narrowed her eyes and slowly reached for the CD player, turning up the volume on the gushing waterfalls and bird calls, to just short of deafening. Requiem tilted her head, watching her every move. She bounced lightly on her heels, waiting. The woman was an unarmed amateur. There was no threat. But she was curious.

Suddenly Mi Na reached for her foot and flipped her sandal over. Natalya saw the flash of metal too late.

She was fast, terrifyingly so, just like her sister had been, and slid the blade up to Requiem's throat. But Requiem had three times the muscle mass on her, and immediately wrenched her hand away and twisted her arm behind her back. She debated whether to snap it. It would be so damned easy. A nice reminder as to who Mi Na was screwing with.

But Mi Na was as fast as Requiem was powerful. She took three light steps up the wall in front of her and somersaulted over Requiem, freeing her arm the moment her body was higher than her limb. On landing, she kicked the hot-rock crock pot at Requiem, who dodged it—barely.

Scorching rocks flew everywhere, tumbling under the table, towards the walls, and at Requiem, who kicked them away. Mi Na picked up a pair of the stones in her bare hands, seemingly not even noticing their searing heat. She hissed in fury, tossing one at Requiem's head.

Requiem snapped her head away to allow it to whistle by, just as Mi Na hurled the other one. Using her forearm, Requiem smashed that away, too, ignoring the thud of pain. The rock flew straight back, slamming into Mi Na's shoulder, and she grunted.

Mi Na threw her arms out wildly. One hand connected with a small, heavy Buddha statue which she grasped in her fist. She held it up like a club, swooping it viciously back and forth through the air. She hurled it.

Requiem spun out of the way. She didn't move quite fast enough. The bronze weight thudded dully off her back, landing on a sore point. She winced. *Again* with her damn back scar?

She yanked the peace mobile down from the ceiling, just as the woman charged at her. Requiem sidestepped her like a bull fighter and wrapped the mess of metal and fishing line around her neck as she rushed by. Mi Na pulled up short and jerked and thrashed as the plastic wire bit savagely into her neck, her face turning hot red.

Requiem yanked hard, as Mi Na, clawing at her throat, desperately tried to free herself. Pulling her close, Requiem leaned into her ear. "One tug and you're dead." She yanked the fishing wire a little to make her point. "You're nowhere near as good as your sister was. If Nabi had wanted it, I'd already be dead. I was aware of her many talents, and she had *so* many. I still think fondly of several of them."

Mi Na growled at the suggestiveness, designed to provoke.

Requiem smiled. The enraged often made mistakes. "So tell me, were you planning to fillet me as we fucked?" Requiem asked. "Or was this seduction routine just to whet my appetite? What you really wanted was for me to agree to meet your fictitious boss somewhere later so you could dispose of my body out of the way? Mm?"

Mi Na cried out as Requiem tightened her hold on the fishing wire. "Answer!"

The woman hissed out a "yes", pain etching her features.

"Well, points for originality. Shame about the execution."

A peace symbol was pressing into the side of Mi Na's face, creating an ironic imprint. Requiem almost laughed. "So why not kill me while I was on the table? Too messy? Harder to hide the stains?"

"With your back turned?" Mi Na said, squeezing out her words with difficulty. "You think I have no honour."

"No honour?" Requiem repeated. "You even sound like her. Who hired you? The dregs of Fleet Crew? Or someone else?"

"No one. This is for myself. For family honour."

Family honour. Requiem's grip eased. She'd been right: this silly girl was no assassin. Great. A civilian on a vengeance kick. Although Mi Na had obviously had some actual training. "Family honour? What does that even mean? Nabi and I were not enemies in the end."

"You broke her heart. She told me. You broke her. Then…I found out later you killed her. You shot her, when she was trying to protect her boss."

Requiem said nothing for a moment, picking apart the anguish in the words, like ligaments from muscles. "I never killed her." She didn't bother denying the rest. The girl's misplaced affections were hardly her fault.

"You used her! Treated her like dirt. And Sal said you killed her. It's my right to avenge her. He trained me to fight you."

Requiem sighed. *Saliya Govi.* The new head of Fleet Crew. Freshly out of jail, if her sources were right. He'd been the smartest gang member left standing when the dust had cleared after Requiem had betrayed the entire Australian underworld. She had wondered how long it would take someone to figure out she'd been the one. Of course Sal didn't know for sure, so he'd manipulated Mi Na and sent her after Requiem. No matter the outcome, his hands were clean.

Slippery little shit.

"I didn't kill your sister," Requiem said in irritation. "Sal has his own agenda. She died of her wounds when police shot her as she was trying to escape."

"Bullshit! And she didn't deserve to die in some dirty alley like she was nothing. She *mattered*. She mattered to *me*."

A burst of scrambling and twisting resulted in Mi Na wriggling out of Requiem's grip. She let the woman go and sat back on her haunches.

Mi Na did the same and rubbed the red lines at her neck as they eyed each other cautiously, four feet apart.

"I didn't kill her, like I said," Requiem said. "Mi Na, your sister was someone I could no more kill than she could kill me. That was our relationship. Dysfunctional and complicated, but for assassins, that counts as downright friendly."

There was a strangled, tortured noise and Mi Na brought her hands up to cover her face. Tears slid out from between her fingers as she wept silently.

Requiem stared at the emotional display with distaste, stomach plummeting. She wasn't any good at this. The failings and frailties of humanity were nothing she'd mastered, beyond how to exploit them. The adrenaline was wearing off as the threat passed. She felt the stillness inside herself, and the seeping away of the part of her that was raw, pure, and dangerous, until Requiem faded.

Natalya lowered herself in front of Mi Na and waited until she had her eye.

"I was there. I held Nabi when she died," she said evenly. "I held her when she made her peace with the universe, and made her peace with me. There was too much blood loss to save her. She died well. She was unafraid, she was strong, and I think her family would have been proud of her. I know I was. I told her so."

Tear-filled, suspicious eyes sought the truth.

"I could have killed you just now," Natalya added. "I didn't. So you know I have no reason to lie. You *know* that."

Mi Na became still, dropping her hands to her lap. Natalya could see their trembling.

"I paid top dollar to get Requiem profiled. Dropped out of med school, used all my savings." The words were a whisper, like a long-held secret, and Mi Na stared at her hands as she mumbled them. "I had to find out how to get to you, how to get you vulnerable. To understand who you are. What mattered to you. To work out what you need. What you desire. The profiler interviewed some of the women Requiem...*toyed* with.

"The report I got back said, over and over, you only want power. Power of the hunt. Power over rivals and those who challenge you. *That's* who you are. But you...you're...not her. I don't understand why you said no. What I did wrong. You *should* have said yes. He said you'd say yes."

The plaintive, confused words echoed in Natalya's head. She sighed and rose.

"Go home, Mi Na," she said, injecting menace into her tone. "Challenge me or anyone in my life again and I will be ruthless. We both know that I know where your family lives. I know your father personally. I know which hospital he's in."

Mi Na's brown eyes widened in shock.

Natalya had never let go of her informants' network for this reason. You never knew which tidbit could pay off. For instance, she had been aware that a profiler had been looking into Requiem about six months ago. His subsequent death had been convenient but, for once, unrelated to her. Requiem's were not the only toes the man had stepped on.

"Do not test me," she continued. "You would regret it for the rest of your life. Tell me that you understand that, at least?"

Mi Na swallowed and nodded.

Natalya pursed her lips. She was getting soft. Mi Na's head was bowed again, tears sliding down her cheeks, mingling with the blood from her injured nose, spattering on the floor in an ugly, sopping red mess.

Glancing around at the destruction in the room, and the human carnage on the floor, Natalya shook her head once, and slipped out the door.

Outside, she paused, wondering which way the linen closet was, and how to liberate an unconscious masseuse without anyone knowing...especially the masseuse herself.

She exhaled in annoyance, flexing her shoulders. On top of everything, now she *really* needed a massage.

Part Two: Bare

Natalya

"Hey, you're early!" Alison's voice echoed down the hall as Natalya arrived home at their two-bedroom penthouse apartment. "How come?"

"My masseuse became unwell," Natalya called back. She hung her keys on a hook behind the door and leaned down to give their slumbering, ancient red heeler, Charlotte, a scratch behind her greying ears. "We cut the session short. What's that interesting smell?"

"Come and find out."

Natalya crossed the parquetry floors, glancing at the white walls and precisely placed modern art, musical trinkets, and framed photos of Alison's family.

Pride of place in the hall was a photo of Alison, her sister, Susan, and niece, Hailey, laughing on the couch in their lounge room. It had felt so strange when they'd come to visit. At the time, Natalya had still been adjusting to having more than one voice in her life. And then suddenly there had been wall-to-wall Ryans. Adding to the surrealness, neither of them called Alison by the name she knew her. It was a dead name from a past that she and Alison didn't speak about.

Natalya had taken to hiding out on the roof of their apartment building for the solitude. "A breath of fresh air," she'd told them, as she'd made her daily escape. She'd sat up there, arms around her bent legs, watching over the city like an avenging angel.

She had even caught a burglar one day while she was there. Natalya smirked at the memory of dangling him over the edge while he'd pissed his pants and swore in three different languages to never trouble her building again. She did miss that—showing vermin the light.

Not that she'd shared that with Alison. Her lover didn't need to know the darkness was still there. What if it frightened her? What if it frightened her *off*?

That didn't bear thinking about.

She headed further along the hall. There was nothing of Natalya here, beyond one photo of her father that gave her pause each time she saw it. It was from before Vadim had migrated to Australia, still wearing his Russian Army uniform. So proud and straight, his eyes direct and cool. She had another photo of him, secreted on the top shelf of her closet, of his wedding day to Lola. But she couldn't bring herself to hang it. The way her former stepmother had died…the way she'd lived…it was all so wrong. Twisted.

Natalya studied her father's bushy brows and lean, long face in this photo. His medals shone. She missed him. He had raised her alone for most of her life, and he had been her only connection with her past. She had been on her tour of Europe just seven months when the nursing home had called her. It had rocked her to her core, hearing of his death, even though it wasn't unexpected.

His funeral had not felt safe enough to attend. The reason lay only a few steps away. Natalya and Alison didn't discuss it, then or now. They didn't discuss a lot of things. What was the point of scraping over the past? It wasn't necessary. They had the present. They had this.

But the ache was there as she studied her father's gentle face.

"I'm making a new recipe I learned in cooking class. Here, come try it." Alison's disembodied voice sounded so excited.

Natalya smiled in spite of herself and headed to the kitchen.

Every pot and pan in existence had been pressed into service in the steam-filled room. Tomato spatters were everywhere, along with eggshells and vegetable offcuts. But all Natalya could see was one thing—the delight in Alison's shining blue eyes. Her hair was sticking up at random angles, and her nose wrinkled as she focused.

Alison held out a wooden spoon to her. Natalya inspected the tomatoey goop on it and her nostrils twitched. Didn't smell half bad. Her tongue inched out to taste it. Bold, primary flavours hit her, as onion, tomato, and garlic punched in. Then the aftertaste hit.

"How much booze did you put in this?" Her eyebrows lifted in surprise.

"Enough to give it a kick. I might have improvised that bit. Why? Did I overdo it?"

Natalya's lips twitched. "I think that could kick a donkey. It's tasty, though, aside from that."

"Damn. I wanted it to be perfect. For our anniversary."

Natalya paused and her brows knitted together. It wasn't quite two years since Alison had moved to Vienna. She remembered the date distinctively, as she did all dates, times, and places. Details were important.

"October 16," Alison supplied. "It's five years to the day that you first met me outside that experimental music club."

Ah.

"'*Met*' is not quite how I remembered it," Natalya said. "I'm fairly certain breath-freshener-as-mace was used as a threat on my life."

Alison gave her a sly grin. "Well, sure, but calling it the anniversary of your stalking me because you wanted to kill me has some unsavoury connotations."

"Well, when you put it like that…" Natalya smiled and decided if Alison could whitewash those days, so could she. She winced as she shrugged out of her jacket and slid it on the back of a wooden chair at the kitchen table.

"Did you hurt yourself?"

Natalya glanced up. Alison's eyes never missed much.

"My masseuse found that scar on my back today, and decided it needed a special kind of pummeling." She wriggled and straightened her back, stretching a little. "Actually, I think she used her entire body weight on it at one point."

"Ouch," Alison said in sympathy, putting the lid on the pot and then turning the heat way down.

Natalya ran her eyes over her lover, taking in the tight jeans and blue shirt rolled up at the sleeves. She felt a familiar tightening of arousal, something she'd never stopped having for this woman. Any thoughts she might become bored with her, or of this life, were fears that had yet to come to pass.

Alison came closer and the smell of her freshly washed hair and scrubbed skin, mingled with tomato aromas, made Natalya want her even more. More than anyone she'd ever known.

What had Mi Na called Alison? A sweet little thing? Actually, she was a woman who had stopped an assassin in her tracks by just being herself.

Alison's keen, interested gaze took her measure. Something of Natalya's desire must have shown in her eyes, because Alison's cheeks warmed. "In the mood, are we?" she asked.

Always in the mood. For this, and for you.

Natalya had never used to *want* like this. But everything was different with this unassuming woman. She had redefined what Natalya's body craved. Natalya allowed a seductive smile to curl her lips, making her interest known.

Alison's lips captured hers immediately, and her tongue sought out Natalya's with enthusiasm. Alison pressed hard against her, pushing her into a wall and grasping fists of clothing as she eliminated all space between them.

Natalya groaned in surprise and delight. She loved it when Alison took the initiative. Oh, Natalya always loved flinging Alison down and taking her until her body was a series of shaking, whimpering trembles. But this, this burning need, was something else. It undid her every time.

She was propelled into their bedroom, *their bedroom*—even after all this time, the shock of that still took adjustment. Natalya had been alone for so long that negotiating things like shared beds, bathrooms, and kitchens still sometimes made her itch with discomfort.

When Alison nudged open the door to their bedroom, Natalya pulled away, her eyes widening.

Red petals. On the floor. On the sheets. The music, playing on an iPod in the corner, was a string duet. Two instruments seemed to be dancing around each other, feeling each other out, flirting, seducing. Philip Glass's *Double Concerto for Violin, Cello and Orchestra*, she noted. *Duet No. 2*. How apt: a cellist and a violinist. She glanced at Alison who gave her a cheeky grin.

Alison's lips were back on Natalya's, claiming her. That magical tongue was doing things to her that were positively obscene. An approving gasp worked its way from her throat. Natalya's eyes fluttered closed and she felt her outer clothes wrenched down her body with desperation. There was little skill; it was pure need.

It brought her back to *that* day.

Their first time together. The *real* first time. Not the earlier time she'd allowed Alison to have a taste of her, a small piece as a farewell because the woman's soft eyes had pleaded for it and Natalya couldn't deny her, despite knowing it was a terrible idea. Risky. She'd held back to protect herself, but it hadn't entirely worked. She'd still given far more than she'd intended. Not all, but more. And she'd thought of little else since.

Natalya had held out for a year. Finally she had returned one night and, heart hammering in her chest, had asked Alison to return with her to Europe. It was a pivotal moment. For the first time in her entire life—a life spent toying with and controlling others—she'd kissed someone. On the lips.

It had been terrifying. And intoxicating.

Afterwards, they'd barely gotten back to Alison's apartment before they'd begun tearing clothes off each other. And then… She swallowed at the memory of a time that had left her so vulnerable she could scarcely breathe.

Alison, hair still wet from the light rain that night, had pushed her down, eyes intense and dark, and smoothed her hands all over her, mapping her naked body with a joy that seemed to come from knowing Natalya was hers. She'd touched her. All of her. For an eternity. Because she could. Because Natalya had allowed her to, as her equal.

Natalya had watched the swaying of her pale, bare breasts, revelled in the softness of her skin, as Alison's burning fingertips teased and touched all around where she most wanted them.

Natalya hadn't asked for more, or for anything, because she'd wanted Alison to take her any way she wanted. It was the most profound and hardest gift she had ever given anyone. Natalya's fingers had curled and retracted, fighting her fierce need to have control, to reclaim her power on that confronting, thrilling, terrifying first night.

Her jaw had tightened each time her body quivered—betraying its weakness of desiring to bend to the will of another. The apex predator side of her didn't want to want this. But, as she'd discovered after roaming Europe alone, not having this was far worse than admitting to needing it.

Natalya's skin and muscles had shone from perspiration in her efforts not to show how hard it was to be so laid bare. Beneath Alison's fervent explorations, and in those eyes watching her so intently, lay a well of desire. *This* was all Alison had wanted in order to be happy.

Even if the fight to surrender killed her, Natalya wanted to give her this night.

Alison's fingers had stroked her muscles, explored her dips and lines, teased her nipples and skidded over her ribs, before worshipping the planes from her hips down. She had laid heated lips upon her most intimate flesh, tasting her with relish. She'd brought Natalya to the edge over and over but never let her cross. Instead, those taunting lips had rushed back up to Natalya's and murmured against her mouth how much she loved this. How often she had fantasised about doing this, *exactly this*, for so long. How having Natalya, this way, having the power, meant so much. How it had meant everything.

And then, finally, when Natalya had been gasping, on the edge again, voice and nerves raw with want, Alison had entered her for the first time. She had nudged her way between her swollen, wet lower lips with a single, long finger. Slow and gentle, with a tiny, sweet smile on her face, she'd pushed in as far and as deep as she could. And in so doing, she'd discovered Natalya's darkest secret.

Natalya had tensed because, like the kissing earlier that evening, this was not something she'd done before. Even when alone, she'd never explored much beyond the surface. Without the thrill of power, there had never seemed much point before.

Thanks to her highly active life, Natalya had no idea whether she even still had an intact "virgin's veil" as they used to call it. So she had lain there, frozen, expecting something—pain, blood maybe… Not everyone experienced these things, but still, she'd tensed, waiting for it.

Alison's shocked eyes had told Natalya the moment she'd worked it out. Because while Requiem had claimed dozens of women over the years—aggressively, powerfully, confidently—no one had ever taken Natalya.

Nabi had come closest; Requiem had indulged her more than most. But it had still meant nothing and hadn't crossed her strictest of lines—she'd never allowed such a liberty as kissing or this particular intimacy.

No one had crossed that line until Alison.

Alison had withdrawn her finger and whispered "Oh," her eyes bright with emotion.

Natalya had found no words sufficient to tell her to stop whatever that look was. How could you put a concept so big into sliced up, rearranged spreads of letters? How could you explain the threats to her body and soul that she'd experienced so young? That in order to feel strong and protected, she'd allowed no one to touch her beyond the superficial?

The act of touching others was nothing to her. Getting people off meant the power was hers, the control hers, and her invincibility was assured. But to allow someone *inside* you—in every sense—that meant something.

Alison's hand had cupped Natalya's reddening face, eyes filled with questions.

Natalya hadn't been able to explain the heat in her own cheeks. It wasn't shame. Not embarrassment. Whatever it was, it had burned across her skin, and she'd wrenched her head away. She hadn't the words for any of this.

But Alison hadn't wanted her words. Instead she had laid herself across Natalya's body, pressing her belly, breasts, and thighs against Natalya's; she'd threaded herself under and through her arms, merging with her. She'd kissed her once more. Thoroughly. Because she now could. Then she'd rocked against her.

Under those delicious, intoxicating, soft kisses that had felt like a fever to Natalya, and against the sweetness of Alison's body, rhythmically sliding against hers, Natalya had burned from the inside out. She had gradually come apart, gasping in a shuddering orgasm that, for the first time in her life, had absolutely nothing to do with power. It had to do with something else entirely. Something she hadn't been ready to think about.

"Where were you just now?"

Alison's voice broke into Natalya's memories, and she blinked back to the present. Her fingers drifted through the rose petals on the sheets and she glanced up. "That night together. After your concert. When I came back for you."

There was a nod, like she already knew. Maybe Natalya always had the same distant look on her face each time she thought of that experience.

Alison pushed her flat onto her back, pressing their bodies together. The weight and warmth was reassuring in its familiarity. "I've been thinking of you all day," she said against her throat between feverish kisses, "thinking of all the ways I'm going to have you. All the ways you'll *know* you're mine."

The words took a moment to penetrate the fog of Natalya's overheated brain. Her breasts were seized by hot, frantic fingers, and then a tongue and teeth asserted their claim on her.

But Natalya was still stunned. How had she known?

"They can look at you," Alison was murmuring. "All your fans, outside the Musikverein every night. All those women, all those men who want you. I see their eyes. I'm not blind. I recognise the look. I see it in the mirror every day."

Alison sucked hard on her nipple, causing Natalya's back to arch. "I see *your* eyes too," she said. There was a pause and only cold air, as her soft lips lifted off Natalya's breast.

Alison's knowing gaze met Natalya's surprised one. Her small hands were suddenly tugging at Natalya's boy shorts, pulling them down, but Natalya did not, could not, break the gaze. Alison's fingers gave one final, sharp tug, and Natalya was naked, exposed. Her arousal on display.

"I see your eyes too," Alison repeated quietly.

Natalya watched her uncertainly, even as she felt a hand dusting her source, tracing her quivers. Finding the telltale wetness betraying her sharp need.

"And I remind myself that your fans can want you all they like, and you can appreciate them admiring you, but they're not who you chose, are they?" Alison studied her.

"No." Natalya looked at her directly.

With a nod of approval, Alison made her way down Natalya's body. She breathed hotly over her intimate flesh that was trembling to be touched, straining for attention.

Natalya closed her eyes, waiting, her breathing harsh and fast.

She felt Alison pause her inspection and heard her almost idle question. "Did you kill her? The masseuse who hurt your scar today? Because I know masseuses. Especially the expensive kind at that fancy salon you like. Unless specifically asked, they leave scars well alone. So I'm guessing that was no masseuse. I'm almost afraid to ask who she really was."

Natalya's eyes sprang open. She glanced down to find Alison watching her closely, her look hard to decipher. Natalya should have known better. It was something they both had in common—a sharp eye for details. She usually appreciated that quality in her lover.

"It was touch and go. But no. Still alive." Natalya left her tone deliberately light. Alison could take it any way she liked.

"Did you have her then?" Again there was the strange expression.

The harsh, unspoken awareness hung between them—that *this* was what Requiem did. Requiem fucked anyone who fucked with her, one way or another. Of course Alison knew that better than anyone. But in some twisted way, this topic usually fell under the category of things from Requiem's past they never discussed.

But today the past was the present. It was a reasonable question.

Natalya licked her lips. "No." She added conviction to her voice. "*No.*"

Alison's eyes glowed, and their faint glint of possessiveness, fear, and tension slipped away. Desire and warmth took their place. "Good," she said lightly, as though Natalya had merely confirmed she'd picked up milk on the way home. "And now I'm going to make you forget anyone but me."

Natalya shivered. Alison's tongue was suddenly driving between her legs, and Natalya cried out at the sensation. Her fingers spasmed and clutched at the sheets as her body was plundered by Alison's nimble tongue.

Natalya hovered between states of being as those demanding lips blew on her, pulled, licked, nibbled, and claimed her. Natalya gasped as the wetness flowed from her. Inside, it felt as if a wolf was howling, as though Requiem was crying out in abandonment, as Natalya twisted, moaned, shuddered, and finally came hard against the feverish mouth of the woman she had claimed as hers.

Hers.

"I feel." Natalya exhaled the words so softly, unaware she'd even said them until the blue eyes halfway down the bed blinked up at her.

"Mmm," Alison whispered against her flesh. "I know that. You pretend it's only ever with a cello in your hands, but I know better. I've seen it. Especially fear."

An objection flew to Natalya's lips at this outrage. It died at Alison's next words.

"When I told you my sister was coming for a visit." Alison's eyes danced with mirth. "Who knew even the scariest assassins have in-law anxieties?" Her look dared Natalya to deny it.

Natalya felt no desire to confirm that unsavoury little factoid. Her breath was still unsteady when she replied, "I meant that I feel love."

It was something else they never talked about. Not since that night, two years ago in the rain, when she'd gone back for her and explained she was terrible at this, that she didn't do love, but they should be together anyway.

She might not do love, but she'd felt it that night. A hint of it, a wisp, swirling around her senses, edging in, like a whisper demanding to be heard. The feeling had almost swallowed her whole when they'd kissed. The knowledge of what this thing between them might be had scared the daylights out of her. Not enough to run, though. She was no coward.

Natalya waited for Alison's reaction, a lip caught between her teeth.

The stillness between them seemed to swallow all the oxygen. The intensity stripped any amusement from Alison's eyes.

Natalya wondered if she'd made a terrible tactical error. A coldness filtered into her veins at the thought that this thing might actually be more one-sided than she'd thought. She'd foolishly exposed herself, stripped herself bare and now…

Alison's eyes softened and lit up with delight. Every emotion in her heart chased across her face. Relief surged through Natalya as Alison smiled and slithered her way up Natalya's body.

"Hey," she whispered. "I thought maybe you did. Hoped you did the way I do. But it's everything hearing it from someone who always says she doesn't do love."

Natalya's eyes fluttered closed and her lips twitched. "Well, I *don't* do love. As a rule. But apparently the rules don't apply to you. God knows, no rule in existence has ever worked in the past."

She felt the weight of Alison, solid and steady, slide across her torso. An arm slipped around her ribs, claiming her. Natalya cracked an eyelid and saw within Alison's blinding smile that addictive essence that she knew she could never give up, no matter what.

Natalya had been right, the night under that soft rain, when she'd gone back for this unexpected woman. Her little mouse. She'd sensed then what she understood now as the truth.

Love is not nothing.

If you enjoyed this short story, check out *Requiem for Immortals* by Lee Winter, the novel in which Natalya and Alison met and fell in love.

Water into Wine

by Roslyn Sinclair

Summary:

Set two years after the end of *The Lily and the Crown*. (Definitely read that first.) Mír's a little restless.

I have never claimed to be a saint.

To be frank, I never claimed to be much of a good person at all, as I told you right from the start. But you, my sweet Ariana, have never quite believed me.

Oh, you've had your eyes opened. In the two years since I stole you away from your father's space station in the dead of night, you've seen what I am capable of. Great things, I hope, as well as vile. And you have adjusted. You have accustomed yourself to your new circumstances, to the reality that you share a bed with a murderer, a thousand times over, while the only thing you've ever killed is a bug. And I daresay you've tortured yourself more over that than I have over all the rest.

But whatever the rest, you believe in one thing: my love for you. You would insist on calling it that, although *love* isn't a word I use, because I'm still not sure what it means, and I don't want to look like an idiot if I misuse it.

For you, on the other hand, *love* is an easy word. It effortlessly rolls off your lips each morning and night. And you believe in it. It is a reality for you.

However wicked I am, however many throats I've cut, however many stations I overpower (always in the name of a higher cause, you are quick to point out), you take solace in the way I return to you at night and hold you close. You are pleased I can say, without fear of mistake, that I love the scent of your hair and the press of your body. You are happy because, out of everyone in the system, I have chosen you and allowed you to choose, or perhaps *demand*, me in return. Yes. You believe that this is love and that it will last forever, and you'll be eternally content at my side.

And whatever it is we have—do you believe it *began* with love, as well? Perhaps you do, no matter what I've told you. Then again, I've never told you the truth.

I never will, either. I'm not a fool. You wouldn't take it well if I told you that in the beginning you were only a game. When I realized you were attracted to me, I wasted no time in attempting to debauch you as thoroughly as possible. (Two years and I have not yet succeeded.) Can you blame me? I was bored to death, tired of gardening—great cosmos, the endless gardening—broken only by looking at the stars. *Restless* doesn't even begin to describe it. And you really were tempting, so unconscious of your loveliness, of how striking you could be if you just took a little time and care with your appearance and bearing.

Then, of course, there was your father to consider.

Your father, whose Imperial forces had slaughtered my troops without mercy; who sat sick and trusting at that humiliating banquet, exposing his naked throat to the open air while I was forced to kneel by your side. Might there have been an element of vengeance in deflowering his daughter, so lonely and vulnerable and unprotected?

No *might be* about it. Your birth and your beauty and perhaps your fecklessness: I thought that was the whole of your appeal, at first.

Well. I certainly learned otherwise in due time. Perhaps I am a little foolish, after all.

Make no mistake, you are precious to me. You matter more to me than any other human being I have ever met or can remember. You matter enough that I compromised years of planning in order to storm your father's station in a ludicrous gesture and snatch you into my den, simply because I hadn't slept well without your warm, slight weight at my side. I honestly don't know what I was thinking, except that your absence was an unendurable lack that had to be remedied posthaste.

And if I should ever know that lack again, if your joy in me doesn't last forever... after all, what joy does? What then?

Would you call these musings *love*? They seem incredibly selfish to me, and you would tell me that love isn't meant to be selfish. Love, to you, is some transcendent feeling, pure and perfect. Although I have my own perfections, I certainly can't call myself pure.

Case in point.

Here I am, lingering alone in a lounge on Ceti Station Three and hungrily watching the limbs and curves of one of the most beautiful women I have ever seen. Not a slave—she's what they call a *paramour* around here. A pretty euphemism for one who spreads her legs for coin. I can see why this one would be rather successful in her trade.

In two years, I have taken no lover but you. This is unprecedented for me. Not that I'm a rampaging monster of carnality; I didn't exactly have harems lying around before you arrived, and I'm not some oversexed young buccaneer. But I've never been monogamous, either. The slave girls—never a free woman, never, until you—pleased me for a few nights and were then sent on their way. If they pleased me well, I freed them. There was no attachment. They were beautiful, fuckable, and that was all. If I felt the need, I called someone to fulfill it and then sent her away. I never stuck with the same woman for a month, let alone two years.

I think it's starting to wear on me.

Don't misunderstand me, my dear. I have never known anyone like you, and I know that no one can do for me what you do. I've known slave girls and paramours, yes: like sweet clouds of incense or potent glasses of wine, pleasing but only a distraction. I have never allowed myself to be distracted for long. I've never kept anything around that dulled my judgment.

But then I met you.

The other girls, lissome and perfumed and well-trained, were incense and wine. You were fresh air and cool water. A distraction, to be sure, but life-giving and sustaining in a way I'd never known before. Something essential, something I needed to have and still need to have. Something that has me in return.

But I'm only human, and as a human, after a while I start missing the taste of wine, no matter how pure the water is. I get tired of all this bracing fresh air and just want to sink back on a cushion and breathe in the incense for a while. So you might say I'm going a bit stir-crazy.

All right. I'll be honest. It's even more than that. If I possess you, then you possess me as well. Our power over one another is disturbingly…equal.

I'm not used to equal. I don't like equal. My success is largely thanks to the way I've never tolerated an equal in my general vicinity. And now, watching this beautiful woman who will indulge my every whim, who will follow all my commands without question, I find myself wishing for someone who is not my equal.

She sees me watching. She's a bold one; she tilts her head to the side and lets her green eyes—yours are huge and dark—blink at me. Golden skin, green eyes, tawny hair. Magnificent. She's one of those girls who has trained as a dancer. I can tell by the way she moves. I can imagine her dancing around me, clad only in a few silk scarves, teasing me until I tire of being teased.

Then she saunters forward, keeping her emerald eyes on the ground, only occasionally flashing them at me. She draws closer, and there it is: the scent of incense. She drops to her knees and presses her forehead to the ground.

Boldness sometimes pleases me. It does tonight. You are so rarely bold.

"Good evening," I drawl.

"Good evening, Your Majesty," she murmurs to the floor.

Your Majesty. My own folk have called me that for years. Soon enough, the whole system will. The knowledge intoxicates me. Like wine. I am so very, very close to my goal.

I reach out and stroke my fingers through her hair. As soft as a silken scarf. It would feel as soft as that on my skin. "Do you dance?"

"I do, Your Majesty." Without my bidding, she raises her face. I see no imperfection there.

"What else do you do?" I ask and wonder, in the back of my mind, if I am really about to do this. If I am about to bed another for the first time in two years.

Well—why shouldn't I? You are my lover, not my official consort. We are not married, you and I. And even if we were, who are you to gainsay my desires? Who is anyone? I have my needs. And given who I am, given what I must accomplish, I think it's only fair that they be attended to.

It's not wrong to do this. It can't be. It was never wrong before.

"I will do anything you desire, Your Majesty," she replies. A rote response, and yet it thrills me. This girl is in my power, in a way you have never been since you said, *"Will you really not let me go?"* A paramour wouldn't dare say anything of the kind. She's not my equal. Not in the least.

She can't just leave me if she happens to feel like it.

Gold studs shine in her earlobes, gold bangles clink around her wrists and ankles. Kohl rims her enormous eyes. Her top is filmy and slit nearly down to the navel; her skirt is little more than a loincloth. What a pretty piece she is. She is petite, shorter than you, but her legs are lean, and her whole body is beautifully neat and compact. It would fit well beneath mine. I know exactly how I would hold her down, splay her, use her. And something about those eyes, the pout of those lips, tells me I would not be disappointed.

She's not the first I've ogled. I've been quite restless in the last month. Perhaps it's because we hurtle so quickly toward the completion of my grand design. Perhaps I just have a lot of nervous energy. But of all the women I've watched, she is the loveliest, the most tempting.

"Anything?" I inquire.

"With joy." It's probably not much of an exaggeration. The chance to service the pirate queen would rocket her to the top of her set. Who wouldn't want to spread for me? Or let me spread for them?

This time, I caress her chin. Her skin is petal-soft. Not a trace of topsoil anywhere. Not a single stray leaf. Her enormous eyes fall shut, her lashes moving like butterflies over her cheeks.

Then, all at once, I imagine your face before me.

I see your brown eyes, so faithful and true, widen with dawning horror. Just like they did on the day I left you, on my last day as a slave, when I saw your heart break right in front of me as I told you I was going away. When you realized I was abandoning you, who had only ever sought to love me, to give me a better and safer life than the one you thought I'd led. And you weren't far wrong.

In my mind's eye, your cheeks go pale. You bite your lip as you look every which way just so you don't have to meet my eyes anymore. You twist and wring your hands, wondering why, yet again, you were not worth enough for someone to keep.

I see you leave. I see you leaving me. Because, tired of being left, you would leave first. I am certain of that.

"Go," I say, my voice thick and heavy in my own ears. The paramour looks up at me in clear surprise, and then in fear, wondering if she has offended. I turn away from her and wave my hand irritably. Her sandaled feet tread lightly on the floor as she scurries away.

I stand up, move to look out the window of the lounge, and try to find peace in the sight of my *Crown Lily* in the main docking bay. My heart is beating with astonishing rapidity, so hard that my body actually shakes from it, harder even than it does in battle.

That was close. I almost—I nearly—

I didn't. I did not betray the only person in the universe who would never, will never betray me. Today I have mastered myself in order to protect what I cannot afford to lose. Even if it does leave the bitter taste of denial in my mouth. Who are you to deny me anything, even without knowing it?

Supremely grouchy, I return to my ship, and from there to our quarters. You're bound to be digging around in the garden, so I should have a few hours of peace and quiet before I assemble my generals tonight for the strategy meeting. I need it. I'm out of sorts and could use a glass of…what else?…wine. Or perhaps something stronger.

But as the door to our quarters closes, I hear you moving around in the bedroom. I sigh. So much for solitude.

"Mír?" you call, your happy, inquisitive tone so different from that of the purring paramour. "Is that you?"

Is it me? Who else would it be? Nobody else can get in without your permission. But I tamp my grumbling down and say only, "Of course," as I head for the bedchamber.

"Oh, good!" you say. "I was hoping you'd come back before tonight. I was poking around the station shops today, and I saw something that made me think of you, so I bought it. Well, I tried to buy it, but then they just let me have it! Did you know that nobody will ever let me pay for anything?"

In spite of myself, I smile. "Astonishing," I reply as I enter the room. You're nowhere to be seen, but then I realize you are rummaging around in the bathroom.

"I mean, I would," you say plaintively from behind the door. "You'd think after two years people would know I have good credit."

I nearly laugh. At the end of the day, you are, in fact, adorable.

"But I don't even have to tell them I'm with you," you continue. "Everybody just…knows."

Of course they know. I circulated your picture within hours of your arrival on my ship so that all could see who you were and would understand that if you came to grief, then the guilty party would be a long time dying. I do the same thing each time we move to a new station or world. And you never, ever travel beyond this ship without being discreetly trailed by a member of my Honor Guard. Not a spy, but a protector: It is other people I don't trust. And I will not let you come to harm.

Shouldn't this be enough for you? Shouldn't this be proof of my affection, above and beyond some silly notion of fidelity or monogamy? Would it really be such a horrible infraction if I just found some pretty woman and got it out of my syst—

"Well, anyway," you say, and emerge from the bathroom, peeking shyly at me from beneath the fall of your hair. My eyes go wide.

You are wearing a gown such as you have never worn before: wine red and low-cut, offering your flawless skin and full breasts to me like gifts. The gown is made of silk and chiffon, and it flutters and clings to you like a lover. You wear no jewelry, no ornaments or gems, save for your two bright, dark eyes.

I'm frozen in place. You bite your lip and smile hopefully at me. "You like it?" you say and pluck self-consciously at the filmy skirt. "The lady said it was a nice fit. She said it was a nice color on me, too." The *lady?* "She was really helpful," you add, and all I can think is, *Someone else has seen you like this? Someone's eyes have touched you, and this sight is not for me alone? You have paraded yourself like a paramour?*

"I saw it in a window, and I thought it was really pretty," you continue, heedless of what you are provoking. I'm having a hard time breathing. "I'm not sure I pull it off, but—"

Then you look at me and blink. I wonder what you see in my eyes. Whatever it is, it causes you to blush.

"Do you like it?" you whisper again and draw closer to me, reach out to touch my arms, to take my hands.

"Where have you worn it?" I ask through numb lips.

You frown. "Just here. Well, I tried it on in the store, but I don't think I could walk around the ship wearing this." You chuckle, and then your eyes widen. "You don't want me to, do you?"

I crush you to me, I kiss you so hard it probably hurts, I grab great handfuls of the silk and rub it all over your skin. Oh, God. You are naked beneath. You squeak and kiss me back. That's a good start, but it's only a start. I'm about to fuck you so hard you won't be able to walk for a solar turn. A long turn. For a really *large* star.

You place your hands on my shoulders and pull your mouth away from mine. I moan, but you gently push at me, step out of my embrace. You are blushing brilliantly, like one of your roses, and you drop your eyes as you raise your shaking fingers to the nape of your neck. Once again, I cannot move.

"There's a clasp," you murmur and look back up at me with your shy smile. "Do you want me to...?"

I can't speak, only nod.

"Okay," you whisper, and pop open this invisible clasp. The halter top falls open, burgundy silk collapsing around your pearly skin, revealing your breasts. Exquisite, luscious. I remember the first time I saw them, when I pressed you up against that tree and showed you what your body could do.

This time I won't be stopped. This time, when I haul you to me, I complete the act by throwing us both down on the bed. You beam up at me, bright as daylight, and say, "You do like it!" before threading your fingers into my hair. Your voice bubbles with delight. You're not wearing any perfume, but I smell *you*, getting wetter and more ready by the second, headier than any incense.

I drag you to the edge of the bed and shove up your skirt. Then I drop to my knees, part your legs, and drink. Fresh water and wine, one and the same. I drink until my face is wet with it and you're moaning. I feel you flutter, I feel you clench around my tongue, I hear you give one final cry, and then I feel it too: that deep throb and swallow inside me, that sublime spasm of pleasure, and I have to stop and pant against your thigh until I'm done.

I marvel at it: I can still come just from fucking you. I remember the first time it happened, which, not coincidentally, was that time I had you against the tree. How it shocked me. It should probably have clued me in, though. I should have known what I was getting myself into, that this was a game I could not win, and that when I tried to stop—after you first told me that you loved me—I was bound to fail. How could I resist this? Resist you?

"Oh golly," you whimper, and I laugh breathlessly against your thigh before raising up on shaky knees. I kneel before you, worshiping you as your humble supplicant. And seeing you lying here on our bed, legs spread and bare breasts heaving, I know I would do it again in a heartbeat.

I am not finished with you yet. I slide my arms around your waist, lift you, drag you into the middle of the vast mattress. You put your arms around my neck and murmur agreeably, dazed with passion. You kiss my sticky cheek and give me a woozy, happy smile, brilliant with innocence.

And how do you pull that off, I want to know. How is it that you can submit with such glee to anything I ask of you in bed, no matter how outrageous, and still remain pure as the snow? How is it that you're *you*? Why can't I work you out? Why can't I ever get to the bottom of you, no matter what I do?

I drive my fingers inside you as if I'm trying to do exactly that. You arch up and groan, biting your lip. You are tender down here now, raw and sensitive, but as you writhe and wriggle on my fingers, you don't seem to mind at all.

"Mír," you sob, giving me my name. Not *Your Majesty*. You never call me that, even in front of others. (Although once you called me *Assistant* in bed and got very embarrassed.) What you are to me, I am to you as well. Equal. And you love me.

How could I ever let you go?

I told you I couldn't, once. You didn't really believe me. But in moments like this, when we are so wholly together, I can't imagine allowing you to be parted from me. You are the only one I cannot lose. If you were taken from me, there is no place in the Empire I would leave untouched, no metropolis or scrubby outpost I would not turn inside out, no world I would not rip apart, to find you.

And there is no sacrifice I would not make to keep you, the least of which is a pretty paramour. Why should I want more than this?

"So perfect," I moan, as I always do, as I've never said to anyone but you. "So beautiful."

"Mír," you whisper again as you open yourself, submit to me, and give me my will.

If you enjoyed this short story, check out *The Lily and the Crown* by Roslyn Sinclair, the novel in which Mír and Ari met and fell in love.

All Wrapped Up

by G Benson

"I lost Toby."

Not sure she'd actually heard right, Anna cocked her head at Lane, who was shifting from foot to foot.

"What?"

"Anna, I lost him."

Finally, it all clicked. Leaning slightly to the left, Anna looked out from the living room where they stood and into the kitchen: Toby happily sat in his highchair, cheeks packed with food and blue eyes sparkling, giggling at his sister. Ella sat with her back to Anna, so she had no idea what Ella was doing to make her brother laugh, but she guessed it had something to do with an open mouth of food. Brows pressed together, Anna turned back to Lane. "Uh, he looks pretty *not* lost?"

As Lane shook her head, Anna felt a shiver trickle down her spine. Lane's trembling lip did not help matters. Anna genuinely had no idea what was going on. Five minutes ago, she'd walked into what seemed like happy kids who'd survived going shopping when suddenly Lane had dragged her away.

Words tumbled out of Lane, uncontrolled.

"We were at the store, like I told you we were going to. I thought I had everything under control—my first time alone with him, and I was feeling kind of smug. I mean, you know, you'd been all unsure when I offered to look after them today, and there I was, all…all over it. I had to pick up some stupid gadget for my stupid dad, and I was standing at the counter, and Toby was right next to my leg. I had my hand on his head, and then I reached into my bag to get out my card. I handed it over in all of ten seconds and dropped my hand back down, and he was *gone*. Like, just gone."

Normally, Lane was calm and relaxed, someone solid to turn to in a crisis. "And I looked around," she said, "and I couldn't see him—he's so damn small. How does he move that quickly? And I felt like I was going to be sick, my heart was beating so fast. When I asked the lady if she saw where he went, she just blinked at me uselessly, and I couldn't see him. I called out like four times, and then he giggled, Anna!"

Lane looked so indignant, Anna almost chuckled but then thought better of it. "He giggled like he hadn't just scared the freaking hell out of me. I turned around, and there he was, standing behind a rack of blow dryers. I almost lost him, Anna, and you only just got them back a few months ago. I almost *lost*—"

There was only one thing she could think to do, and Anna wasn't sure if it was going to get her hit. She kissed Lane, hard, and didn't let go of her mouth until she felt Lane relax slightly.

"You didn't lose him. He was right there." She looked Lane straight in the eye.

"Yeah, but what if—"

"But nothing happened. He was right there."

"Anna—"

"Lane. He did that to me a few weeks ago. He hid in a rack of coats, and it was only the damn giggle that let me find him."

Visibly, Lane let out a breath. "Yeah?"

"Yeah. And his sister's no better: When Ella was two, the shopping centre guards had to go find her, because she'd pulled a Houdini on Sally; she was missing ten minutes."

"But, what if he…what if—"

This time, Anna simply pulled Lane against her and wrapped her in a hug. They stayed that way, Anna's head buried into the softness of Lane's neck, until Lane's body relaxed, tension seeming to fade from her muscles.

"Kids are hard work."

In spite of herself, Anna chuckled. "Yeah. They are. They have the ability to scare the crap out of you and make everything really good, all in the same minute."

Lane nodded.

"Lane, you don't have to take them again like today, I really appreciate it, but—"

"No. No, I had fun. After the horror feeling that Toby was gone, we had fun. It was hard, and I hadn't realised how much entertaining they need. Did you know Ella hates picking up her stuff?"

"Oh yeah."

"We had a ten-minute discussion about why it was her job."

"Yeah, I've been working on that one." She tried to put on her best expression of gravitas, pretty sure that showing amusement right now was not the best option here.

"I almost lost Toby."

Slowly, Anna kissed her again, softly. This time, Lane returned it. It was easy to fall into this feeling, to not stop until Lane let go first. When she did, Anna rested their foreheads together. "Lane, you didn't lose him," she said. "You found him."

"Well, I *did* lose him. *Then* I found him."

"Which is all that matters." Still, trying to be reassuring was getting difficult. Laughter threatened to spill out of Anna.

"What?" Lane's eyes narrowed at her, and Anna knew she was busted.

"What, what? You're laughing!"

The whiny tone made Anna smile even harder.

"I'm sorry—you're just adorable when you freak out."

"Am not." Lane's bottom lip was practically sticking out.

"Are too. Normally it's *me* freaking out."

"Shut up."

"Aunty Na!"

Both of them jumped at Ella's shout from the kitchen.

"Aunty *Na!* Toby just threw the last of his potato at me—oh! That means we're both finished. Can we have ice cream now?"

They waited, looking at each other.

"*Please?*"

"There it is." Anna shook her head in mock weariness, then raised her voice. "Only if you've actually finished everything!"

Silence was her answer.

"Lane—thanks for taking them today; I really did appreciate it."

"It was okay—in the end, anyway. Did you get everything for the party?"

"Uh…"

All Lane had to do was cross her arms and raise an eyebrow for Anna to feel sheepish.

90

"I got called in to work! I couldn't." But even Anna knew her protests were falling on deaf ears. "I'll do it tomorrow."

"You better. Don't want you panicking the night before."

"I'm not the type to do that, Lane."

The bark of laughter was sufficient to show Lane's thoughts on that.

"What if—"

"Stop it, Anna."

"But he could—"

"Stop it."

"But Kym—"

"Anna! It's fine. Everything is going to be fine."

Embracing her inner child, Anna *humphed* and leaned back on the couch. Sitting to either side of Anna, Kym and Lane exchanged a glance over their wine glasses and made a poor show of trying not to laugh.

Anna opened her mouth, and Kym clapped her hand over it. Unable to speak, Anna tried to convey her displeasure at the motion by tugging at the offending hand, then glaring at Kym. Finally managing to pry it away, she wrinkled her nose.

"Why does your hand smell like ice cream?"

Looking everywhere but at Anna, Kym gave an overly exaggerated shrug. "It doesn't."

"Uh, yeah it does." In full detective mode, Anna raised her eyebrows. "Did you feed them ice cream?"

"Uh, no. I had some after they went to bed."

"You're my best friend, Kym, but you're a terrible liar. They'd already had some before you got here, and I told you that. You let their big cute eyes wear you down."

Squaring her shoulders, Kym sipped her wine. "What Ella, Toby, and I do when you're not here is between us."

"Oh, really?"

"Really."

"The three of you are a combination that terrifies me."

"You love it."

"I wouldn't say as much, but thank you for taking them tonight, you saved me. I had no time."

"You know I don't mind, goober."

Clearing her throat to attract Kym and Anna's attention, Lane put her glass onto the coffee table and stared Anna down. "Weren't you going to sort everything on Tuesday?"

"Uh, yes, but then I had that emergency, remember? I even had to have Mum pick up Toby, and I was stuck at the hospital until nine."

"And Wednesday?"

"You were going to take them for me, but you got called in, even though it was your day off."

"Right—but I thought your mum was helping yesterday?"

"She had to take Dad to an appointment. So that left the last minute."

With a laugh, Kym nudged her. "You're so type A. Tonight wasn't the last minute; tomorrow morning would be."

Anna raised her eyebrows. "I *am* type A, so, therefore, yes, it was last minute."

A pointed sigh was all Lane had on offer. "I can't believe I went through being traumatised by Toby the other day for nothing. You didn't even get anything done."

"It still helped—"

"Wait." Kym sat forward. "Traumatised by Toby? The chubster with angelic blue eyes?"

The glare Lane pointed at Kym made Anna snicker.

"I *was* traumatised," Lane said. "Those angelic eyes are more demonic sometimes."

"What did he do? Smile you to death?"

"He...*nothing*."

Looking from Anna to Lane, Kym poked Anna in the leg. "What happened?"

"All right, all right." Lane broke in before Anna could answer. "I lost Toby in the shopping centre. Happy now?"

Anna spoke up quickly. "Toby lost *himself* in the shopping centre."

Kym grinned. "You must've been freaking, Lane."

"Yes, I'm glad you find it so amusing. And I wasn't, I didn't—I didn't *freak*."

Taking a quick sip of her wine, Anna shrugged. "You, uh—you freaked a little."

"Anna!"

Laughing loudly, Kym flopped back against the sofa. "I knew it."

"He *hid* from me. What's up with him doing that at the moment?"

"He likes your reaction."

The smirk playing at Kym's lips prompted a pout from Lane.

"Great. What a special thing to share with Toby. Anyway—did you get everything you need?"

"Yeah, but—"

"But what?"

"What if I forgot something?"

Kym rolled her eyes. "You made a list and checked it three times."

"But, we still have to—"

"Anna!" Lane and Kym said in unison, and Anna gave in.

"Yes, okay, we'll sort the rest tonight, and it will be fine."

Kym raised her glass. "Atta girl."

Even still, Anna sat chewing her lip as Lane sighed dramatically. "Anna, it's a two-year-old's birthday party. He won't even remember it."

"Okay, he may not remember it in detail, but these experiences shape kids! We still have to make the pass-the-parcel and goodie bags, the fairy bread, and the cake! Shouldn't *I* be making the cake? We could always cancel the order, and I could make—"

"No!" Lane and Kym both smirked in unison again.

Making a cake could not be *that* hard. Anna huffed and leaned back into the couch again, pushing Lane's hand off her knee, pointedly crossing her arms over her chest. "My cooking is *not* that bad."

Kym choked on her wine, and Lane looked the other way.

Anna gave them both the glare of death, even though they were studiously avoiding her attention. "You both suck."

Putting her wine glass on the table, Lane turned to look at her. "*You* have got to calm down." Lane gestured widely to the bags and bags of things Anna had returned with. "We are going to make the goody bags and games tonight while polishing off this wine. And we have already assembled his damn present. We have blisters to prove it."

"This is a big deal. He's turning two."

Kym rolled her eyes. "And he's going to have an amazing day at the park and play games and eat sugar and have lots of attention and presents. He barely knows what a birthday is. *He* is going to have a great time. *You* need to have another glass of wine and calm the hell down and tell me if I should have said 'no' to a date tomorrow night."

Anna felt her mouth dropping open of its own volition. She looked over at Lane, who was simply staring at Kym, her face a mirror of what Anna imagined her own to be.

Plastering a determined smile on her face, Anna got her act together first. "You—you said 'yes' to a date?"

For months, Anna had been tempted to nudge Kym to get out there but had restrained herself, thinking it probably wasn't the best idea. Pushing her wouldn't help anyone. She would start that process when she was ready and not a minute before.

Disappearing behind her glass, Kym took a long sip of wine.

Across from her, Lane was doing a terrible job of hiding her delight. "Kym… that's awesome."

Kym finally detached from her glass. "Is it, though?"

"It is *such* a good thing." Anna leant over and squeezed her knee.

"I was going to cancel."

"No." As always, Lane's voice was soft, reassuring. "Don't cancel. Just—just think of it as dinner; dinner with a manly shaped friend."

Grateful that Lane was there and knew what to say, Anna nodded. "Exactly. Don't put pressure on it." Kym looked from one to the other as if she wanted them to keep talking. "And if you feel like shit, come over here afterwards and have a Toby cuddle, and we'll consume our body weight in wine and watch *Friends*."

Kym let out a slow breath. "Okay."

"What are you going to wear?" Lane was almost bouncing in her seat. As she visibly paled, Kym's eyes widened again, and Lane quickly backpedalled. "Nope, never mind, that's pressure."

"What *do* I wear!"

This time, Lane looked desperately to Anna.

"You wear your black dress pants and killer black heels with your dark green shirt. Leave the top two buttons undone, and wear it tucked in with that thin black belt."

Lane and Kym blinked at her.

"What? You look good in that outfit."

94

"Okay," Kym said again.

"Do we get to know who he is?" Lane asked.

"I met him at the supermarket. He took the last tub of ice cream I was going for but then insisted I take it."

"Aw!" Anna nudged Lane in the ribs none too subtly. Clearing her throat, Lane pursed her lips. Anna suspected she was holding back an excited grin. "I mean, *continue*."

"Anyway, I ran into him there a few times, and he eventually asked me. I meant to say 'no', but 'yes' fell out, and then he had my number, and now I'm going out tomorrow night."

"Do you need distracting?" Anna could see in Kym's wide eyes that she was near panic, even as Anna had to bite down her excitement.

"Yes, please."

Standing up, Anna started gathering bags. "Right. Lane, you're putting the toys in the goody bags. Kym, you're putting in the lollies."

With a soft thump, Lane slid off the edge of the couch to sit on the floor and pulled more bags towards her. "And what are you going to do?"

"I'm going to make the pass-the-parcel."

Already sorting non-choking-hazard toys into a pile, Kym grumbled under her breath. "Why do you get the fun one?"

"Don't challenge that," Lane said. "She's planned every layer of that thing."

Across from them on the floor, Anna sat with one leg out in front of her and the other bent, foot pressing against her opposite thigh. She grabbed the scissors. "Don't support her idea that I'm being too pedantic about all this, Lane."

Kym shook her head. "Anna. It's a two-year-old's birthday."

"It needs to be perfect."

"Why? It's a birthday. You told me you hate birthdays."

"Because." Anna started tearing opening packets of lollies and various fillers with vigorous intent. "Toby is a kid. He should love his birthday. And Sally always made a really big deal of it all. She'd invite her entire mothers' group and half of Ella's school, and she'd bake for three days." Her voice lowered slightly, fingers fiddling with a chocolate. "At Ella's party, a few weeks before Jake and Sally died in the accident, all the cupcakes were little frogs, and her cake was made to look like an art box. Their parties are—were—always like the ones you see in movies."

Anna started cutting wrapping paper to various sizes, jaw clenching. "And, well, now Toby just has me. I can't bake, I'm the professor of hating birthdays, and I've never thrown a child's party before." She blew some hair out of her eyes. "I want him to have what he would have had if his mum and dad were here."

There was silence except for the sound of Anna's scissors cutting through paper. She could feel their stares on her. Gently, Lane's fingers wrapped around Anna's foot, giving it an affectionate squeeze when Anna looked up with burning cheeks.

"Toby's birthday will be amazing. And he is *incredibly* lucky to have you. Your brother would be so happy to see what a great job you're doing with his kids."

Throat tight, Anna managed a small smile.

Kym poked her in the leg. "And Toby's getting a *Thomas* cake; you just didn't make it. Let's not joke, Anna: that's a good thing."

A plastic whistle flew past Kym's ear.

"Hey! Don't throw your party supplies. It's not like you bought enough to supply four schools or anything."

"Kym, I'll put you on games duty tomorrow."

That shut her up.

Her chin thrust out in victory, Anna went back to her paper. "That's what I thought."

Lane smirked and leaned over Kym to top up all their glasses on the coffee table. She raised hers up in toast: "To Kym and her date we're not mentioning, to Anna and the first birthday party she's in charge of, and to Toby, who has no idea what any of the weeks of effort mean—Oh, and to Ella, who is more excited than everyone else combined."

Laughter rang out as glasses clinked together to celebrate the night ahead, of organising a *Thomas the Tank Engine*-themed two-year-old's birthday party.

Hours later, they all staggered upstairs, exhausted and a little tipsy. Anna checked on Toby and Ella while Kym stumbled blurrily past her to the guest room. When Anna walked into her bedroom, she smiled to see Lane already under the covers. After brushing her teeth, she crawled into bed, the euphoria of soft sheets enfolding her. With a chuckle, she remembered Kym going on about 'bedgasms' the week before. Nothing beat this feeling. Falling next to Lane, who was half-asleep lying on her side, Anna sighed contentedly as Lane blindly groped around, grasping Anna's hand from behind and pulling her against her back. Wrapped around the warmth of Lane, the band around her chest eased. Eyes already closing, Anna curled around Lane's back, kissing warm skin under her lips as Lane mumbled sleepily.

"What, Lane?"

Voice husky, Lane murmured, "All good romances start in the supermarket."

Humming her agreement, Anna buried her face into Lane's hair and fell asleep almost instantly.

What felt like only hours later, a noise that no one wanted to hear that early in the morning assaulted them.

Children. Very, very awake children.

Hair everywhere and squinting from the brightness, Anna sat bolt upright. Next to her, a groaning noise was Lane's only contribution as she rolled over and pulled the pillow over her head.

Anna's bleary eyes finally focused on Ella, holding on to Toby's hand and kneeling on the edge of the bed, both of them giggling and jumping.

"Aunty Na! You're awake, and it's Toby's birthday!"

If one didn't know better, they would assume it was Ella's birthday.

"Is it?" Grinning, Anna pulled him onto her lap, tickling him and planting kisses all over his face and head. He squealed and squirmed until she stopped, and he sat up, grinning and flushed, hair like a nest atop his head. "Happy birthday, little man!"

"Birfday."

Attempts to smooth his hair failed, so she cupped his cheeks, pulling him in to kiss his forehead. "Yup, it's your birthday."

Wasting no time, Ella crawled up the bed and flopped onto Lane, who made a loud "oof" noise without moving or otherwise acknowledging Ella's presence. Sprawled over Lane, Ella said none too quietly, "Wake up, Lane!"

A whimper came from under the pillow.

"Wake up!"

Finally, Lane seemed to realise there was no escaping. Wild and tangled hair emerged from under the pillow when she pulled it away from her face. Anna had the urge to bury her hands in it and kiss her. With a glance at the two kids, though, she realised that at this rate, she'd have to wait until tonight.

"I'm awake." Not even attempting to sit up, Lane turned her gaze onto the bundle in Anna's lap.

"Happy birthday, Toby!"

Far too enthusiastically for morning, Toby waved his hands at her. Anna wrapped her arms around him and hugged him against her. "Do you know what birthday boys get?"

Before anyone else could say a word, Ella beat them to it: "Presents!"

"Yes, Toby gets presents, but he also gets birthday breakfast."

"Panks!"

That word was always a disaster. Smiling, Anna repeated, "Yup, pancakes."

Trying again, he said, "Panks." He nodded very seriously, as if there had been a difference.

"Did I hear 'pancakes'?"

Kym rounded the doorway into the room and flopped on the end of the bed, both Ella and Toby crawling over to land on her in a hug.

"Whoa! Morning, guys. And happy birthday, Toby!"

With a grin, she blew a raspberry on his neck and he squealed, crawling back, giggling, to Anna. Changing his mind partway and heading for Lane instead, he lay on her and snuggled into her neck. Lane rubbed his back, and he wiggled closer against her.

Anna patted his bum, which was sticking up in the air. "Mister Toby, how did you get out of bed?"

A giggle was his only answer as he burrowed further into Lane, who did nothing to discourage him.

Another giggle, higher pitched and telling, made Anna turn around to raise her eyebrows at her niece. "Ella?"

Green eyes widened. "Yes?"

"How did Toby get out of his cot?"

Kym suddenly became extremely interesting as Ella, her lips curving up in spite of herself, made zero eye contact and played instead with Kym's fingers. "Um…"

Making Ella crack was easy. All Anna had to do was stare at her. It worked every time, even when she just felt Anna's glare. Ella lasted all of five seconds, and Kym visibly smothered a laugh.

"Well, I woke up, and I was so excited for Toby's birthday. So I maybe went into his room and woke him up."

Yet another giggle came from Toby. Lane poked his ribs and made him yelp and laugh loudly.

"So how did he get out?"

"Uh—"

"Did you help him again?"

Ella squirmed. "I maybe, last time, helped him, but he did it mostly himself. And this time, he kind of just climbed out after I woke him up and sang 'Happy Birthday' to him."

With a heavy sigh, Anna said, "Great. I was waiting for that."

Ella looked up at her, visible relief across her features. "You were? I'm not in trouble?"

"Not really, missy. It's normal he'd learn to get out."

Kym wrapped her arms around Ella and tickled her. "It's a good thing. You just helped the process, Ella."

Pushing at Kym's fingers and giggling, Ella's eyes glinted with mischief. "I'm his big sister. I like teaching him to get into trouble."

There were times like this where Anna was grateful that somehow, Ella had still stayed *Ella* after her parents' death. More contemplative, quieter at times, but still her. She squeezed Ella's knee. "That's true. Well, lucky for *you*, Toby's present is about that."

"What did you get him?"

"Hmm, I don't know. Maybe we should have breakfast before we do presents."

Ella shook her head, and Toby sat up, interested in the conversation now that a word he knew well had been mentioned. Ella gave her a pleading look. "No, Aunty Na, presents. *Please.*"

Never in the history of pleases had there ever been such an elongated one.

Looking from Anna to Ella and back, Toby then pushed off Lane's stomach, making her groan loudly in protest as a little knee sunk in. He ended up on Anna's lap and knelt in it, smiling, dimples prominent. "Na, pease?"

Anna wrapped him up in her arms and scooted to the edge of the bed, standing up and moving him onto her hip. "All right! Everyone to the guest room."

Easily scooting off the bed, Ella said very seriously, "Don't be silly; it's Kym's room."

With a groan, Kym followed Ella out. "Kym's room?" She huffed. "I need to get me a life."

A pillow hit her in the back, and Kym turned to glare at Lane. With a shrug, Lane grinned. "Just move in and admit defeat, Kym."

"That's rich."

"Excuse me?" Lane asked. "What was that?"

Kym smirked. "That's rich, directed at me, the woman who barely sleeps here anymore, from the woman who probably can't remember the last time she slept two nights in a row at her own apartment."

"I—but, you—oh, shut up."

"Hm. Nice comeback."

They followed Anna, Ella, and Toby to the guest room. After sliding a squirming and delighted Toby to the ground, Anna joined the others in watching him run the few steps to the bed they had assembled in there to keep it hidden from him when he woke up.

He stopped at the end and stared, taking in the *Thomas the Tank Engine* toddler bed. It was bright blue and red and in the shape of Thomas, and Anna quite possibly had spent a lot more money on it than she should have for a bed that would last him five years at a maximum.

Though right then, the look of utter delight on his face made it worth it. A knot formed in her stomach as she watched his bright eyes, so reminiscent of her brother's, as they stared in utterly transparent disbelief.

"Happy birthday, Toby!" they all said together. Ella was bouncing and looked just as happy as Toby.

"Cool!"

Turning to look at Anna, Toby asked, "Mine?"

Anna nodded. "It's all for you, Toby. A big-boy bed."

With his eyes back on the bed, he ran his hand over the wide *Thomas* face. Slowly, the smile disappeared from his lips. He looked from the bed to Anna. As one, they all stood aside while he walked past them and stared down the hallway. He looked down, then back at his new bed, then down the hall again.

Eventually, he focussed back on Anna. "Bed!" He looked to the *Thomas* bed and pointed at it. "Mine?"

And finally it clicked.

He was looking at her as if she was a crazy lady putting his bed in the wrong room. Easily, she scooped him up to her hip. "I know; it's in the guest room."

Ella's voice chimed in. "Kym's room!"

With a nod, Anna said, "Right. Sorry, Ella—Kym's room."

"Oi!"

"It's in Kym's room so it would be a surprise," she told him, acting as if she hadn't heard Kym. "We'll move it into your room after your party, okay?"

For a moment, he eyed her, until a grin plastered on his face. "Toby's bed!"

The lisp on his *s* was cuter than it should have been. Her brother had lisped for years.

"Exactly. Toby's bed. Now, breakfast?"

Ella took Lane and Kym's hand and dragged them down the hallway.

"You're cooking, though. Right, Nurse Lane?"

Ignoring Anna's indignant "hey," Lane said, "I sure am."

They made pancakes, with Ella helping and Toby thinking he was helping.

When Lane and Kym gave Toby his presents, his delighted shouts filled the house. Once he got the idea of ripping the wrapping paper off, his little fingers made quick work and quick mess of it all. Ella had chosen Toby a new backpack for day care that came with pencils and stationery inside. It was something Anna had the sneaking suspicion Ella knew she'd end up using herself, as Toby wasn't yet big on colouring in. A new box of toddler Legos from Kym was upended in seconds and spread over the floor, the colours brightening the normally dull white linoleum. At one point, Toby wandered into the kitchen with the *Thomas the Tank Engine* pyjamas Lane had bought him pulled on back to front and clutched at Anna's legs, flushed and grinning. She ran her fingers through his silky hair, grateful that, at least for now, he was having a good birthday.

"Hello, big birthday boy!" came calling down the hallway just as they were sitting down to breakfast, and Toby squealed. Anna had just managed to get one of his legs into his high chair, but as Andrew wheeled in a bright green tricycle, Sandra right behind him, all hope of him sitting vanished. Instead, they ate standing around the room as Ella taught Toby to use his newest present.

The rest of the morning passed with getting Toby's new bed into his room, now that Anna's parents were there to help, and dismantling the old cot. As soon as his new bed was ready for him, Toby grinned at Anna and lay down, pulling his new blanket up and completely over himself. All that was left was a wriggling lump under the cover.

There was a pang in her stomach as she looked at the pieces of the cot on the floor.

He was growing up.

A hand cupped her shoulder, and she nearly jumped. Her father stood behind her, an odd look playing over his features as he watched the lump wriggle further down the bed.

She put her hand over his and watched Toby.

"Right now, it's like I'm watching Jake when we put him in his first bed."

The grip she had on his fingers tightened. For a moment, she almost didn't breathe, as if she could scare him off with the slightest movement.

"Jake called me when they got Ella in her first bed, asking if it was legal to sedate kids."

Andrew gave a startled laugh. "My son did that? Really?"

"It was the second week, and the new freedom meant getting her to stay in her bed was a nightmare. He called saying they found her in the kitchen playing with her tea set at two a.m. He said that if he had to sit down and pretend to be 'Mrs Bird' in the early hours of the morning one more time to pacify her into going back to bed, he'd scream."

"He'd do that with her?"

She nodded—of course he had. Her brother had done anything for his kids. "It settled after a few weeks, but Sally sent me a photo of him on the kitchen floor downstairs wearing a purple feather scarf and blearily eating fake biscuits."

Andrew gave a small chuckle, and his hand stayed on her shoulder, as heavy as a promise.

As Toby became bored with what he was doing, he scooted on his bottom to the gap at the end, past the small guardrail that ran along the edge of the bed. After a moment of staring at it with a furrowed brow, he figured it out, managing to slide down and grin at them, his sense of triumph unmistakable. With a final pat of the sheets, he walked up to take Anna's offered hand.

"Ella?" His *l*'s still came out more like *y*'s.

"Want to find your sister?"

Toby nodded, then held out his hand to his grandfather, who took it, giving him a small smile. "Ganpa."

Andrew's smile only grew as they were tugged downstairs.

Giving up on getting Toby down for his usual late morning rest, they instead all sat on the front porch, watching Toby ride his tricycle up and down the front path while Ella followed on her scooter.

Her leg bouncing slightly, Anna asked her mother, "And you picked up the cake?"

"For the third time, 'yes'. And I brought the cupcakes I made."

"Sorry, just—what if all the mums there judge me? What if I throw a crappy birthday party?"

Kym snorted into her mug. "As if."

"What does that mean?"

"You spent three weeks researching toddler's birthday parties on the web, Anna. You made lists. You bought half the grocery store and the toy store. We were up until all hours sorting the prizes and the bags and everything." She raised her eyebrows at her. "We've checked everything off list one."

From where she stood leaning against the railing next to Andrew, Sandra coughed. "List one?"

Anna's cheeks warmed as Lane fought through her laughter. "There's three lists: *pre*, *during,* and *post*."

Andrew joined in, and immediately, Sandra cocked her head at him. "Uh, excuse me, why are you laughing? You made an itinerary for Anna's first week home from the hospital that you expected the newborn to follow."

Lane snorted, and Kym elbowed her, biting her lip to smother what Anna assumed was a laugh. Rubbing the back of his neck, Andrew looked anywhere but at them.

With a tightly pressed grin, Anna turned back to Lane and Kym. "See, there's a reason I am how I am."

Amusement brightened Sandra's expression. "Honey, if you expect to have time to check off a list during a toddler's birthday, you're in for a horrible shock."

"I was at Ella's parties; there'll be time."

Sandra smirked, a look that didn't quite fit her. "You think there's time because you were being cool aunty giving awesome gifts and playing with them? Sally was running around like a headless chook ensuring soccer Mums didn't bitch each other to death, that no one fell over and damaged themselves, and that the kids didn't implode from too much sugar."

Anna's eyes went wide, and Sandra sipped her tea with a grimace. "That probably wasn't the calming thing I was meant to say."

Lane and Kym snickered.

At one thirty, they all walked to the park, except for Andrew, who drove the car filled with the party supply boxes they'd packed the night before. While Toby and Ella played, the adults blew up balloons and hung them with streamers all over the barbecue area. Anna clutched her clipboard and gave her mother a smug look.

Infuriatingly, her mother only responded with a benign smile.

Come two o'clock, people were arriving, and the park filled with screaming and laughter.

Anna had invited some of Ella's friends from school and pretty much the entire day care population. Pretty soon, she didn't have time to even think of her list. As Toby pulled apart wrapping paper, Anna had to ensure everyone got a 'thank-you', that food was distributed, and that introductions were made. It was hectic and exhausting, and why did children squeal so much? Anna barely remembered to sit. It wasn't until Lane floated past and pushed a couple of the cut-up sandwiches into her hand with a chuckle that Anna realised an hour had already passed and she hadn't eaten anything since a few pancakes early that morning.

During games time, the various ages of the kids clashed, with the older ones who understood the rules exhibiting increasing signs of frustration at the younger ones who kept wanting to play with the boxes the presents came in or throw wrapping paper at each other. One red-cheeked five-year-old even hit his younger brother on the head with a sauce bottle. But eventually, prizes were handed out, and Anna gave silent thanks that there were only three incidents of sugar-hyped tears.

As she stood over the cake box in exhaustion, Anna pulled it open with a long, relieved breath. Cake meant it was almost over. Next year, she would take Toby to the cinema or pay her mother a million dollars to do it for her.

"Hey."

The soft words trickled over her, and she leant back against Lane's chest. "Hey," she said. "Fancy seeing you here."

When Anna finished putting candles on the cake, careful not to destroy the overpriced design printed upon it, Lane stepped out from behind her, gazing at her with a soft look.

"You okay?"

Across the park, Ella was patiently showing Toby how to use the bubble blower someone had bought him. She had a crowd of kids around her, all in their best party clothes, jaws hanging open as the bubbles flowed out around them. Inevitably, they started trying to slap and step on them as the bubbles flurried in the wind.

"Yeah. I'm okay."

Lane nodded. "It's been a great party."

"It has." Yet, Anna looked back down at the cake, even as Lane pushed Anna's hair back off her shoulders and rested her fingers atop the dampness along Anna's neck. "What is it?"

How did Lane always know?

"For Toby's first birthday, Sally made a bunny because he was obsessed with them. And now it's trains, but they knew about his love for those. Next year, though, it'll be something new. Maybe dinosaurs. Maybe princesses, or princess-dinosaurs—whatever he wants. And they'll miss it." She gave a shrug and picked up a lighter. "It's all just weird."

Those fingers stayed against her neck, soft and reassuring. "But you're okay?"

This time, Anna smiled at her. "Yeah." She lit the candles and looked back at Lane. "I really am."

Lane leaned forward and gave her a quick kiss.

When they pulled apart, Anna was still smiling. "Thanks for putting up with my crazy."

"I like your crazy."

"And I love you."

Lane grinned. "Me too."

"Ready?"

"Ready."

Anna picked up the cake, and they walked towards the main bench, Lane starting to sing and everyone joining in, the kids flocking to the table. Wide-eyed, Toby was held over the cake by Sandra, his cheeks covered in cupcake icing. When they finished singing, Lane's arm around Anna's waist, Ella showed him how to blow out the candles while everyone clapped and cheered. Toby looked proud, even though he couldn't have any idea why.

The candles were lit another six times so all the kids could have a turn.

Cake was passed out, and everyone said how amazing it was. Someone even congratulated Anna on how well she had made it. Anna didn't correct them, smiling sweetly and saying, "Thanks. Old recipe."

Before Ella could completely open her mouth, Kym clapped her hand over it and gave her a wink, pulling her hand away to reveal a huge grin on Ella's face as she caught on in an unsubtle, six-year-old way. She tried to wink back at Kym but only managed an exaggerated blink.

By the time four rolled around, kids were starting to crash, and people were drifting away. At four fifteen, everyone had left. Thankfully, with the five of them remaining, it wasn't long before the clean-up was done. Anna was putting some Tupperware into a storage box when Sandra walked up next to her, adding a cupcake rack to the contents and sliding her arm around Anna's shoulder. Gratefully, Anna leant into her. Nearby, Ella propelled herself sleepily back and forth on the swing, the bright yellow party dress she had chosen covered in grass stains from playing soccer with her friends. She looked to see if Toby was still where he had been for the last half hour. There he was, curled up on Lane's jacket where he had put himself and promptly fallen asleep, hands and face covered in cake. At her mother's squeeze, she turned her head and kissed Sandra.

A cheeky expression more befitting Toby crossed her mother's face. "How'd your list go?"

Anna groaned. "Yes, okay, you were right."

"I'm your mother, I'm always right."

In the swing next to Ella, Lane sat pumping her feet, getting her swing up into the air, and Anna smiled at them. Kym soon began pushing Ella to let her compete with Lane and see who could swing higher.

She turned back to her mother. "You are."

"Well, that was far too sincere."

Anna gave a shrug and kept her gaze on the swing set. "You said I could do this."

More tightly than before, Sandra squeezed Anna to her. "As your mother, I am biased, but I think you can do anything."

At the face Anna made, Sandra laughed, dropping her arm. "Let me know if you still think you're coping tomorrow after trying to keep Toby in his new bed, especially since he's currently having a late afternoon nap."

"Oh God."

"It's karma." The delight in her tone did little to make Anna feel better. "When we got you in yours, you used to go into Jake's room in the middle of the night and wake him up by patting his face. Only, we clued in and tried to stop you. I could never get you back to sleep, but whenever your father was home, you became like butter. He'd pick you up and put you back in bed and read to you until you fell asleep. When he was gone, you were a horror."

Watching the man in question pull down streamers, a warmth spread through Anna. "I didn't know that."

"Oh please. As a toddler, you were a typical daddy's little girl."

Grabbing a box, Anna held that information close.

When Sandra and Andrew finally made it into their car, they waited to give Kym a lift, while Kym hugged Anna as if she was never going to let go. When she finally pried herself off Anna, Anna grinned and elbowed a bouncing Lane standing next to her.

"We aren't making a big deal," Anna's face arranged itself into what she hoped was a neutral expression. "But just—have some fun, okay?"

After untangling herself from Lane's hug, Kym nodded, her lips pressed together in a thin line. "I'll try. That, or I'll be at your house with wine in a few hours."

Anna squeezed her shoulder. "Either one."

As she walked away, Anna thought she looked small and a little lost.

"Kym!" When Kym looked back, Anna waved a dismissive hand at her. "You could wear a sack, and he will think you're gorgeous. Strut your stuff tonight."

With a wave and a coy, definitely cheerier expression, Kym slipped into Anna's parents' car.

A sniff made her turn to Lane, who then sniffed theatrically again. "Our little girl is all grown up."

Laughing, Anna grabbed her shirt, pulling Lane against her, trying to kiss the smirk off her lips. When she withdrew from the embrace, Lane grinned and grabbed her, bringing Anna to lips that were soft against her own.

"If you two are going to be gross, can we go home now?"

Hands on her little hips, Ella stared at them with her eyebrows raised. Letting Lane go, Anna poked her tongue out. "Yeah. Let's go home."

Anna ruffled Ella's hair and walked over to Toby, scooping him up and holding him against her chest, his head on her shoulder. The weight of him in her arms was solid, almost heavy. He grew too fast to keep up with, surprising her every day with new words and new skills. There were moments he took her breath away as he'd look up from an accomplishment, eyes lit up like her brother's once had as he discovered a new talent.

Now in her arms, Toby murmured but didn't wake up. His eyelashes left shadows against his cheeks, and he smelt like grass and sugar and baby shampoo. At that moment, watching Ella take Lane's hand and start chattering, Anna didn't care that she had two overly tired, sugared kids to try and settle that night.

There wasn't much else she'd rather be doing.

With Ella's sticky hand in Anna's left hand and the right under Toby's bottom in order to carry him, they started the walk home. Between Lane and Anna, Ella swung their hands back and forth.

"Nurse Lane?"

"Yeah, Ella?"

Lane winked at Anna over Ella's head.

"You're staying tonight, right?"

"Yeah?"

"Can we have pancakes in the morning?"

With a snort, Anna grinned at Lane, who looked back down at Ella. A smile played at the edges of her lips, and Lane let go of Ella's hand to wrap an arm around her small shoulders.

"Sure."

If you enjoyed *All Wrapped Up*, check out *All the Little Moments* to really get to know Anna, Lane, Ella, and Toby.

No Going Back

by Cheyenne Blue

"The world number one does not lose in the first round of a grand slam tournament." Her coach crouched beside the ice bath, his gaze dispassionate on Alina's nearly naked body.

Alina sank lower in the frigid water and tried not to shiver as the cold bit into her aching muscles. "This number one just did." She shrugged, striving for a nonchalance she didn't feel. Nausea rose in her throat, forced up by the crushing disappointment of her failure and she blinked fast to control the tears that threatened. "It happens."

No chance of a kind or consoling word from Anatoly. Her coach treated her like a machine. A *thing* to be fuelled efficiently, brought to peak fitness, and doubtless discarded once it was no longer profitable. Her emotions were irrelevant.

Anatoly's lips tightened to a thin line. "The number one ranking is now achievable for five players from this tournament. Jelena Kovic or Simona Halep have only to reach the semi-finals. Serena Williams can retake the ranking if she wins the final."

"Even Serena has lost in the first round of a grand slam." Alina winced as her aching hip spasmed. Was this the start of her slide in the rankings? She forced her mind away from the negative thinking. That was a loser's mindset. And she was a winner—next time. She had to be.

"Serena's loss was the 2012 French Open. Not since then. You would do well to study her determination." Anatoly rose, his face a blank mask. "Tonight, we will analyse your loss, pinpoint where you went wrong. Tomorrow, we will work on your weaknesses."

Alina closed her eyes momentarily. She hadn't had a day away from tennis in nearly three months. Even the off-season—December—had been spent at Delacourt Academy in Florida. She'd spent Christmas Day doing footwork drills. She clenched her fist under the water. She would *not* spend another evening with Anatoly listening as he picked apart her game, her tennis skills, her fitness, and then, invariably, he would focus on the personal—her looks and what she needed to do to gain better sponsorship. No. Anatoly could go hang himself.

"I have a date. Mikhail and I are going for dinner." It wasn't true, but she was sure she could talk Mikhail into it. His first-round match wasn't until late the following day.

Anatoly grunted. "Be back early. I've reserved a practice court for 6:00 am."

She didn't reply, simply sank lower so that the ice water circled her neck. It was as frozen as her heart.

Mikhail was predictably delighted when Alina asked him to dinner. Men. She snorted to herself. A tiny hint of flirtation, the barest insinuation that this time he wouldn't be going home alone, and he fell into her palm like vending machine candy. As the number eight seed, he was expected to cruise through his match. No doubt a sexual dalliance the night before wouldn't put him off his game.

She tightened her lips. That was never going to happen.

One advantage of the Australian grand slam being held in Melbourne was that there was no shortage of fantastic restaurants. Mikhail's choice though, was as plain as could be. A steakhouse, where she already knew he would order the largest steak on the menu, cooked well done, and served with a mountain of green salad, no dressing.

She arrived first, and was shown to a prominent table in the centre of the room. The restaurant was almost full and there was a background buzz of chatter and the subdued chink of cutlery. Alina fixed a smile to her face and strutted to her seat. It seemed the room fell quiet as she walked past. Every eye in the room was on her: assessing, caressing, lusting, scathing, dismissing. The world number one, dumped out like a rank qualifier. The censor in the gazes cut her like grains of sand on a windy beach.

She sat, ordered a sparkling mineral water, and pretended to study the menu. Mikhail was late. Where was he? She took a swift glance around the room under the guise of summoning the waiter. No Mikhail. Most of the patrons had returned to their meals, except for one woman who, like her, sat alone. Her black hair hung loose in an asymmetrical bob, and her copper skin was set off beautifully by the cream-coloured dress she wore.

The woman was, quite simply, stunning. She sipped a glass of wine and glanced around the room as if she, too, was waiting for someone. Her gaze caught Alina's and stopped. The woman's mouth tipped up at one corner and she raised her glass to Alina.

Alina looked away. Suddenly it hurt to breathe through the tightness in her chest. Caught looking. Her nerves jangled and she resisted the urge to glance around the restaurant to see if anyone else had noticed the interest in her gaze. Instead, she looked back at the menu, flicked a page, and studied food choices she had no interest in eating. Fillet steak or chicken in mushroom sauce? She didn't care. Food was fuel for her body, seldom more. She ate the nutritionally balanced diet that her health and fitness coach recommended. Years of lean meat, protein, salad, and platefuls of pasta the night before a match. No dessert. No wine. Even her mother's pierogies were a distant memory. Except for the other night, when she'd woken from a dream of potato and chive pierogies and sour cream sauce. The hunger pangs had made it hard to sleep after that. Other players went out to dinner together. Sometimes, by chance, Alina ended up in the same restaurant and she'd seen them: a group of laughing girls, drinking wine, ordering lavish desserts even. Alina's lips compressed. That had never been something she'd done. Maybe that was why she was number one in the world and they were not.

When she looked up again, the black-haired woman was still staring at her. She smiled and it seemed as if she might rise to her feet to approach Alina. Then another woman hurried up to the table and bent to kiss the woman's cheek. The moment passed.

Alina looked down at the tablecloth, at the heavy silver cutlery. What would she have done? And why was she even wondering? The woman was probably a tennis fan, someone who'd recognised her, nothing more. She'd probably been summoning her courage to ask for an autograph.

"Alina." Mikhail stood next to the table. She hadn't seen him approach. He stood waiting, as he always did, for her to rise and kiss him. Other players might want to pass unrecognised during a tournament. Not Mikhail—he thrived on the recognition.

She stood, kissed his cheek, and let him usher her into her seat as if she hadn't just risen from it a second ago.

"You look stunning." Mikhail covered her hand with his own. "That blue dress is my favourite."

"Thank you. You look delectable too. Very handsome."

"We make a good couple." He tapped the menu. "Have you already decided?"

She nodded. Mikhail summoned the waiter and ordered fillet steak, well done, and salad, no dressing. Exactly as she'd known he would. The waiter was looking at her patiently. Chicken or steak? Did it even matter? She ordered steak simply to avoid a lecture on nutrition from Mikhail.

He was a good conversationalist, which was one reason she was happy to spend time in his company, and he knew more of the tour gossip than she did.

"Michi Cleaver is now sponsored by Nike," he said. "Watch out. She may be after your number one ranking."

"There's not a player alive who isn't," Alina replied. The tender steak turned to cardboard in her mouth. Someone was likely to take the top spot at the end of this Australian Open. Not Michi, not yet, but one of the others. She looked down at her plate. Maybe she should have spent the evening with Anatoly, and let him pick apart her game. If she was to retake the top spot, she'd need all the help she could get.

"—over there." Mikhail's head tilt was barely noticeable. "She hasn't taken her eyes off us."

She peeked where he indicated. The black-haired woman was looking in their direction. What did Mikhail mean: write about? Then the woman turned to her companion and her very classical profile sparked faint recognition. "Where have I seen her before?"

Mikhail reached across the table, took both of Alina's hands, and brought one to his lips. "That caught her attention. She's Tova Wright, the sports journalist. Magazine pieces, not the usual run-of-the-mill post-match interviews."

That must be it. The press often had access to the players' areas. No doubt she had seen Tova Wright there. Alina glanced again. Just quickly. No one would think anything of it.

The glance she'd intended stretched as Tova's gaze held Alina pinned. Her shallow breathing barely moved her chest, and she reached for her water glass to give her shaking fingers something to do. Tova's expression was curious, and it flicked from Alina to Mikhail and back again. A tiny frown wrinkled Tova's forehead. Her lips curved in a faint smile, as if she knew all there was to know about Alina.

A sick feeling churned Alina's stomach. It was as if Tova knew a secret.

Even though Alina had been summarily dismissed from the Australian Open, as the number one ranked player, she was comped a luxury hotel room for the first week. There was nowhere else she had to be, and Anatoly could put her through the refined torture he called "training" anywhere. It made financial sense to remain in Melbourne.

Alina headed to the practice courts. Her racquet bag weighed heavy on her shoulder, and even at nine in the morning she sweated lightly from the scorching summer sun. It would be sub-zero at home, the ground frozen to a depth that wouldn't melt for several months yet. She rotated her shoulders, enjoying the heat of the sun.

Alina pushed through a knot of fans, some holding programs and pens in the hope of an autograph. She didn't stop; she seldom did. Fans thought they owned you. They were just another distraction she didn't need.

Anatoly waited for her, and for the next hour, he made her work on her smash, lobbing ball after ball high into the air for her to smash back.

Alina fought to keep her expression neutral as Anatoly then proceeded to dismantle every one of her returns, one by one, criticising her footwork, court position, line up, and execution.

"You are positioning yourself too far back from the ball." His eyebrows lowered in a frown. "It is the sign of a lazy player."

She gritted her teeth so hard her jaw ached. Lazy. She was many things; lazy was not one of them. But arguing the point had never worked in the past. Anatoly demanded total obedience to his routines.

He reeled off a list of strength exercises to keep her occupied during the afternoon. The number of repetitions alone would deaden her mind.

I can't do this. Alina drew in a deep breath. Her legs ached, and the racquet was a dragging weight in her hand. She summoned her courage and lifted her chin. "I am not feeling too well. I will do as many as I am able, but I intend to have a few hours off this afternoon to rest. I will see you tomorrow." Without waiting for his answer, she spun on her heel and marched back to the bench. She stuffed her racquets back in the bag, wiped her face with her towel and slung it around her neck. No doubt Anatoly was staring at her back, gasping like a stranded salmon. In the five years of their professional relationship, she had never walked out on a coaching session.

Alina flashed a small smile to the fan who held the gate open for her.

"Alina." The voice was low and mellow. Even the rather nasal Australian accent was softened at the edges.

Alina slowed and turned toward the voice.

The dark-haired woman let the gate swing closed and held out her hand with a smile. "I'm Tova Wright, sports journalist. I'm pleased to meet you. I saw you last night in the restaurant."

Alina stopped. Up close and in casual clothes, Tova was more intriguing than she had been last night. Her hair gleamed in the sun, and she wore a scarlet polo shirt with a pair of white tailored shorts. The glow on her skin seemed natural. "I remember. My companion told me who you are."

Tova smiled, showing slightly uneven white teeth. It added to her natural look. "Then maybe Mikhail told you I like to profile sportspeople in-depth. Interesting people, not just jocks."

A knot of teenage girls approached, giggling and nudging each other. They clutched oversize tennis balls and marker pens. They were too close, inside her personal space, with their grins and hopeful faces. Alina took a step back and moved so that Tova was between her and the fans. "Walk with me to the locker room," she said to Tova, and started off without waiting to see if Tova agreed.

Quick footsteps sounded on the path and Tova drew alongside. "Most players like to engage with fans, at least some of the time."

"I prefer not to. It makes me uncomfortable, to be honest." She clutched her racquet bag tighter to her body and snuck a glance sideways at Tova.

Tova raised an eyebrow. "Why so? You're world number one. This tournament aside, you've got a fantastic record. Thirty-odd million in career prize money. Is the adoration so strange?"

"People will always look up to the most unlikely people. But I'm happy for it not to be me." The more people knew about her, it seemed the more they wanted to know. *Keep them out. Keep flying below the radar.*

"You don't engage much with your peers on the tour either." Tova's voice was musing, not accusatory. "I wonder why that is?"

"It dulls my competitive edge. It must be very hard to demolish a friend in a match." Alina stopped outside the door to the competitors' area. "If you'll excuse me, I need a shower. It was good meeting you, Tova." She swiped her pass and stepped inside, closing the door behind her, and blew out a deep breath. She wasn't sure why, but Tova—and her questions—unsettled her. Questions to which Alina was sure Tova knew the answers to, maybe even before Alina did herself.

The door opened again, and Tova stepped through. She held up her own pass. "You don't get rid of me so easily."

"What do you want?" Alina put a layer of coolness in her voice. *Keep her at a distance.*

Tova rested one hand on the wall, effectively cutting off Alina's exit.

Alina drew herself up, tilted her head, and raised an eyebrow.

"I want to interview you, Alina Pashin. You're an intriguing person, quite apart from your incredible tennis talent. I'd like to shadow you for a few days while you're in Melbourne."

"Such requests need to go through my agent. If you'll excuse me." Alina brushed past Tova's arm. Tova was too perceptive. Her questions, innocuous as they seemed on the surface, put her off balance. It was like being poised on a precipice, waiting for Tova's next question, the one that would surely make her fall.

"I've approached your agent. He knocked me back."

"Then why are you here? You already know the answer." Alina stopped and turned to face Tova.

The corridor was an artery for the Australian Open. Players moved swiftly to and from the locker rooms. Coaches, tournament officials, and umpires hurried to wherever they had to go. Nerves prickled Alina's skin. What would Tova say in response? What was it about her that unsettled her so?

"I want to get to know you. I want to write an article that shows the real you, not the superficial version that is trotted out for the press." Tova's voice was steady. There wasn't the urgent demand Alina heard from other sports writers.

"Most journalists say that." She should keep walking to the locker room where surely Tova couldn't follow, but something kept her feet rooted to the floor.

"Consider it a chance to say what you want to say. Maybe, what you need to say. I report honestly, Alina. I don't sensationalise." Her gaze skewered Alina, so that her skin prickled. "Here's my card." Tova pressed the rectangle into Alina's hand. "Check my articles on the internet. You might be interested in my interview with Andy Murray on his life after surgery. Or Viva Jones about the reasons for her retirement. Talk to Viva if you wish. She's here, commentating for Tennis Australia. Then, if you want, call me. I hope you do."

Alina watched Tova's lithe figure stride down the corridor in the direction of the café. Her fingers clenched on the card in her hand. She wouldn't call. Women like Tova were dangerous.

She slipped the card into the outside pocket of her tennis bag.

"I don't know what I'm doing here."

Across the table, Tova sat silently. A half-smile graced her face, and she turned the coffee mug around in her hand to cup it.

"My agent says you're dangerous. That you get people to say what they shouldn't. He told me to stay away from you." Alina heaved a breath. "I read your articles. They are excellent. You humanised Serena, whereas so many interviewers make her out to be some sort of machine."

"Did you talk to Viva?" Tova moved her own mug a few centimetres across the table into Alina's space.

"No. Viva and I never got on that well. As you pointed out, I don't have friends on tour. I read the article though. It was well done."

"Viva is a good person. Her decision to retire was made with difficulty, at some personal cost. Yes, her wrist injury was pushing her towards retirement, but her relationship with Gabriela Mendaro, a tennis official, was the deciding factor. It was, at its roots, a case of choosing love over career. That was the human angle I wanted to emphasise."

Alina closed her eyes and pushed down the twist of shame. Viva had followed her heart. Wasn't that what everyone should do? *Except me. Never me.*

"Let me shadow you for the next few days. We'll talk, yes, but I won't interrupt your routine. Then I'll write my article. You'll have the right to veto anything you don't agree with."

"Do people veto much?"

"Serena vetoed a couple of things about her daughter. Andy didn't like how I talked about his potty mouth. Viva vetoed nothing." Tova watched her closely.

It was like being pinned by a searchlight. Alina heaved a breath. She wasn't sure what was pushing her this way, why she was going against the advice of her agent, but something deep and visceral was telling her she could trust Tova. That this was something that she needed to do.

"I'll do it." Anxiety twisted deep in her belly. *This is a mistake.*

Tova nodded as if she hadn't expected anything different. "Can we start tomorrow? What's your routine?"

"I'll be at the gym at six. A light breakfast. Then I'll work with Anatoly until lunch. Later I'll work with my fitness trainer."

"The tennis centre gym?"

Alina nodded.

"I'll meet you there." Tova hesitated, then laid a hand on Alina's arm. "Thank you for agreeing. I hope to get to know you a lot better."

The light touch of Tova's hand seemed to radiate fire. *Danger!* But despite the alarm bells clanging in Alina's mind, Tova's smile seemed sincere. Genuine. It wasn't the fake, practised expression that she saw in so many people who wanted a piece of her.

"Six." Alina finished her mineral water and stood. With a nod at Tova, she turned and left the café. She wouldn't think about it now. Right now, her fitness trainer awaited her.

Tova was waiting for her the next morning. She was dressed in a loose t-shirt, and her tanned thighs under the bike pants were as toned as any top ten player's. Without makeup, with her hair scraped back in a ponytail, Tova looked like any workout partner Alina's fitness trainer might throw at her.

But none of them had made Alina's belly clench, had made her avert her eyes from the shape of her breasts under the loose t-shirt.

Alina nodded a greeting, and moved to the treadmills. She set the program and started at a brisk walk.

Tova glanced over Alina's shoulder at the display, stepped onto the neighbouring treadmill, and set the same pace.

"I know the basic information." Tova flicked her a glance from under lowered lashes as she strode at Alina's pace. "You're twenty-six, born in Russia, trained in Florida. Your… boyfriend is Mikhail Kreshnov. You have possibly the best power game on the tour right now—"

"Serena Williams might not agree." Alina increased the speed and broke into a jog.

Tova matched her. "Ten years ago that comment would be true. Now, not so much. I stand by my words. Tell me what you did last night."

"That isn't relevant."

"I disagree."

Alina increased the pace again. Four minutes thirty seconds per kilometre. "I ate the meal my nutrition coach had ordered for me from the hotel menu. I did 45 minutes of yoga and mental conditioning exercises." She flicked a sideways glance. Tova, too had increased her pace.

"Is that all? Did you call anyone? Watch TV? Read a book? Check your socials?" There was no pity in Tova's voice, just mild curiosity.

Tova wasn't even breathing heavily. For a second, Alina considered upping the treadmill pace even more, but she resisted. Her warm up called for 20 minutes at this speed. "Sometimes I call my mother. Not often. She lives in a small town and the internet is not good there."

"TV," Tova persisted. "You must turn it on at some point."

"Yes. During a tournament, I watch my next opponent's matches." Her footfalls thudded on the belt and she kept her gaze on the ticking timer. Seventeen minutes to go. She'd spent maybe five minutes in Tova's company. She'd asked the simplest questions, but already, Alina found herself evading Tova's piercing blue gaze.

"And at other times? Now, for instance, when you don't have a next opponent."

Alina shot her a glance. Was that a dig at her early loss? But Tova was running steadily, lightly for such a tall woman, her gaze focussed on the TV screen on the wall of the gym.

"Sometimes I'll watch an old series, if there's one I like."

"Such as?" There was a smile in Tova's voice. "How old are we talking? *Neighbours? Home and Away? I Love Lucy?*"

"Not those. Sci-fi. *Battlestar Galactica. Stargate.* Even *Star Trek.*"

"Favourite captain?"

"Janeway."

"Mine too." Tova directed a quick smile at Alina. "Why do you like sci-fi?"

Alina held her gaze for a moment longer than she should. A sheen of sweat glistened on Tova's shoulders, and her t-shirt clung damply to the small of her back. "Exploration. People working together as a team. There's a theme too in most of the shows of working towards a greater good."

"Yes. And there's seldom any discrimination for species, gender, planet of birth." A sideways glance. "Sexuality, age."

"That too."

"I hadn't pegged you for a Trekkie. I wonder how else you will surprise me, Alina Pashin?"

The days fell into a pattern. Every day, Tova would be waiting at Alina's early training session: the practice courts, the gym, or the pool. Tova would keep pace with her on the treadmill, or perch on a bench typing fast with two fingers on a tablet as Alina worked through her strength exercises with her fitness coach. If Alina looked her way, Tova would glance up with a bright smile and open expression, holding Alina's gaze until, discomfited, Alina would have to look away.

At lunchtimes, they would go together to the players' café. Alina would eat her usual chicken salad, Tova would order something different each day: burritos, a ramen noodle bowl. Dessert. She would shoot questions at Alina, interspersing questions about tennis, and life on the tour with other, seemingly inconsequential things.

"What would you have done with your life if you hadn't been successful as a player?" she would ask. Or, "How do you see the future of this planet?" Tova seemed to accept Alina's answers, but Alina still tightened in nervous anticipation when she spied a certain faraway look in Tova's eyes that often preceded a more personal question. "Do you want children some day?" or "How important is it for a person to be true to themselves?"

Alina couldn't answer that question. She sat for a second, an eternity, her heartbeat pounding in her ears, staring at Tova, completely unable to form a pat answer. Tova had waited, and then asked a different question, something about her favourite player from past generations.

Tova's eyes were kind as she stood after lunch. She touched Alina's shoulder. "Don't worry. You don't have to respond to a question if you don't want to."

Alina nodded, mute, and watched Tova depart, her shiny black hair and yellow polo shirt standing out in the lunch crowd. She focussed down at her plate and pushed a piece of tomato to one side. Her pulse still pounded from the tension. Tova was dangerous. Alina should never have agreed to the interview.

But somehow, somewhere in the last few days, she'd found herself looking out for Tova in the gym, anticipating her bright laughter, wide smile, and her calm, all-knowing eyes.

Mikhail lost in the third round. He asked Alina if she would like to go out for dinner. "You can console me for my defeat."

Alina gritted her teeth. No doubt he expected her consolation to include the bedroom. But it would keep her agent happy, and Mikhail would have some entertaining tennis gossip.

"The steakhouse, like last time?" he asked.

She opened her mouth to agree, but a spark of rebellion made her change her mind. For once, she would *not* do what everyone wanted. "No. Let's try somewhere different. Do you like Greek food?"

His surprise hung in the air. "I will try it. Where do you want to go?"

The suggestion had sprung into Alina's head without conscious thought. She didn't even know if she liked Greek food—but in the locker room, she'd overheard one of the players mention a good Greek restaurant. "There's a place in Smith Street," she said. "I'll make the booking for seven."

The restaurant was brightly lit, with a blue and white Mediterranean décor and checked tablecloths. It was very different from the places she normally ate. Next to her, Mikhail was tight with disapproval at her choice.

They were shown to a tiny table, and a carafe of water was brought. There were no menus. Alina looked around. Almost every table was full, and a muted buzz of chatter filled the air.

The waitress returned. "Have you been here before?"

"No. I had a recommendation." Alina gave her a quick smile. "Can we see a menu?"

"No menus." The waitress smiled at her surprise. "You tell me if there is anything you don't eat, and I will bring you food until you tell me to stop. Okay?"

Mikhail shifted restlessly in the chair opposite. "I would prefer—"

"Okay," Alina said, and this time the smile she gave the waitress was wider, more genuine. "We both eat everything."

She touched Mikhail's hand. "You said it yourself; you don't have a match for a while. Live a little." It was all very well dispensing advice like this, but could she follow it herself? Steak or chicken. Chicken or steak. Somehow she thought neither would be on tonight's menu, at least not cooked in any way she was used to.

There was grilled lamb with herbs, marinated octopus, a creamy moussaka unlike anything she had ever tasted. Cubes of grilled halloumi nestled next to glossy, black olives. There was even grilled kidneys that were unbelievably tasty and tender.

Mikhail refused the kidneys with a grimace, but ate heartily of everything else.

Alina devoured everything put in front of her and sat back with a sigh. Her nutrition coach would admonish her tomorrow, but she pushed the thought away. When had she last eaten whatever she wanted, with no concern for food groups or portion control? The last time was a visit to her family three years ago. Her mother had clung to her, patting Alina's hair and face and crying tears of happiness. Then she had sat her down at the old kitchen table and piled her plate with potato pierogies until Alina had thought she would burst.

Food made with love tastes better, her mother always said. Maybe, this café also went by that.

Opposite, Mikhail smiled and reached across for her hands.

Alina bit back a sarcastic comment. Now the real business of the evening was over, he moved on to the next thing he wanted—her. He was as predictable as his cross-court backhand.

"Hello Alina, Mikhail." The voice came from above them.

Viva Jones stood there, a hesitant smile on her face. "I was surprised to see you here. This place is one of Melbourne's undiscovered gems."

Alina swallowed her surprise—not that Viva was here, but that she'd come over to say hello. "I overheard another player mention it."

Viva nodded. "I think word is spreading. I was here a few nights ago with Jelena Kovic and her girlfriend. I'm here with Gabriela now. I'd invite you to join us, but of course Gabriela cannot socialise with an active player." She nodded towards a table on the other side of the room.

She knew, of course. Three years ago, Viva's relationship with the umpire, Gabriela, had caused a minor scandal in the tennis world. Alina's belly clenched in shame. She'd been less than pleasant to Viva over it. But, it seemed, Viva wasn't one to bear a grudge.

She glanced over to Viva's table. Gabriela Mendaro was a striking woman, one who had often umpired Alina's matches. Gabriela inclined her head in acknowledgement and offered a small smile.

Alina nodded in return. The code of conduct for umpires was strict. Gabriela was not being rude; she was simply abiding by the rules.

Viva followed Alina's gaze and her eyes softened. "Gabriela is umpiring the men's final this year." Pride shone in her voice.

Alina closed her eyes briefly and a yearning for what Viva had closed her throat momentarily so that she couldn't speak. Viva had always had it all: a hugely successful tennis career, and now, against all odds, a girlfriend whom she obviously loved with all her heart.

Girlfriend. Even thinking the word was difficult.

"In a way, this café is part of how Gabriela and I got together," Viva said. "I don't suppose you remember, but three years ago, a picture of us having coffee in a little café in Clifton Hill was leaked to the press. This restaurant belongs to the niece of that café owner. She invited us here when her niece opened the doors. Now we recommend it to everyone!"

"I remember," Alina said through stiff lips. The incident had first deepened, then gone some way to healing the animosity between herself and Viva.

"I'm glad I caught you. I was hoping to set up an interview with you for Tennis Australia. Although you're very much in demand these days. I hear Tova Wright is shadowing you this week." Viva pushed her thick chestnut hair behind her ears.

"That's right."

Beside her Mikhail shifted restlessly.

"She's good." Viva's gaze clung to Alina's. "You can speak freely with her. She's trustworthy. That's not true of all journalists, but Tova has integrity."

There was an intensity in Viva's expression that was unnerving. What was Viva trying to say? Memories of a locker room, three years ago, surfaced. Herself, Viva, and Michi Cleaver. Alina had said too much, revealed a weakness—one that could be dangerous. Alina swallowed hard, picked up her fork and speared the last piece of grilled lamb. It would probably choke her, but maybe Viva would take the hint and leave.

"I'll let you enjoy your dinner. But I hope you'll grant me an interview. Nothing in-depth—I'm no Tova—just some chit chat about your upcoming tournaments. That sort of thing." She grinned. "Maybe I'll ask you for a restaurant review. It was good to bump into you both." Her glance encompassed Mikhail. "I'll get back to Gabriela before she eats all the dolmades."

Alina watched Viva's upright back and springy stride as she weaved her way back to her table. Viva sat, leant over to Gabriela and snatched the final dolmade from the plate in front of her. Gabriela laughed and batted at Viva's hand. The sound was a ripple of infectious pleasure.

Alina closed her eyes momentarily. *If only.* When she opened them, Mikhail was studying her with a strange expression, more intently than he'd ever looked at her before.

"Was there something between you and Viva once?"

Startled, Alina set the untouched piece of lamb back on the plate. "Viva? Not at all. We didn't like each other much when she was on the tour. Now though, she's okay."

Mikhail nodded, a short up and down. "I wouldn't mind if there had been. I'm not one of those people who find such relationships objectionable."

Keep breathing. He means well. Alina stared down at her plate. The solitary chunk of lamb was still in the middle. "I'm glad you're not homophobic, but in this case, your concern is unwarranted. Viva has never been of any interest to me except as an opponent." She forced a smile. "I don't think I can manage any more. Do you want dessert?"

"No, I won't. Too much sugar. Maybe instead, we could have coffee somewhere else? A café. Or—" His thumb caressed the back of her hand "—my room?"

No way in hell. She bit back the instinctive response. Mikhail had done nothing wrong. "I have an early start in the morning. I'll take a raincheck."

He nodded, as if he hadn't expected her to say different.

"We had a deal." Tova stood courtside, her arms folded across her chest. She waited while Alina pummelled the final few balls from the ball machine, then Tova stalked across the court towards her.

"What do you mean?" Alina bent to pick up a stray ball.

"You agreed I would shadow you for the rest of the week. Every night you've eaten dinner in your room, but last night, you snuck off for a romantic dinner."

"You're being ridiculous." Alina hit the ball in a high lob that landed in the stands. "I have a private life. I don't want you in it."

"My article is about the person inside the tennis dress. Your hopes, your dreams, who you really are. For that, I need to be with you."

Alina shrugged. "You don't. My hopes and dreams are to win another grand slam and retain the number one ranking. You don't need to watch me eat Greek food for that. How did you know what I was doing anyway?"

"I had coffee with Gabriela Mendaro this morning. When she stopped talking about Viva, she mentioned seeing you and Mikhail last night."

"Then you must realise why you weren't welcome. Did you want to lie between us in bed as well?"

Tova snorted and came closer. She took the racquet from Alina's suddenly weak hands and set it on the ground. Her fingers closed around Alina's own. "We both know that didn't happen. I'm not pushing you to say anything, Alina, but if you were minded, this is a good chance."

"What do you mean?" Her mouth was dry, the words stuck to her tongue. She knew, of course, but she wanted Tova to say it.

Tova's fingers tightened. "You're from a country that puts all sorts of pressure on its sportspeople to play at the highest level, even if getting there skirts the boundaries of what is acceptable. I know you're told to conform, and what to say in interviews. I know it's hard for you. You have family there; you need to consider their well-being."

Tova took a half-step forward. It was just a small shuffle but it put her firmly in Alina's personal space. Too close.

Tova's skin was smooth, silky. Touchable. Her lips, bare of makeup, formed words, but Alina barely heard them. She was transfixed by Tova's mouth and the potential it offered.

Tova moved closer. Alina's heart thudded in her throat. Tova was going to kiss her, and, she shouldn't, she mustn't, she wouldn't… but God only knew how badly she wanted to, even though they were on a practice court at the Australian Open with players, coaches, officials, and thousands of fans were milling past.

Tova stepped back. "Daria Gavrilova took Australian citizenship. She came here for the exceptional tennis facilities, but she stayed for love. Martina Navratilova defected to the US from communist Czechoslovakia. Asha Bulbogan now plays under the French flag. Players switch allegiances all the time. That is all I will say." She bent and picked up a ball. "Now, what is your schedule for the rest of the day? I will follow you around, but this evening you will spend with me."

Alina glanced around Tova's choice of restaurant as she entered. It was in a Victorian cottage in a quiet part of Melbourne marked only by a discreet gold-coloured plaque on the door. It was like walking into someone's living room. But she was greeted politely by a waiter wearing a red suit and a yellow bow-tie and shown down the timber-floored hallway to a tiny room with three tables. Tova was already there, and she stood to greet Alina. The other tables were empty. When they were seated again, the waiter handed them menus handwritten on stiff card, and poured a glass of wine for Tova from the bottle that rested in an ice bucket next to the table.

"No wine for me, thank you," Alina said. "I'll have a sparkling mineral water when you're ready."

The waiter nodded and disappeared.

"I took the liberty of ordering a local Yarra Valley chardonnay. Do you drink wine?"

"I think I had a glass of something when I was home last," Alina said. "I don't drink at all during the tennis season."

"Why is that?" Tova arched an eyebrow. "Many players allow themselves the small pleasure of an occasional drink."

"My nutrition coach generally picks my food choices. They do not include empty calories."

Tova inclined her head. "So be it."

Alina bit her lip. In any other universe, this intimate little restaurant would have the feel of a date. A beautiful woman on the other side of the table. Soft music and candles. It was a romantic place, not the sort of place a journalist would take

125

someone for an interview. She glanced at the menu. The three options per course offered eclectic dining choices. There was no chicken or steak.

Tova was right. There was no reason for her not to enjoy some good food, interesting conversation and yes, even a small glass of wine. *This is not a date.* Tova was probably softening her up, building a rapport so that she would talk more freely. Tova's words of earlier came back: *Players switch allegiances all the time.*

What if she approached another country for citizenship? She knew there were fast track programs for sportspeople. The United States, a European country, Australia? What if, as well as developing her tennis potential to the fullest, she was free to be herself? State her opinions freely? Have more control over her own career and the fitness choices made to achieve it? Be free of state control in so many things. Date whomever she wanted without fear of censure or repercussion. And her family? What of them? Were families allowed to migrate too? Would her mother and brother even want to?

Tova stared at her with a quizzical expression. "Penny for them?"

"What?"

"A penny for your thoughts. You seemed suddenly so far away."

"I was thinking of my mother. She lives in a small town. She has heat and power and a small garden to grow vegetables. Because of me, she's well off. She is content where she is."

"Does she ever come and watch you play?"

"Yes, sometimes. I paid for her to come to Wimbledon last year."

"You reached the semi-finals."

"The last semi-final I've reached. You don't need to say it."

"I wasn't going to. Has your mother met Mikhail?"

"No. There's no need for that. Mikhail… Mikhail is…" She couldn't bring herself to continue. Viva had said Tova was trustworthy. Tova herself had said Alina could veto anything she didn't want in print.

Tova watched her across the table. She radiated a calmness, a stillness that was reassuring. The urge to talk, finally to spill what was in her heart without fear swelled in her chest. The words rose in her throat, until it seemed they would either erupt out into the quiet air or choke her. She glanced around. The other two tables were still empty. There was no one to hear, no one except Tova, sitting so quiet, her eyes radiating empathy.

"Are you ready to order?" The waiter's words startled her. She hadn't heard his soft-footed approach.

"Do you need more time?" Tova asked.

Time. More time for what? She shook her head and studied the card. Food was food. Chicken or steak? She stifled a laugh. Neither of those were on the menu. Which was the healthiest option… Did it even matter? She looked again with fresh eyes. "I'll have the duck pancakes and then the sea perch. Thank you."

Tova ordered oysters with a caviar topping and then lamb shanks with wasabi mash.

The waiter departed.

"The service is relaxed here," Tova said. "It will be fifteen minutes or so before our entrées arrive. You have time to talk."

Nerves jumped in her belly, an anticipation worse than any match point. "May I have a glass of wine?"

Tova lifted the bottle from the ice bucket and poured Alina a glass.

Alina took a large gulp. The dry wine registered on her taste buds and she took another, smaller, sip. She set the glass down.

"Mikhail," Tova prompted.

"I was advised by my agent that it would be beneficial for me to date Mikhail. Show my more human side. And glamourous couples get a lot of press."

"Why Mikhail?" If Tova was pleased to finally get some personal details, she wasn't showing it. Her expression was serene and inviting. A small smile crinkled her eyes.

"We've known each other a long time and we share the same agent. For me, it is just for show. For him though, I think he wishes it to be real." She shot Tova a glance. "Be kind to him, please, if you mention him in your article. He is a good person, if a bit—"

"Predictable? Overbearing?"

"Yes, both of those."

"Do you date anyone for real?"

"No." The pressure in her throat eased. Tova was not going to put her on the spot. "Tennis is my life, and dating—falling in love—is a distraction I can't afford."

"That's not necessarily true. Plenty of players have relationships or marriages. Michi Cleaver is married to her coach. Jelena Kovic travels with her long-time girlfriend. Serena Williams is married with a child."

"I don't think I could do that. Love is such an all-encompassing emotion. Something would have to give so that love could take its place."

"When were you last in love?"

Alina's hand trembled on the stem of the wine glass, and she tightened her grip and took a sip to steady herself. "A long time ago. When I was seventeen."

"At the Delacourt Academy?"

"Yes. There was another junior player there. An American. We fell in love."

"What happened?" Tova turned her wineglass a quarter turn and studied the contents as if they were somehow new and strange.

"We kept our relationship secret, and I don't think anyone ever found out—except my coach of course. He told me to end the relationship. He said it wasn't acceptable in my country, and it could be dangerous both for me and my family. I've always believed I didn't have any choice."

"Do you still see them?"

Them. Could she do this? She took another sip of wine. The glass was nearly empty. If she did this, if she confirmed what Tova so obviously suspected, then there would be no going back. Oh, she could veto any mention of it, but if she said the words aloud to another person, then she couldn't keep them inside ever again.

Alina took a deep breath. Her heart pounded in double time at the enormity of what she was going to say. "Stacy is no longer on the tour. She had a couple of years on the Challenger circuit, but she wasn't good enough to make tennis her career. The last I heard, she works in politics as some sort of campaign advisor."

Tova was silent. Then she reached a hand across the table. "Alina, you know this is off the record if that's what you want—need—it to be. You can talk to me. I don't think you've talked to anyone for a very long time."

The compassion in Tova's voice was nearly Alina's undoing. *I won't cry.* She dragged a deep breath, and then another, until she was sure her voice would remain steady. "Nothing has changed." She closed her eyes momentarily at the unfairness of that. "My coach, my agent, my country… Tennis must come first in everything I do. If I date, it must be a suitable man."

"If it were up to you, would you have a personal life that went beyond tennis?"

The ache of longing in her chest bit deep. She nodded. *If only…*

"Well then." Tova sat back in her seat as the waiter approached and set down their entrées.

Alina stared at her duck. The aroma made her mouth water. How long had it been since she'd been excited about her food? How long had it been since she'd been excited about a lot of things? "What about you?" she asked. "You travel a lot following the tennis tour. Do you have a partner?"

"No. My last girlfriend was a physiotherapist who also spent a lot of time with the tour. But we split nearly a year ago. It was a mutually amicable decision."

The duck tasted as delicious as it looked. Suddenly, there were new possibilities in the evening, in the remainder of the week in Melbourne. Beyond that? Alina didn't know.

The boulder that had lodged in her chest for the past few months shifted. It wasn't gone, not yet, but in the flickering candlelight, the haze of an unaccustomed glass of wine, there was the potential for it to dissipate in a starburst leaving her free of its weight.

Free to be what? Alina didn't know. But maybe, she was about to find out.

She leaned forward and raised her palm.

Tova placed hers against Alina's without hesitation.

Tova's hand was warm, and the touch sent sparks along Alina's palm, travelling the nerve pathways towards her heart. She linked their fingers together. "Tell me how players go about changing their citizenship."

If you enjoyed this short story, check out *Code of Conduct* by Cheyenne Blue, where you'll be able to meet Alina for the first time.

What Happens at Game Night...

Alex K. Thorne

"Game night!" Ava announced with excitement.

Gwen looked at her as if she'd just grown a second head (which, considering Ava's alien DNA, was not entirely out of the question). She forced herself to repeat the words, making sure to inflect them with an appropriate amount of disgust. "*Game night?*"

It was the first time in weeks that Gwen was home before dinner. The table read for her new HBO show had ended earlier than anticipated, and Gwen was excited about the prospect of spending the evening with her fiancée and son. Between Ava's writing and Gwen's shooting schedule, it felt like eons since they'd had time together. Except now Ava was ruining it by proposing the preposterous.

"Oh, don't sound so affronted!" Ava bent down to retrieve a pint of ice cream from the freezer.

If Gwen had not been on the defensive, she would have appreciated the perfect curve of Ava's ass in her jeans. Instead, she was running through the hundred or so reasons why a repeat of game night was an absurd death wish.

"The last one was fine," Ava insisted, twisting open the ice cream.

Gwen reached for the small tub before Ava could just plunge a spoon into it. "I seem to recall an argument, someone storming out, and…a house fire."

Ava winced. "All of those things did…technically happen. But I put the fire out before it caused any real damage."

Gwen plucked a bowl from the dishwasher and started scooping ice cream into it. She licked some off her thumb before handing the bowl to Ava, who took it a little sheepishly.

"Darling, I think the damage was done when you suggested Jenga."

"I just… I know that you and Nic don't exactly get along and—"

"You can't swoop in and fix this one, Swiftwing." Gwen shrugged. "Nicole and I are just…different people. I certainly respect her and her…opinions." That last part might have been a lie. Many of Nicole's opinions were unfortunate. "I just don't…"

"Like her."

"Understand her. And forcing us into insipid group activities certainly doesn't help."

"Was the last one really that bad?" Ava asked, licking peach gelato off the spoon.

"I'm surprised nobody died."

"Of fun?"

Gwen leaned in to kiss the sticky sweetness from Ava's lips. "You're adorable when you're being obtuse."

Ava clutched onto Gwen's shirt, keeping her close. Gwen could feel the smile against her lips before Ava deepened the kiss. Gwen sighed and melted against her. Three years and Ava still managed to undo her with a single kiss. They stumbled back against the fridge, causing a few of the magnets to fall and clatter against the kitchen tiles. Ava wrapped her free, non-ice-cream-holding hand around Gwen's waist, and for a glorious moment, Gwen forgot what it was they were talking about.

Until Ava pulled back and said: "You know we could do it for my birthday?"

Her expression was all innocent and hopeful, and Gwen hated herself for being so easily manipulated just because her fiancée happened to be sunshine incarnate.

Gwen's sigh was deep and long-suffering. "And how long would this game night take? Because I have plans for your birthday that do not involve cards and dice." Gwen licked her lips slowly, making sure Ava got the point.

"Like two games, definitely not more than three. And…no Jenga this time, promise." Ava smiled sweetly. "And after I'll let you shower me with naked gifts and birthday sex."

"Oh, you'll let me?" Gwen leaned in again and pressed her lips against the space under Ava's ear, earning a little shiver. "How very generous of you."

Ava laughed softly as Gwen's mouth moved down her neck, placing featherlight kisses as she went. "I can be very gen—"

The front door slammed shut, followed by, "I'm coming in. Don't be doing anything gross!"

Gwen immediately broke into a smile. She hadn't expected Luke home so early.

"Too late," Ava yelled and buried her face in Gwen's neck before making exaggerated smacking sounds. "Grossness abounds!"

Luke walked in and dramatically covered his eyes with his forearm. "Is it safe?"

Gwen huffed in faux annoyance and shoved Ava off her. "Sweetheart, I thought I was fetching you."

Luke shrugged off his backpack and tossed it on the couch, where it promptly slid off onto the floor. "Jake's mom was coming this way, so she dropped me off."

Gwen sized her son up and decided that he was definitely taller since that morning. It was getting out of hand, this growing thing. He allowed her to gather his tall, gangly teenage body into a hug and even wrapped his arms around her. He was almost fourteen and had not yet succumbed to the role of sullen teenager, something she was eternally grateful for. Gwen never would have imagined, when she adopted Luke all those years ago, that he'd grow into such an incredible kid.

"I saw your billboard while we were driving down Vine," Luke called over Gwen's shoulder before she finally released him. "It looks sick! Your name is on it and everything."

Luke had always been vaguely supportive of Gwen's career, but Ava's new show found him obsessed. She supposed it was appropriate that her superhero fiancée was writing a show about a group of immigrant aliens who discovered their powers in a detention centre. It made even more sense that her adolescent son, whose biological mother was an alien refugee, would be excited about it.

Ava grinned and came around the kitchen island. "Aw, jealous! I haven't seen it yet. I'll make sure to fly past tonight."

Gwen looked between them and felt an overwhelming tug of affection. It was a sort of blurry, hazy love that filtered her vision, a squishy, warm feeling that—Ava's voice reached her through this love haze and effectively acted as a record scratch.

"…decided to do game night."

Luke's face fell in disappointment. "But I'm at Dad's this weekend!"

Ava must have known this—they had Luke's schedule stuck to the fridge. To her credit, she managed to sound disappointed. "I'm sorry, bud. I'll make it up to you with an epic game of Forbidden Island. Loser clips Garbo's claws."

"Deal." Luke seemed mollified and then started planning the birthday lunch they'd have once he returned from his father's. "And then after, you, me and mom can have our own game night!"

Gwen sunk down onto the couch and sighed, wondering if there was a way to fireproof the curtains.

Nic finished off the last of her beer and watched her best friend save the world. Today, she was helping put out the fires on the 405. This time of year, the combination of dry heat and wind turned most of LA into kindling just waiting to burn. By the time Ava landed on Nic's balcony, she had changed into her street clothes but still smelled like Nic's childhood backyard on the Fourth of July.

"Take a load off, hero." Nic tossed her a cold can of LaCroix, which Ava caught and downed in a second.

"Thanks." She wiped her mouth with the back of her hand. "That was intense."

"You got it contained though." Nic pointed to the TV, where the local news was interviewing one of the families who had to be evacuated. "Could have been worse."

"Could have been better." Ava fell onto the couch beside Nic and exhaled an exhausted breath. "I should have been there sooner. I was in a meeting, and I thought I could get there faster than I did."

"Oh, so it took you point-six seconds instead of point-two?" Nic flipped the channel to Netflix. "Don't beat yourself up. You did good." The burden of being a superhero's confidante was providing constant validation...and snacks.

Ava pointed to the empty beer can. "Got another one of those?"

This was a weekly routine they both tried hard to maintain, especially since Ava moved out. Wednesday evenings after work were reserved for *The Great British Baking Show*. It was a night of beer and takeout from the Thai place across the street, and feet propped up on the coffee table while they commented on the choice of shortcrust pastry over choux and rolled their eyes at Paul Hollywood's hate of everything matcha. It was one of the highlights of Nic's week.

Soo-Mi, intrepid journalist and girlfriend extraordinaire, showed up halfway through the night. She came in through the door, a whirlwind of papers and boxes and a half-drunk cup of tea. Before they had met, Nic would have bet her life that she'd be the messy one in a relationship. And yet here they were. Soo-Mi and Nic had met when she had interviewed Nic for an article about women in STEM. They hit it off and were living together three months later. Nic was pretty sure that Ava would have relentlessly teased her about the U-Haul of it all if Ava hadn't done the same with Gwen.

"Hey, babe! Hey, Ava!" Soo-Mi shuffled through to the living room before dumping everything on the kitchen table.

"Work okay?" Nic called over her shoulder, angling her cheek up for a kiss. Soo-Mi obliged.

"Same old." She snatched a spring roll from the coffee table and munched on it. "Padma is going home." She gestured to the screen. "Her profiteroles were pathetic."

"They were…okay," Ava tried lamely. "And anyway, after Henry's pie, it's anyone's game."

Soo-Mi made a sound of agreement. "I'll leave you guys to it. Let me know if I was right."

Another kiss for Nic, and she disappeared into her little office, taking her haul of paperwork with her.

She got that this was a Nic and Ava thing. She was good like that. Also, Ava really liked Soo-Mi, which was cool. Then again, Ava liked almost everybody. She was like the golden retriever of people.

"Padma is definitely leaving now." Nic clucked her tongue in disappointment. "That extra layer of ganache was a terrible choice."

"Speaking of terrible choices." Ava turned to Nic with a sunny smile. "I wanna have a game night for my birthday."

The words echoed in her head. Nic went through all the stages of grief before finally landing on begrudging acceptance. She fixed Ava with a hard stare. "It's your 30th birthday. You're the world's most beloved superhero. You're engaged to one of the most famous women on the planet, and instead of a Kanye-level party on a boat, you want to do game night?"

"Yes?"

Nic pointed to the window behind her. "You know the curtains have barely recovered."

Ava laughed. "Look, we'll have it at our place. Just you, me, Gwen, and Soo-Mi. It'll be fun. I promise."

Nic took a long sip of her beer. "I love you, girl. But do not make promises you can't keep. Last time—"

"It won't be like last time."

"Last time," Nic continued, trying very hard to sound casual about this whole thing, "your girlfriend called me a quixotic millennial, so..."

Ava cringed. "She went too far. I know. To be fair, that was after you called her walking white privilege."

Nic shrugged without apology.

"I just... I want you guys to get along. You're both my favorite people, and it sucks that you don't like each other."

"I don't not like her, I..." Nic struggled to find the most diplomatic way of putting it. "I think we're from different worlds, and—"

"Ha!" Ava pointed a finger at her. "You and I are literally from two different worlds, and we get along."

Nic rolled her eyes, barely repressing her smile. Ava was a dork. "You know what I mean, Eisenberg. Your girl and me... We have nothing in common. But," Nic continued as Ava's face fell. "I will come to your dumb game night, even if I wish it was an 80's themed pool party on Beyoncé's boat."

Ava fell onto Nic with a squeal of excitement, enveloping her in a hug until she gave in and succumbed to the inevitable. "Yeah, yeah," Nic mumbled, smooshed against her favorite superhero. "There better be fancy champagne."

Gwen watched Ava flit about the apartment like a hyperactive bee.

They had spent a very lazy morning in bed, during which Gwen had wished Ava happy birthday in so many delicious ways until around noon, when Ava realised they hadn't acquired anything in the way of snacks for that evening's game night.

Gwen's assistant, Cari, came by around three that afternoon, having ticked everything off Ava's shopping list, with at least twenty paper bags filled with everything from crackers to sangria.

"I see you bought out Whole Foods," Gwen quipped at Ava in amusement.

"I couldn't decide between a cheese board or a charcuterie board, so I told Cari to get enough for both." Ava looked panicked. "Too much?"

Gwen bit down on her lip to keep herself from smiling. Ava was adorably flustered. "No." She kissed her softly. "It's fine. This is your day."

Ava smiled, nerves calmed by the simple kiss. "Okay. I just want it to be perfect."

"It will be." Gwen leaned in for another kiss, hoping it would soften the lie.

"Hold on! Is that legal? Can she just take my sword?" Nicole looked as if she was about to stand up and punch something, so Gwen tightened her grip on her item card.

"The rules say that I can pilfer anything that you haven't already added to your vault, and as of your last turn, your sword was still in the common area."

"She's right." Ava shot Nicole an apologetic look that annoyed Gwen for some unfathomable reason. "You should have put your weapons in the vault."

"Well, that's just stupid." Nicole huffed and slumped back in her seat. "How am I supposed to do that and attack Gwen's pillar?"

"Um, you're not. This is supposed to be cooperative, babe." Soo-Mi, whom Gwen liked immensely, put her hand over Nicole's.

"But she took my sword," Nicole grumbled and directed a scathing glance at Gwen who took a sip of her wine, determined to remain unruffled. "You took my sword."

"I needed your sword because I have the orb card, which allows me to move us through the Tombs of Wisdom." Gwen felt ridiculous spouting this nonsense, but if she was going to play, then she was going to win, and winning meant having fastidiously learned the rules half an hour before their guests arrived. She also wanted Ava to see that she was trying. Trying, however, was definitely the mood since Nicole had arrived.

It wasn't that Gwen set out to dislike her. It was that Nicole made it so difficult to be liked. She was prickly and insisted on always being right. It was frustrating. But Gwen could have forgiven all of it, if she was supportive of Nic's relationship with Ava, which she wasn't. Three years in, and Nicole still seemed to be waiting for Gwen and Ava to break up and for Ava to move back in to her shabby little Studio City apartment.

Gwen had once asked Ava if there was any chance that Nicole was in love with her, to which Ava had laughed so hard that she'd given herself hiccups. "It's definitely not like that," she had said, once she'd finally caught her breath, and Gwen had to admit that Nicole's hostility was not jealousy so much as possessiveness.

It was ridiculous, really. Nicole had known Ava all her life. There was nothing to be possessive about. If anything, Gwen was the one who constantly felt left out of their inside jokes and silly meme references.

"I don't get it," Nicole was saying. "If there's an item card on the board, but a quest card is not in play, then can we still pick up a token?"

"I think." Soo-Mi looked lost. "Maybe? Ava, what do you think?"

"I think." Ava looked around the table with a panicked puppy expression. "Maybe we should play Jenga instead?"

"Not again." Nicole cried out, beating Gwen to it.

"Okay, okay." Ava held up her hands. "Maybe we should read the rules ag—" She stopped midsentence and cocked her head slightly. Gwen knew what that meant.

"Trouble?" Both Gwen and Nicole asked, then looked at each other, startled.

"There's another fire," Ava answered, already standing. "But...it's arson. I think."

"Arson?" Soo-Mi jumped up as well. "You're sure?"

"I've gotta...." Ava flashed to the bedroom in the blink of an eye. When she came back, she was in her suit and at the living room window. "I'll be back soon." And then she was gone.

Gwen looked at Nic; Nic looked at Gwen, and Soo-Mi said, "Well, shit."

Gwen watched the strangely familiar scene unfold in front of her, but this time, she wasn't one of the players.

"Are you sure you'll be safe?" Nicole was asking, as Soo-Mi furiously typed something on her phone, barely looking up.

"I will." Soo-Mi looked up at Nicole somewhat distractedly, already inching towards the door. "Look, babe. My feed is already going crazy. I have to get down there."

Emotions played across Nicole's face—panic, fear, and ultimately, resignation. Gwen understood those feelings all too well. Which is perhaps why she felt compelled to say, "Take my car. My driver will get you wherever you have to be. That way Nicole will still be able to get home safely, and—"

"I'm staying," Nic interrupted, "until Ava gets back."

Gwen sighed. "I'll open another bottle of wine."

It was only after the door closed on Nicole's goodbye that Gwen realised what she had committed to—alone time with Ava's best friend, a woman who by all accounts was not a fan.

"Red or white?" Gwen called from the kitchen.

Nicole's voice answered back from the living room, muddled with the sound of other voices from the TV. "Got anything stronger?"

Arsenic? She was tempted to call out but instead opened the freezer and got out her favorite bottle of gin, gifted to her by Ryan Reynolds. Martinis then.

By the time she got to the living room, Nicole was sitting at the edge of the couch, remote in hand, eyes glued to the screen.

"Anything?" Gwen set the tray with drinks down on the coffee table.

"Nah. The fire isn't even that big. Nowhere near as big as the one on the 405 last week. I don't understand the urgency."

"But if Ava said it was arson, it might mean—"

"A Keela."

A shiver ran up Gwen's spine at the name. Keelas were known as a particularly volatile race from a sulphuric planet a galaxy away. They had been on the same ship that crash-landed and brought Ava to earth. Unlike most of the alien races that had been on the Andromeda, Keelas had no desire to play nice with earth's law enforcement. Many of them disappeared into the world of undocumented immigrants and were never heard from again. Some, however, reveled in destruction, their preferred method being fire. Ava had gone up against a Keela a few years back and barely made it out of the fight alive.

The reporter on-screen said, "Again, we're coming live from Porter Ranch, where a number of properties have seemingly spontaneously caught alight. Firefighters are calling it arson, but so far nothing has been—" She paused mid-sentence and looked to the sky. "We have reports that Swiftwing is on the scene. She seems to be in mid-combat above the fires."

They watched the fires rage for a while, squinting at the screen. Gwen vaguely registered the sound of Nicole's phone alert.

"Soo-mi is on her way there, but traffic is insane," Nicole reported and then paused. "She says…"

Gwen tore her eyes away from the screen to look at Nicole. "What? What does she say?"

"She says two male Keelas have been seen on the site."

The blood drained from Gwen's face. Ava had struggled to fight one of them the last time. The helplessness was overwhelming. It had been a long time since Ava had been in a fight. It had been a long time since Gwen had been faced with these very specific fears. These days, it was mainly natural disasters and crime around the city.

"Hey." Nicole's voice reached her from very far away. "Hey, Gwen. Listen to me."

Dread swirled heavily in the pit of her stomach, and it took everything she had to focus and give Nicole her attention.

"There are two." Gwen's voice trembled. She was usually better at this. She was good at keeping her calm, at waiting, at watching how things played out. But it was Ava's birthday. It was her goddamn birthday, and she was out there, fighting those monsters.

"Yeah, I know," Nicole was saying. "But she's going to be okay."

"How do you know? She's never had to go up against two of them before."

"She's smart. She'll use their strengths against them. We've done something similar in training. A sort of simulation where she was overwhelmed."

"You've..." Gwen cleared her throat. "The two of you have prepared for something like this?"

Nicole nodded. "What do you think we do in my geek lab all day? I have a whole training facility down there."

"I thought you just ate junk food and discussed *Stranger Things* fan theories."

"I mean, that too. But Ava knows what to do if she's physically overwhelmed. You should have seen her when she first started. She was terrible. She could barely fight her own shadow. She'd come home all bruised and bleeding and—"

"Not helping," Gwen interrupted.

"My point," Nicole continued, "is that she's worked like hell to get stronger and faster and smarter. And if I know Ava's tactics, which I do, she'll lead them through the smoke, get a few hits in while they're blind, and then force them into close range. Then, she'll create a sandstorm and bury them before they can even think of igniting."

Gwen was hanging onto her every word, imagining the fight going down as Nicole narrated. She could see it. "How do you know all this?"

Nicole shrugged. "Because I know Ava. And look." She pointed at the TV.

"…a sort of sandstorm to presumably douse the fires." The reporter on scene was pointing behind her, where a tornado of sand and debris swirled through the air before landing on one of the estates, effectively drowning the fire.

The camera tilted upwards, where a blur of blue and yellow flitted across the canvas of night so fast, it got lost between the stars and smoke. Up and down the figure dipped, the force of the wind from the velocity acting like breath to a candle flame. The fire itself was monstrous—it heaved and spat as bright orange flames licked up into the sky. But Swiftwing was persistent, and the blaze slowly dimmed until there was nothing but thick black smoke. She was silhouetted against the sky for a moment before diving back down into the billowing plumes, only to shoot out of the darkness like a pebble from a child's slingshot.

"That was a punch," Nicole murmured, leaning closer to the TV. "They're in there."

Without thinking, Gwen reached out and took her hand. Together, they watched Swiftwing zoom back into the murky fray. Nicole's grip on Gwen's hand tightened.

The reporter then began interviewing an evacuated family with a little girl who spoke about how Swiftwing saved her cat.

"Sod the cat," Gwen muttered. "Where is she?"

An explosion behind them caused the camera to focus back on the smoke. From the blackness, two columns of humanoid-shaped flames emerged. Someone screamed, and Gwen's heart began a heavy thud. She felt sick. Two Keelas alive and no sign of Swiftwing.

And then those burning bodies were flung through the air, each one raised high and dropped from a tremendous height. It was like watching matches fall from the sky. By the time they hit the ground, the flame was extinguished.

Then, finally, the smoke cleared, and Swiftwing was there, hovering above the charred carcass of the property. Below, on the ground, were two unconscious figures.

"She did it," Gwen breathed and then looked to Nicole, who was shaking her head in something akin to disbelief.

"She fucking did it," Nicole echoed and flashed Gwen a smile.

They sat there in silence, watching the footage over and over until it cut to a newscaster in a studio, who gave a play-by-play of the events. It was only once they cut back to an image of Swiftwing giving the camera a sooty smile that Gwen's heartbeat returned to normal.

Ava called her seconds later. She was fine, if a little banged up. She was going back to the precinct to do all the necessary, boring paperwork that came after saving the city. She'd be back in an hour. She hoped they hadn't eaten all the cheese and crackers because she was starving.

Gwen found herself laughing in relief before telling Ava to get back as soon as possible. When she looked up, Nicole was standing rather awkwardly in front of the TV.

"Okay, well…" She shrugged. "I guess I can go now. I'm sure you guys have plans once she gets back." Nicole looked as if she was struggling before she finally said, "I'm sorry if I overstayed my welcome. I know you weren't particularly excited about me being here tonight."

Gwen wanted to tell Nicole that she might not have gotten through that without her. She wanted to tell her that she very much wanted her there. For the first time in maybe forever, Gwen looked at Nicole and really saw her. In jeans and a t-shirt, she was casual and very pretty. Brown eyes, brown skin, and dark, curly hair. She was the polar opposite of pale blonde Ava, but they complemented each other so well.

Gwen found herself reaching for their forgotten drinks.

"Stay for a drink," she said, handing the glass to Nicole. "God knows we deserve one."

"Wait, wait, wait!" Nic snorted in glee. "Gillian Anderson said that. To you. In George Clooney's bathroom." She took another sip of her martini. This was her second one, her third one? It was hard to keep track once Gwen brought the bottle out. Nic was aware that her knees were a little tingly and her head pleasantly fuzzy. Maybe this was her fourth one.

"She did." Gwen giggled.

Nic blinked and replayed the moment in her head. Gwendoline Knight, Academy Award winner and Hollywood's head-bitch-in-charge, just giggled in her presence.

Maybe it was the fact that they had known each other for years and this was the first time they'd ever been alone together. Maybe it was the fact that they had shared some weird, indelible moment while watching Ava. Maybe it was that fourth martini. But something prompted Nic to cut through the bullshit and just ask, "So why don't you like me?"

The smile fell from Gwen's face. "I..." She looked almost panicked. "I don't not like you," she said, as if the notion was ridiculous, which made Nicole feel ridiculous.

"I know you don't like me, Gwen. *Why?*" Nic meant to sound detached, disinterested, as if she didn't really care one way or the other. Instead, it came out sad and sort of whiny. Nic cringed but kept her gaze steady.

Gwen opened her mouth once, as if to speak, but then seemed to think better of it. She sighed, knocked back the last of her martini, and straightened.

Nic could wait. She didn't realize how much it meant to her until now, and found that she was weirdly nervous. She *wanted* Gwen to like her. She wanted this person who meant so much to Ava to see her as worthy. A part of Nic hated herself for it. She'd never sought out anyone's approval before. But this felt so important.

Eventually, Gwen said, "I don't dislike you, Nicole. I honestly don't. I just..." Gwen gave her a small, rueful smile and shrugged a shoulder. "I think I'm a little jealous."

Nicole wanted to laugh out loud. She'd expected...not that. "You?" Nic shook her head and reached for the bottle of gin. "You're jealous. Of me?"

"Hmm." Gwen hummed in confirmation and took the bottle from Nicole. She reached for the vermouth and poured them both another drink. "Of your relationship with Ava."

Nic made a face. "Oh. Oh, gross. Ava and I are totally platonic." She stuck her tongue out. "Ew."

Gwen actually looked amused. "No, I don't mean... You have history. You... you know her in ways that I..." Gwen made a little sound of frustration. "I'm usually a lot more articulate than this."

Nic didn't say anything. She'd never seen Gwen this sincere. It was slightly alarming. Gwen looked almost distressed as she tried to get the words right. "What I mean is...you've been there for her throughout it all. You were, you are an integral part of this journey she's been on. She trusts you in ways..." Gwen trailed off and took another sip of her drink. "I treated her like a lowly assistant for years. It took me so long to see the spark that you've always known. Sometimes I feel like you'll always know her better than I will. And I'm...I'm a little jealous of it."

Nic watched her for a long time. Gwen's cheeks were a little flushed, her eyes a little glassy. She was most definitely drunk. This was the most human, most fragile Nic had ever seen her, and while Gwen was not her type — *at all* — Nic could almost see who it was that Ava had fallen in love with.

She made sure she had Gwen's full attention when she said, "You're an idiot."

Gwen blinked. Frowned. "Excuse me?"

"An idiot, a dolt, a simpleton," Nic said. "Sure, I have history with Ava, and yeah, I knew her when she was all pigtails and braces. Believe me, it was not a pretty sight. But she chose you. Despite your weird work power-dynamic thing, which, by the way, I'll never understand. Despite all the fake-dating stuff and the fact that, in the beginning, neither of you could get your heads out of your asses long enough to admit your feelings. You're the person she chose to share her life and secrets with. For the longest time, it was just the two of us, you know? We had our families and our traditions and our stuff. We dated people, but it never really affected our lifestyle. It was different with you." Nic took a long sip of her drink. Gwen did make a damn good martini. "It is different with you."

Nic sighed and gritted her teeth, not wanting to make the next admission but knowing she had to. "I guess I was a little jealous too. Not of you or, or this." She waved her arm around the room. "Although, we have got to discuss why you have not yet introduced me to Chris Evans. I am gayer than a fairy riding a unicorn, but that man..." She gave a little shiver then continued. "I...I didn't really get why she was willing to give up so much and change so much for you. Now, after being with Soo-Mi and after tonight, I get it. And...I guess we're both idiots."

Gwen watched her for a long time, until Nic felt almost uncomfortable beneath the intensity of her stare. And then Gwen raised her glass and clinked it against Nic's. "Well, cheers to that."

After a comfortable silence settled between them, Gwen said, "You know, I think what you do is remarkable. Ava comes home and tells me about the things you've thought up. The ingenuity and science of it all. I play pretend on set all day, and you think of ways to better the future. You're very impressive, Nic."

An unexpected warmth bloomed in Nic's chest. She did not expect Gwen's validation to mean this much. It was stupid how much her respect meant to Nic, but here they were. And so Nic's smile was small but genuine. "Of course I am."

Ava was tired, sore, and ravenous when she landed on the balcony of their home. The lounge light was still on, as well as the kitchen light, which meant she wouldn't have to worry about waking Gwen up when she fixed herself a snack. She smiled to herself, remembering the birthday cupcakes Gwen had ordered. She wondered if there was still a strawberry one.

She opened the giant French doors quietly and let herself in. Her suit smelled of smoke and burnt kevlar. She'd have to ask Nic to look at it. Ava wondered if her best friend had made it home safely. She suddenly realised that Nic and Soo-Mi would have left immediately after. So much for game night. It was sort of fun while it lasted. She sighed and supposed it was an inevitable end to a night no one except Ava really wanted anyway. Whatever. She was tired and ready for a bath and a long, long sleep.

The sound of laughter and the clink of a glass made Ava stop and listen. Was the TV still on? But then a familiar voice said, "And that thing she does with her socks. Like, oh my God. Balled up socks in the weirdest places!"

More laughter. Definitely Gwen's laughter.

Ava turned the corner to the living room and stopped dead, blinking as she tried to get her brain to catch up to what her eyes were seeing. Nic and Gwen were on the lounge floor, kneeling on opposite sides of the coffee table, with a tower of small tiles between them. Also on the table was an empty bottle of gin, a half empty bottle of vermouth, and a recently opened bottle of the fancy champagne that Gwen had told Ava she never planned on opening.

"Uh…" Ava stepped into the light, and two pairs of eyes turned their blurred visions towards her. "What's uh… what's happening?"

"Isn't it obvious?" Gwen asked, using her champagne glass to motion towards the table. "We're playing Jenga."

"Jenga!" Nic yelled, pulling at a tile and causing the rest of the tower to collapse around them. Both women broke into silly giggles, and Ava wondered if that Keela had given her a concussion.

"You wanna play?" Nic slurred a little as Gwen collected the tiles.

"I…" She laughed incredulously and shook her head. "I think I'm good."

They were still stacking tiles when Ava left to go find a strawberry cupcake. Game night, she decided, had been a rousing success.

If you enjoyed this short story, check out *Chasing Stars* by Alex K. Thorne, the novel in which Gwen and Ava met and fell in love.

Two Hearts—One Mind

by RJ Nolan

"Hey, McKenna."

Sam's fingers froze on her uniform shirt buttons. She stepped to the end of the row of lockers and peered toward the door.

Kowalski, a fellow officer, stood with the locker room door propped open with his foot. He motioned Sam over.

Buttoning her shirt as she went, Sam made her way to the door. "What's up? I already signed out."

Kowalski smirked. "You're a sly dog, McKenna. You better hope Christy never finds out."

Sam scowled. Just the mention of her girlfriend was enough to sour Sam's good mood. She waved Kowalski out into the hallway and followed him. "What the hell are you talking about?"

A smile that could only be termed lecherous covered Kowalski's face. "There's a smoking-hot blonde asking for you at the front desk."

Sam wasn't expecting any visitors. "What does she look like?"

"She's got a killer body." He brought his hands up and mimed the woman's breast size. "Hot damn."

Sam smacked him on the back of the head. "That's not what I meant."

"Kill joy," Kowalski muttered. "Fine. About five-nine. Shoulder-length curly blond hair. Blue eyes." He waggled his eyebrows. "And like I said, she's smoking-hot."

She knew one woman who fit that description perfectly. *Kim.* "Did you leave her in the lobby?"

"Yeah. I—"

Sam waved him off. "Thanks." She headed for the front desk at a fast walk. *What's Kim doing here in the middle of the week?* Fear shot through Sam. *Has something happened to Jess?* Even as the thought crossed her mind, Sam discounted it. There was no way Kim would be anywhere but at Jess's side if that were the case.

She shoved open the door to the lobby and scanned the packed room. Every chair was filled, and people were lined up in front of the main desk. Kim was sitting in a chair against the far wall. A poster on domestic violence hung on the wall above her head. The woman sitting to Kim's right was leaning way too far into Kim's personal space for Sam's comfort.

Sam quickened her pace. "Hey, Kim," she said as soon as she got close enough to be heard.

The woman next to Kim jerked back. Her gaze bounced between Sam and Kim.

Crossing her arms over her chest, Sam gave the woman a stern look.

With one last glance at Kim, the woman got up and scurried away.

Sam tried not to smile at the relieved look on Kim's face. While Kim dealt with more than her fair share of strange characters as a psychiatrist working in L.A. Metro's ER, she looked uneasy and out of place in the police station.

"Sam," Kim said. She smiled as she rose from her chair.

"Everything okay?" Sam gave Kim's hand a quick squeeze.

Kim hesitated, then nodded. "Um…sorry to just show up like this without talking to you first. I tried to call you last night, but your phone went straight to voice mail. I tried again this morning but just got your voice mail again."

"Sorry about that. My phone got broken last night at volleyball practice. I haven't had a chance to replace it."

"Oh. Okay." Kim shifted in place and stuck her hands in her jean pockets. "I planned on coming down regardless." Her gaze dropped to the floor. "I hope you don't mind."

Sam peered at her. *What's going on?* Something was off. It wasn't like Kim to sound so unsure of herself. *She knows how much I care about her. I'm always happy to see her whether my sister can come with her or not.*

A commotion broke out near the front desk before Sam could question her further.

Sam stepped in front of Kim, shielding her from the fracas. She made sure her fellow officers had the troublemaker under control before turning back to Kim. "Come on. You can wait for me in the back while I change and secure my gear. Then we can go grab a cup of coffee and you can tell me what's going on."

"I need to do some shopping," Kim said.

"Shopping? But…" That didn't make any sense to Sam. She couldn't think of anything that would be available in San Diego that wouldn't be in Los Angeles, where Kim and Jess lived. Before Sam could ask any questions, Kim headed toward the back of the coffee shop. Sam trailed in her wake.

Kim settled into an overstuffed chair in a quiet corner of the shop.

Sam pulled the chair next to hers closer and angled it so they could talk somewhat privately. Thankfully, at this time of the afternoon, the coffee shop wasn't crowded. "So Jess couldn't get the day off to come with you, huh?"

Kim shook her head. She looked everywhere except at Sam. Kim popped out of her chair, making Sam jump. "I'll go get our coffee." She practically bolted from Sam.

What the heck? Between Kim coming to San Diego alone for a shopping trip and her unusual behavior, things just didn't add up for Sam and that stirred her cop instincts. *I hope she's not upset with Jess.*

Jess had been keeping a secret from Kim for weeks now. *Please don't let anything mess up Jess's plans.* She was drawn out of her thoughts by Kim's return.

"Here you go," Kim said. She handed Sam a cup of coffee and a small brown bag.

Opening the bag eagerly, Sam smiled. *Oh, yeah. She knows me well.* Unlike Jess, Sam shared Kim's chocolate addiction. She pulled out the chocolate croissant and took a big bite. Sam groaned, and her eyes closed as the rich chocolate and pastry melted in her mouth. She opened her eyes and grinned at Kim. "Are you trying to bribe me into going shopping with you?"

Kim flushed. "Maybe." Her expression turned serious. "I really do need your help."

"Anything," Sam said. "You know that."

"I know." Kim touched Sam's knee. "And I appreciate it."

"Tell me what I can do to help." It bothered her to see Kim, who was usually so outgoing and vibrant, acting so subdued.

"Well, Valentine's Day is next Friday."

Since that's all Jess has talked about for the last month. Oh yeah. I know. She couldn't wait to see Kim's reaction to Jess's surprise. Sam fought to tame a smirk. "Really? That's next week?"

"Sam!" Kim's tone left no doubt she wasn't in the mood to be teased.

"Okay, sorry. Go ahead."

Kim scrubbed her hands up and down her thighs, then sighed. "The Valentine's Day present I planned for Jess," her voice hitched, "well, it didn't work out." She looked up at Sam with tears glimmering in the corners of her eyes.

What the hell is going on? This has got to be about more than a present. Sam leaned close. "Hey. It's okay. I'm sure Jess will understand. She'll love anything you get her."

As Kim brushed her hair back from her face, she blew out a breath. "I know. It's just…complicated. Anyway, I want this Valentine's Day to be extra special—for both of us." She met Sam's gaze, and the confident spark Sam was used to seeing in Kim's warm, blue eyes finally made an appearance. "I'm going to buy her a ring and ask her to marry me."

Holy smokes, Batman! There go all of Jess's plans up in smoke. Now what do I do? "Um…Well…"

Kim's expression fell.

Ah. Crap. "That's great. I'm sure Jess will be thrilled."

"You're sure?" Kim's brow furrowed. "Do you know something I don't?"

Oh, shit! Jess warned you Kim was getting suspicious. Sam put on her best cop face. "No."

"You're positive?" Kim stared at her hard as if trying to gauge her sincerity.

"Absolutely positive." Sam was sure Kim would forgive her once she found out why Sam lied. *Jess will kill me if I blow the surprise she's been planning for weeks.*

"Then you'll help me?"

"Of course," Sam said, finally over her shock at what Kim was proposing—literally. A little half-smirk tugged at the corner of her lips. *Looks like Jess is about to get a surprise of her own.*

"Great. Thank you." Kim's smile lit her face. "You're the same ring size as Jess, so I wanted you to make sure the ring would fit her."

Well, now I know why she wanted to come to San Diego. "Did you have a specific jeweler in mind?" *I know a good one, but I'm sure as hell not suggesting that one.*

"Yes," Kim said. "That's the other reason I needed to come down here. I want to go to Aberdeen Jewelers in La Jolla."

Panic raced through Sam. Aberdeen was the same jeweler where Jess had purchased Kim's ring. *Could this get any worse?*

"It must be around here somewhere?" Kim glanced at the piece of paper in her hand, then up at the number on the store nearest them. "We're still twenty numbers off. Must be farther on."

Sam knew they needed to go to the end of the walkway where they were and then around the corner, but she couldn't very well say that. Aberdeen's was tucked into the back corner of an outdoor mall filled with run-of-the-mill tourist shops. It was not in a location you would stumble upon by accident. "So where did you hear about this place?"

"Do you remember Lindsay Bower? She's the social worker you met at Sid's."

"Right." Sam nodded. "I remember."

"She bought her partner a ring here last year. She just raved about the place."

Ah. Same way Jess heard about it. Thanks a lot, Lindsay. They must get lots of word-of-mouth business because the place sure doesn't fit in with the rest of the low-end shops here.

"There it is!" Kim said.

Sam kept a smile plastered on her face as she held open the door to the exclusive jewelry store for Kim. She scanned the small store. *Oh great.* Sam bit back a groan. *You just had to ask if things could get worse.* There, standing behind the counter, was the same salesman that had waited on Jess.

The man's smile brightened when he spotted Sam. "Welcome ba—"

Sam coughed loudly. "Excuse me. Hello."

A frown marred the salesman's face. "Here to pick—"

A coughing fit overtook Sam. Or at least that's what she hoped Kim thought.

Kim was instantly at her side. She stroked her hand soothingly up and down Sam's back.

Sam straightened up and cleared her throat. She met Kim's concerned blue eyes. Guilt stung her for worrying Kim and taking advantage of her caring nature. But under the circumstances she had little choice.

"You okay?" Kim asked.

"Yeah. Don't know what happened there." Sam motioned toward a water cooler she had spotted on her initial perusal of the room. "Would you mind getting me a drink of water?"

"Of course, Sam."

As soon as Kim walked away, Sam moved close to the counter and the salesman. She had to be quick; the shop wasn't that big, and Kim would be back momentarily. She lowered her voice. "You don't know me. I've never been in the store before. Got me?"

"Here you go, Sam."

Sam jumped and spun around toward Kim. "Thanks." She took the small cup, grateful for the chance to regain her composure.

"It everything okay?" Kim asked.

"Good. Everything's good." Sam barely resisted the urge to squirm under Kim's sharp gaze. *Calm down. She's way too perceptive, but it's not like she can read your mind.* "Mr. …." She turned to the salesman. "I'm sorry. I didn't get your name."

"Redmond. David Redmond."

"I was just telling Mr. Redmond."

"David. Please. Call me David."

"Okay, David. That you are interested in seeing some wedding bands without stones. That's what you wanted. Right?"

Kim looked back and forth between Sam and Redmond.

Please don't ask questions. Sam held her breath.

"Yes. I'd like to see some wedding bands in white-gold and platinum if you have any," Kim said.

"Great." Sam caught herself before she walked straight to the case where the bands were. She looked at Redmond. "Where would those types of rings be?"

When Redmond pulled two trays of rings from a display case, Sam moved away. She stared unseeingly into a display case several feet away. *You know she's going to ask your opinion. So how do I keep from giving it without hurting her feelings or making her suspicious?* Her brain was running a mile a minute, trying to come up with a solution. As much as she loved her sister and Kim, Sam couldn't help cursing her involvement. *How the hell did I end up in the middle of this?*

"Sam. Come take a look. Please."

Damn. Here we go. Sam made her way toward Kim as if she were dragging a fifty-pound weight.

"I've narrowed it down to these rings," Kim said. "Which one do you like?"

Two rings lay on a piece of black velvet on the counter.

When she got a good look at the rings, Sam struggled to hide her reaction. *No way!* She glanced at Kim.

Kim's bright smile abruptly faded. "You don't like either of them."

"That's not true." Sam picked up each ring and made a show of examining it. "They're both beautiful." And it was true. The rings were fantastic.

"So what's wrong then?"

All these rings and those are the two you picked. Just kill me now, 'cause there is no way in hell I'm giving my opinion. "Nothing—"

"Sam."

She flinched at the irritated tone in Kim's voice. *She knows you too well.* Sam forced herself to meet Kim's gaze. *Don't ruin this for her.* "They're both beautiful rings. I'm sure Jess would be thrilled and proud to wear either one. It's just that… It's such a personal thing." Sam shifted and stuck her hands into the pockets of her jeans. "I mean this ring is supposed to be your expression of your love for Jess. I don't feel comfortable giving an opinion." *Especially not on those two rings.* She tensed, waiting for Kim's reaction. Her breath almost whooshed out in relief when a stunning smile graced Kim's face.

"You're absolutely right." Kim placed a quick kiss on Sam's cheek. Without hesitation, she reached for one of the rings.

Sam bit her cheek to keep from laughing. *Unbelievable. Looks like you're in for more than one surprise, Jess.*

Come on. Kim tapped the pen against her teeth. *It shouldn't be this hard.* She stared at the blank sheet of paper, willing the words to come to her. The din of the busy hospital cafeteria was not helping her concentration any. Blocking out the sights and sounds around her, she focused on what she wanted to say. *It's not like*

it's the proposal. Jess had almost caught her twice trying to write that. *You just don't want her to worry that you left work early.*

Kim had been surprised that morning. She had expected more of a protest when she suggested they take separate vehicles to work. While it had made things easier for her plans, it also worried her. Jess had been uncharacteristically distracted and a little distant over the last two weeks. *Ever since she found out you weren't pregnant—again.* Kim wanted it so desperately that she convinced herself that this time she was going to be able to fulfill her and Jess's wish for a child. That was to be her Valentine gift to Jess. She had been devastated when once again she failed. Anxiety twisted Kim's stomach. *Maybe she's regretting her commitment now that she knows I can't give her a child.*

Sliding her hand into her pants pocket, Kim felt for the ring box. She had taken to carrying it with her like a talisman. Her fingers tightened around the box. *Now you're just projecting your own fears onto Jess. She's never been anything but sympathetic and encouraging that you try again.*

She blew out a breath, then glanced at her watch. *Write her a note so you can go home and get everything ready for her surprise.* With that pep talk, Kim set to work on her missive.

Someone pulled the chair next to her away from the table.

Kim started. Instinctively, her hand covered the note to Jess.

Chris set down his tray and slid into the chair next to her. "Hey, Kim. Sorry. I'm running a little late."

"That's okay." Kim withdrew a twenty-dollar bill from her pocket and offered it to Chris. "I appreciate your help."

Laughing, he waved off the money. "I was just kidding earlier. You don't have to pay for my meal."

"I don't mind. You're really helping me out. I know you're not fond of covering the ER." Under normal circumstances, she wouldn't have asked him, but she needed to get home before Jess and she could only do that if someone covered the ER for her.

"I promise to be on my best behavior."

Kim flushed. "I didn't mean anything—"

"Relax, Kim. It's fine. We both know I'm not a big fan of the ER, but it has gotten a lot better since you've been down there full-time. I wouldn't have agreed if

153

I didn't want to do it." He cocked his head at Kim and grinned. "Want to tell me what the big secret is?"

A flash of panic struck. *How does he know I've got a secret? Could Jess know too?* She forced herself to meet his gaze. *Get a hold of yourself. He can't possibly know anything.* "Nothing secret about it. I just need to take care of some things." Kim silently cursed the stress modulation of her voice.

"Right. You just happen to need me to cover for you on Valentine's Day." He pointed to the pen in her hand. "You've been tapping that pen since I sat down. And don't think I didn't notice you covering that note when I walked up."

Kim jumped when his hand stilled her bouncing knee. A blush heated her face. *Damn. Now I know how Sam feels. Psychiatrists are just too observant.* She had been completely unaware of the body movement.

"You're practically vibrating with repressed emotion." He wagged a finger at her and chuckled. "Careful, Doctor. Your 'tells' are showing."

Kim's gaze darted to the tables closest to them. If someone had overheard Chris… When he placed his hand on her forearm, she jumped.

"No one heard me. Sorry. It's so unusual to see you flustered, I couldn't resist teasing you. Normally it's hard to pick up anything from you that you don't want someone to see." He gave her arm a squeeze, then retreated. "Whatever you're doing, I hope it works out like you want."

"Thanks, Chris."

Using the doorway for cover, Kim scoped out the nurses' station. *No sign of Jess.* She squinted, trying to read the two-sided intake board hanging above the far counter. If she could make out Jess's name, she would know if she was busy in a room or not. *No such luck.* She was just too far away to read the board.

Kim had intentionally left her coat and purse locked in her trunk this morning. All she needed to do was leave Jess's note with Penny and get out of there before Jess saw her. She had thought of putting the note on Jess's desk, but there was too big a chance Jess might not see it.

Keeping her eyes peeled for Jess, she made her way toward Penny, who was staffing the desk. "Hey, Penny. Could you do me a favor, please?"

"Oh. Hey, Dr. Donovan. I've been looking for you."

Oh, no. Not today. Kim sighed. *Patients come first, no matter how bad you want to get out of here.* "What's up?"

"Dr. McKenna asked me to give this to you before she left." Penny held out a plain white envelope with Kim's name written on the front in Jess's bold script.

What? Jess left? Where would she go?

"Dr. Donovan?" Penny was still holding out the envelope.

"Sorry. Thanks," she said as she took the note. Her curiosity was killing her, but she needed to take care of business first. "Before I forget, I'm leaving as well. Dr. Roberts will be covering the rest of my shift. Make sure everyone knows, please."

"Sure, Dr. Donovan." Penny eyed the envelope. "I guess with you both leaving early you must have some special Valentine's Day plans."

Kim gave a noncommittal shrug. Some information about their personal life being known at work was unavoidable since they worked together every day. But they made a point of never giving out any details of their private time together. *Although when Jess accepts your ring, that's going to be kind of hard to hide.*

Unable to wait any longer, Kim tore open the envelope Jess had left for her. She pulled out the single sheet of paper and started to unfold it.

Penny, not so subtly, leaned on the counter.

Kim raised an eyebrow in her direction.

Penny's cheeks pinked. She took a step back and seemed to find the counter top of sudden interest.

Assured Penny couldn't see it, Kim read the note. *Huh?* She read it again.

Kim,

A wheeled conveyance holds scents to stimulate your senses. A sight pleasing to your eyes. And tastes to delight your palate.

Love, Jess

Kim smiled when she figured it out. "Penny. I need to get going. Don't forget, call Dr. Roberts if you need anything."

"Sure thing, Dr. Donovan."

Kim turned and set off with a purposeful stride.

Kim peered in the window of her car as she unlocked the door. Grinning at the sight that met her eyes, she slid into the driver's seat. There, on the passenger seat, were a bouquet of red roses and a heart-shaped box of chocolates. She breathed in the scent of the roses, then, unable to resist the lure of the chocolate, opened the lid of the box.

A second note, resting on top of the chocolate, awaited her. *Pretty confident I'd open the chocolate right away.* She popped a piece of chocolate into her mouth. *Like I could resist.* She hummed when the rich confection melted on her tongue. *Oh yeah. Almost as good as sex.* She chuckled to herself. *Almost.*

A surge of anticipation gripped her. Jess had never done anything like this before. *What's next?* She read the new note. It was even more cryptic than the previous one.

Kim,

Let your heart be your guide. The eye in the sky will lead you to your fated destiny.

Love, Jess

What the heck? Kim indulged in another piece of chocolate to stimulate her thought process as she puzzled it out. She picked up the heart-shaped box filled with chocolates. Not finding anything, she put it back on the seat. She looked out the windshield at the sky. *The eye in the sky?* She glanced around the car. *Did I miss a clue?* She looked closer for anything she might have missed. Her gaze landed on the lid of the chocolate box resting on the dash, right next to her GPS unit. *Oh. That's sneaky, Jess.* She laughed.

She flipped on the unit and sure enough, a new destination had been entered. All she needed to do was press Go. Her eyebrows shot up at the sight of the address. *Wow, Jess. You're really going all out. The Beach House Hotel.* As she picked up the lid to put it back on the chocolates, she spotted something written on the inside of the lid in Jess's distinctive handwriting. *Room 377.*

I can't wait to see what else she has up her sleeve. Kim started the car, then froze. *Dang.* She had been so excited about Jess's surprise, she had forgotten about her own plans. She glanced at her watch. It was too late to cancel the elaborate dinner she was having delivered to the house. *Maybe Debbie and Joel would like the meal. If not, at least they could take delivery of some very expensive leftovers.* On such short notice, Kim wasn't sure who else to ask except their closest neighbors.

Dinner doesn't matter. Jess had obviously put a lot of thought and planning into making the day special. Kim's hand went to the ring box in her pocket. *She's done a great job of surprising me, but I still have a big surprise of my own.*

Her heart was light and overflowing with love as she headed to fulfill her destiny. *I'll be there soon, love.*

Jess leaned against the balcony railing, the soothing sounds of the surf washing over her. The sun had begun its final descent. Vivid hues of red, orange, and purple painted the darkening sky. She was barely aware of the stunning vista laid out before her. Her thoughts were focused on one person. *Kim.*

Her hand went to the ring box in her pocket. While she had planned for over a month to ask Kim to marry her, it had become imperative after Kim's latest attempt to get pregnant had been unsuccessful. Jess would never forget the sight of Kim curled up on their bed, her beautiful face streaked with tears. Or the sound of her cries and repeated apologies. Jess had never felt more helpless. With Valentine's Day looming, it had seemed the perfect opportunity to avow her commitment and propose.

I wish she were here to share the sunset. Jess glanced at her watch for probably the thirtieth time in the last thirty minutes. Kim would be leaving work soon. *Wonder what she thought of my riddles?* Jess grinned. *Hope she figures them out.* She snorted at the ridiculous thought. *Of course she will.* Her anxiety flared anew. *I just hope she didn't think they were too dumb. I suck at riddles.*

Unable to stand still, Jess walked back into the hotel suite and checked her preparations one more time. A table covered with a snow-white tablecloth waited just inside the glass patio doors. It was already set with two place settings. An unlit candelabra with rose petals surrounding its base graced the center of the table. A gas log was burning brightly in the fireplace opposite the couch. *Looks good.* She wanted everything to be perfect for Kim.

Jess made her way into the bedroom that was separated from the rest of the suite by a waist-high wall. She ran her hand over the thick terrycloth of one of the robes draped across the bottom of the bed.

157

She glanced at her watch. The waiting was making her anxious. Barely resisting the urge to pace, she returned to the balcony doors.

A knock on the door made her heart race. *Relax. It's too early to be Kim. She's probably just now leaving work.*

Jess peered through the spyhole in the door. Her heart, just starting to calm, shot into overdrive. *Kim. But how?* She pulled the door open. "Happy Valentine's Day," she said as she stepped back to let Kim enter.

"Hi." Kim walked past her and into the room.

No kiss?

Kim set her flowers and chocolates down on the small table just inside the room. Free of her burdens, she spun around and pinned Jess against the door.

Jess moaned as Kim took her lips in a searing kiss. When Kim's tongue slid into her mouth and she tasted chocolate, Jess smiled into the kiss. She was panting by the time the kiss broke. *Wow.*

"Happy Valentine's Day."

Jess took Kim's hand and led her into the suite. "Do you like your surprise?"

Kim looked around. "Wow, Jess. This place is amazing." She headed for the balcony doors.

Following her outside, Jess smiled at Kim's reaction. The sun was almost down, but she could still make out the fading colors of the sunset. The roar of the surf added to the ambiance. Jess moved behind Kim and wrapped her arms around her, pulling her close to her chest.

Despite the chill, they watched in silence until the last sliver of the sun had disappeared.

Jess rubbed her hands up and down Kim's arms, trying to warm her. "Let's go inside. The fireplace will warm you right up."

"Good idea." Kim headed straight for the fireplace. She sat down on the raised stone hearth and stretched her hands out toward the fire.

Jess joined her. She took up a spot on the carpet near Kim's feet.

Kim bent down and kissed her gently on the lips. She stroked her fingers though Jess's hair. "Thank you for doing all of this. It was a wonderful surprise."

"It's not over yet." Jess let a little half-smirk appear.

Kim narrowed her eyes at Jess. "What else do you have up your sleeve?"

Jess laughed and made a show of looking up her sleeves. "Nope, nothing there."

"Maybe I should check for myself."

The smoky timbre of Kim's voice sent shivers down Jess's spine. *Check anything you want.* She leaned toward Kim.

"Maybe I should check your pockets as well."

Oh. Yeah. Kim's words finally sank into Jess's aroused brain. *Whoa! Not a good idea.* She pulled away from Kim's questing hands and stood. She resisted the urge to check her pocket to make sure the ring was still there.

"What's wrong?"

Jess gazed down into Kim's passion-filled eyes and bit back a groan. It took every ounce of her formidable willpower to keep from giving in to the want in Kim's vivid blue eyes. Jess took a big step back and bumped into the coffee table. "I just realized dinner will be arriving shortly." Her gaze bore into Kim's. "And once I start making love to you, I don't want anything to interrupt us."

Kim growled. "Cancel dinner."

Laughing, Jess offered her hand to Kim. "You better eat. You're going to need your strength for later." She tugged Kim up to stand next to her.

Kim pressed close and nipped at her pulse point. "Is that a promise?" she husked close to Jess's ear.

Arousal pulsed though Jess. *So help me, God.*

It's time. Nervous energy made Jess feel as if she were going to jump out of her skin. She forced herself to be still. She didn't want to disturb Kim, who was snuggled against her side with her head on Jess's shoulder. "Tired?" she asked.

"No. Just incredibly content."

"Would you like some more wine?"

"No. I don't want to fall asleep on you."

Jess laughed. She gave Kim a quick squeeze, then pulled away. *Okay, this is it.* She swallowed heavily as she turned to face Kim. *Don't mess it up.* She had been working on her proposal for the last week. "Kim...I want to—"

"Wait. I have something I need to say."

"But."

"Please." Kim put her finger on Jess's lips, stilling any further protest.

Jess kissed the finger pressed to her lips and nodded.

Kim clasped both of Jess's hands in hers, then ran her thumbs over the backs of Jess's hands. "You've made this evening so special. First, the notes with the riddles." She laughed. "That was great. Then the roses and chocolates. And finally, all this," she spread her arms, encompassing the room, "and a wonderful dinner. There is only one thing that could make this day even more special." Kim slid off the couch and onto her knees in front of it.

What is she doing? Jess's heartbeat picked up speed.

"I struggled to come up with the perfect speech to express everything in my heart." Kim removed a small jeweler's box from her pocket.

Is that...? It felt as if her heart was trying to escape from her chest.

Kim met Jess's gaze and held it. "Turns out it was really very simple." She opened the box.

A ring was nestled in a bed of black velvet.

Oh. My. God. She's going to ask me.

"I love you." Kim tugged the ring from its velvet nest and offered it to Jess. "Will you marry me?"

Rendered speechless, Jess could only stare at the ring in Kim's hand. Her thoughts whirled through her head like a pinwheel set in motion by the wind. She knew her mouth was hanging open but couldn't seem to move.

"Jess?"

Her gaze darted to Kim's face, then back to the ring. *That's not possible.* Jess felt for the ring box hidden in her own pocket. All of her carefully laid plans were blown away in seconds, but Jess didn't spare them a moment's regret. *She asked me to marry her!*

A heavy sigh from Kim tore Jess from her euphoric stupor.

Kim's hand dropped, and she sat back on her heels. She curled her fingers around the ring.

Wait. My ring! "Kim—"

"It's okay, Jess. You don't like it. I'll get you something else." Distress twisted Kim's beautiful face. "Or...if...I mean." She cleared her throat. "If you'd rather wait and not..." Tears glimmered at the corners of Kim's eyes.

A surge of panic so strong she felt sick to her stomach hit Jess. She slid off the couch and onto her knees in front of Kim. "I was just shocked. I wasn't expecting this." Jess tugged Kim's clenched hand toward her and urged her to open her fingers. She took the ring from Kim's palm. "It's beautiful." She offered it back to Kim. "Will you put it on me?"

Kim shook her head. "I can't."

What?

"You didn't answer my question yet."

Relief washed over Jess. She sank down onto her heels. "Yes. Forever."

A stunning sun-out-from-behind-the-clouds smile lit Kim's face. "Funny you should say that. Read the inscription."

Jess tipped the ring, trying to make out the inscription in the dim light. When she did, her smile rivaled Kim's. *Amazing. Fated indeed.* Jess locked gazes with Kim and repeated the inscription. "Forever."

"Forever." Kim slipped the ring on Jess's finger, sealing the vow.

As Jess gazed down at her ring, the incredulousness of the whole thing struck her funny bone. She burst out laughing.

"What's so funny?"

The tone of Kim's voice drove the laughter from Jess. She flinched at the look on Kim's face. *Fix this fast, or you're going to spend the most important night of your life on the couch—alone.* Jess took both of Kim's hands in hers, pleased when she wasn't rebuffed. "You wouldn't believe it if I told you."

"Try me."

Jess allowed her trademark smirk full rein.

Kim arched an eyebrow, making Jess laugh.

"I had one more surprise for you tonight." Jess pulled the ring box from her pocket.

Kim's eyes went wide.

Jess opened the box. She took great satisfaction in the gob-smacked look on Kim's face. *Now you know how I felt.*

"But…that's…" Kim's gaze darted between the ring in the box and the one on Jess's finger.

"Exactly," Jess said, suppressed laughter in her voice. "They're identical." She lifted the ring from the box and held it out to Kim. "Read the inscription."

Kim's hand shook as she reached for the ring. She tilted it and read the inscription. "Forever yours." Her eyes brimmed with tears. "Put it on me. Please."

"Guess it's kind of a moot point now. But since I'm only ever going to do this once, I want to do it right." Jess rose up onto her knees. "Kim, will you marry me?"

"Yes. Forever." Kim said, echoing Jess's earlier vow.

Jess slipped the ring on her finger. She pulled Kim into her arms.

The kiss they shared was one of love, devotion, passion, and hope of a bright future.

If you enjoyed this short story, check out *L.A. Metro* by RJ Nolan, the novel in which Kim and Jess met and fell in love.

The Brutal Lie

by Lee Winter

Power and intimidation oozed from the New York penthouse office of Bartell Corp's international headquarters, with its sleek, round floors, chrome, and tinted glass.

Maddie Grey padded along the thick carpeted floor, one hand tight around a bottle of champagne, in search of the fashion-editing world's newest conqueror.

The first time she'd been here, two years ago, Maddie had felt like a boot scraping, out of place and lost. Tonight, wearing a grunge T-shirt, leather jacket, and worn jeans, Maddie wasn't a much better fit, but she was no longer awed. This space was now as familiar to her as the imposing woman who ruled it. Elena Bartell: Media mogul and the founder, President, and Chief Operating Officer of Bartell Corporation.

Elena didn't stalk the corridors of this building often anymore, having divested the day-to-day running of her company to her deputy. Her heart and focus had shifted, as had her home base. These days she was engaged in a furious magazine war against iconic fashion bible, *Catwalk Queen*. Elena had been in the trenches, from Sydney to London, trying to make her fashion magazine, *Style International*, the world's number one.

Eighteen months later, it was official. The latest circulation figures had landed a few hours ago while Elena had been holding Bartell Corp's annual general meeting. *Style* hadn't just beaten its rival, it'd ground it under heel.

This was definitely cause for celebration.

Maddie found Elena scribbling notes at her desk, still wearing a cocktail dress from the party after the AGM, as if she'd been distracted and forgotten to change.

Maddie leaned against the door, appreciating her lover's dress—a scarlet second skin with a plunging neckline that hinted at the delights within.

Dear God. Elena did wear red well. It reminded her of a particularly sinful garnet dress that had undone Maddie once. She'd been a junior night-shift crime reporter and had made a total fool of herself, face-planting in front of her then-boss. And Elena had seemed...amused.

"Hey, sexy. When you didn't come home, I brought the party to you." Maddie placed the champagne on Elena's glass, designer desk.

Elena's head lifted in surprise. Regret darted into her eyes as she glanced at the clock. "I'm sorry. I didn't intend to be so long."

"Time flies when you're vanquishing your mortal enemies."

"Now there's a pleasant thought." Elena's eyes lit up. She tapped a sheet of numbers. "Almost as pleasant as my figures."

"Well, I do like one of your figures in particular." Maddie's gaze lingered. "God, *that* dress. It reminds me of a certain other creation."

"You remember that?"

"Is that a trick question? I'm astonished I could still walk after the first time I saw you in it."

"If I recall, you spent more time on your face than walking." Elena rose, smoothing the dress down her hips and thighs. "I also recall you watching me in the reflection of the window." Moving toward it, her hips gave a languid sway. "I was standing right here, staring outside."

Maddie came up behind her, close enough to feel Elena's warmth. "Gazing at me in the glass you mean."

Elena's eyes twinkled at her in the reflection. "I distinctly remember the impressive New York City skyline."

"Uh-uh." Maddie pressed herself into her lover's back. "Fess up: What *were* you thinking that night?"

"Truthfully?" Elena's expression in the reflection became distant. "I was transfixed by how hungry your eyes seemed. You surprised me."

"And me. I had an epiphany that night."

"Oh?"

"Mmm. How hot my boss was. How I wanted my hot boss. And a few other unspeakable things."

"Unspeakable?" Elena's voice dropped a register lower.

"Mm-hmm. You know…" Maddie licked her lips. "We could re-create that night. I may have suggested to Tony on the front desk not to interrupt you except for emergencies."

"That seems somewhat presumptuous." Elena's voice warmed.

"It's late. Barely anyone's left in the building." Maddie paused and added slyly, "I mean…unless you have other plans?"

Elena pretended to consider that. "Well, I am rather busy. One doesn't destroy *CQ*'s circulation in a day. It must be ongoing. There's planning."

Maddie dropped a kiss at the base of Elena's neck, then another under her ear. "True, but today you're a golden goddess who can ignore her work and accept her glorious reward."

"What form does this reward take?" Elena's voice was low and interested.

Maddie slid her hands down that sleek dress, and then reversed course, bringing the hem up with her. Her fingers slid to between Elena's thighs. "Well, the usual accolades and tributes. Plus sexual favours, naturally." She rubbed Elena's thong pointedly.

Elena's mouth parted slightly. Her eyes became half-lidded, and there was no mistaking the arousal in her expression.

Fingers dancing and teasing, Maddie listened to the shift in Elena's breathing. Oh, how she loved this bit, where Elena wouldn't ask for more, not yet; because she enjoyed the games and foreplay as much as the sex. Elena's jaw clenched, biting back a gasped moan, and her eyes pleaded for things Elena's lips would never ask for.

Maddie played with her lover for long minutes, soaking in the naked want on the beautiful face in the window: high cheekbones, pale skin, jet-black, sculpted short hair, and arching eyebrows that always seemed mocking. But there was nothing but desire in those hooded eyes tonight. All for her.

She loved seeing Elena in a way no one else did. Emotionally naked and vulnerable. *Mine.*

"Take this off for me." Maddie tapped Elena's soaked thong.

Sometimes Maddie ordered Elena to do intimate things just to watch her wordlessly obey. That was arousing. Telling the woman who controlled almost a billion-dollar empire what she *had* to do.

Elena always seemed to know what that meant for her. That this was where Maddie had power too. After a delicious pause, Elena reached under her dress and slid her lace thong down. She met Maddie's eye and her need was clear.

"Madeleine." She drew out the word until it sounded French and naughty, becoming a demand. Elena's way of saying, *enough playing.*

Smiling at her impatience, Maddie reached for her soft thigh. She trailed higher. Without a barrier, Maddie's fingers moved easily across swollen skin.

"Tell me something," Elena said, voice breathless. Her eyes became far too knowing.

A shiver skittered down Maddie's spine at that taunting, devilish gaze. *Uh-oh.* Elena did love to fight back, to try to wrestle the power away from Maddie when she felt her own control slipping too fast.

"What did you wish you could have done that night two years ago?" Elena asked. "When you watched me in this window?"

Maddie parted Elena's folds and slid her fingers through wet flesh. "That night, I wished you'd kissed me. Pushed me against a wall and kissed me senseless." Her nipples tightened at the reminder. *God, that night.*

"Is that *all* you wanted?" Elena rolled her hips forward, pressing harder into Maddie's fingers. She quivered and bucked into Maddie and seemed to struggle to keep her arousal in check as she finished the deliberate words designed to crack Maddie's restraint.

If only Elena knew how pitifully close Maddie already was.

"You just wanted a kiss from me that night?" Elena's hands landed on the window, bracing herself. Her fingers shifted a little, leaving steamy, smeared imprints on the glass.

"Well, maybe my fantasies included you flinging me on your desk, tearing off my jeans, and—"

"On my desk?" Elena's eyebrows lifted to cocky heights. "My desk is only for work, Madeleine."

Jesus. The soft, playful timbre of her voice would kill her yet.

"You know that," Elena finished, adding a soft growl as Maddie pressed harder.

She *did* know that. It's why it was so fun to tweak her about desk sex. Maddie smirked, then dipped inside her. "God, Elena, you're so wet. So needy."

Elena bucked into Maddie's hand and muttered, "I am *not* needy."

Sure she wasn't. Maddie lifted her other hand up the dress, tracing heated skin within the deep vee. She slipped her hand under the silken material and lifted Elena's bare breast outside the dress. They gazed at the sight in the window.

Maddie's breath hitched. It seemed so naughty, so daring, that pale, soft breast lying against a blood-red dress, an erect nipple crinkling in the air. *Jesus.* Maddie rubbed the tight nub while moving her other hand through coarse, trimmed hairs, to Elena's clit, circling it. She shifted her legs trying to alleviate the rising heat between her own thighs. One touch, hell, one pointed look from Elena, and she'd fly apart in seconds.

Elena moaned.

"Not needy? Are you sure?" Maddie tongued the salty skin of Elena's neck until she shivered. Then she drove her fingers deep inside her, curling them up, at the same time pinching her nipple hard.

Elena choked out a gasp, pushed a hand between her legs, and rubbed herself frantically. She shuddered, trembled, and slumped her forehead into the glass with a pained groan. "Oh God. That was… Oh, Madeleine, I had to. Couldn't wait."

Maddie would never get used to this arousing sight, no matter how many times they'd made love. Elena unable to stop herself. Elena lost. Whimpering. Finally, irrevocably undone. She smiled. "I love it when you do that. Lose control so completely you can't help yourself."

Maddie withdrew her fingers, pausing to spread the wetness around Elena's most intimate flesh until she twitched again.

Turning Elena around to face her, Maddie kissed her deeply. The response was hungry, heated, and arousing.

When they parted, Elena's mussed hair, smudged lipstick, and bare breast pushed Maddie right to the edge. Her swallow was shaky.

Elena's smile was cocksure. She trailed a fingertip down Maddie's neck. "Now then. What to do with you?"

"The desk?" Maddie croaked hopefully, already knowing the answer, as she unbuttoned her jeans.

"Absolutely not." Elena's cool gaze raked Maddie's form as if deciding exactly how to devour her. "How would I ever be able to work if all I could picture was me debauching you all over it?" Pushing a hand inside Maddie's jeans, she cupped her heat through the boy shorts. "Well, well. Speaking of needy."

"It's not like you work a lot on *that* desk, though," Maddie protested weakly, as Elena rubbed with determination. Her underwear was soaked through. She was helpless whenever Elena's fingers got anywhere near her. Maddie couldn't get enough, and her moans were soon filling the room. Just her touch, combined with the thought that Elena might consider flinging her down on her desk, where she ruled her almost billion-dollar empire… *Gah.* "*Style Sydney*'s desk gets most of your attention these days," Maddie gasped out. "We could just…"

Elena pressed against her clit with unerring accuracy, and oh God, Maddie was about to…

The desk phone started ringing.

Both women froze.

Maddie frowned. She'd been clear to Security about no interruptions.

Elena yanked her hand out of Maddie's jeans, adjusted her breast back into her dress, and stalked to the desk, irritation sharp in her stride. Wiping her fingers on a tissue, she then stabbed the speaker button. "Yes?"

"Ms Bartell, sorry to bother you, I have Perry Marks here to see you. He says he has urgent business. Shall I send him up?"

"One moment." Elena stabbed the Hold button. She glanced over at Maddie. A speculative, dangerous look crossed her face. Elena perched on the edge of the desk and leaned back, which pushed her ample breasts hard against red silk. "I suppose I *could* take you on the desk," she said as though considering it. "Spread you out, strip you bare. Splay you before me. Then I'd roll up to you in my chair, lick my way up those delightful thighs, and feast on you. Would you like that? *Madeleine?*"

Oh fuck. Arousal surged through Maddie. Elena loved to do this to her, describe in detail her erotic plans. She searched Elena's daring expression and came closer. "Y-you mean now? B-but—"

Elena gave her an imperious look. "Well?" She moved in front of her and rubbed the seam of Maddie's jeans, hard, between her legs. "*Would* you like that, Madeleine?"

The pressure and positioning were perfect—as Elena well knew given the look in her eyes.

With a sharp, startled cry, Maddie came on the spot. Her knees and thighs trembled as warmth spread through her nerve endings. "You'd actually agree to that?" Maddie gasped out. "Next time, I mean?"

Elena's smile was equal parts triumph, amusement, and delight. "Of course not. My desk is for work purposes only."

Maddie groaned. God damn it. Elena could play her like a fiddle. She used her power so perfectly in their sex life, with such precision, it should be a crime. Maddie both hated and loved how well Elena knew her weaknesses and every turn-on. It was arousing, powerful, and probably a little pathetic if she bothered to care, which she absolutely didn't. Maddie was, quite simply, putty in Elena's hands, and they both knew it.

Heat flooded her, and only part of it was to do with that magnificent orgasm.

Elena smirked, dropped a kiss on Maddie's cheek, and then stabbed her phone. Her voice was stern and dry: "Send my global art director up."

Elena made it into her chair with seconds to spare when the elevator dinged announcing Perry's arrival. Madeleine—teasing, intoxicating Madeleine—had insisted on distracting her with further passionate kisses, leaving barely any time to fix her appearance. Elena squirmed in her chair, self-conscious about what was missing, and darted an appalled look toward where a tangle of thong still lay. She hadn't had time to reclaim it. Still, those kisses had been quite something. She prayed Perry wouldn't notice what lay at the foot of her office window.

Madeleine followed her gaze and mouthed "sorry", just as Perry swished into the office in an elegant, lilac Brioni suit.

He stood in front of Elena and ran a hand over his dark-skinned bald pate. "What *did* you say to Tony for him to give me the third degree about sending me up?" He almost pouted.

"A better question is what has you in here so late? And what constitutes enough of an emergency for him to override a Do Not Disturb?" Elena drawled. "Especially after Bartell Corp's dividend that'll see half its shareholders off to Aspen, and a certain fashion mag's destruction." She leaned forward. "Do *not* tell me you're here to ruin my famously good mood with bad news."

He snorted at that characterization of her mood. "Yes, well, it's *CQ* I'm here about." He sagged a little. "Emmanuelle Lecoq specifically."

Elena's pulse kicked up at the mention of the rival magazine's editor. "What's she done now?"

He opened his mouth, then caught sight of the visitor's sofa. "Sorry, Maddie, didn't see you there. Hello."

"Hey, Perry. Great to see you again." Madeleine grinned, and her genuine affection for the man was infused in her voice.

Then again, her warm, affectionate lover seemed to like pretty much everyone. Elena could not relate to that in the least. She folded her arms. "Perhaps if you just spat it out."

"Fine." Perry reached into his briefcase. "You know I have contacts everywhere. This is out tomorrow." A newspaper hit her desk.

Madeleine joined Elena to read over her shoulder.

'NO PASSING FADS FOR ME!' LECOQ DISHES DIRT

Elena scoured the page. Just a shallow profile about the *CQ* editor's style, beauty, leadership, and, *Christ*, genius. The puff-piece was designed, no doubt, to take the heat off her circulation figures.

Perry tapped a paragraph. "Here's where the bile begins."

Unlike some, I'm not into fickle fads. You won't see me having a desperate, midlife-crisis Sapphic fling with my empty-headed secretary-turned-reporter to feel young or relevant. I also don't need the obscene trappings of success to prove I'm powerful. What would I want with a round, monolithic office and a helipad, any more than I need some ambitious, gold-digger lesbian lover? I'm as classic as my Jimmy Choos. I've been around longer than any other fashion magazine editor, and I will endure long after certain others get bored and move on to their next toy.

Elena stiffened. *Of all the nasty, underhanded...*

Madeleine hissed in an outraged breath. "She stuck a neon arrow on your head with all those clues. Round office? Helipad?"

Elena didn't answer. She stared at the insults. *Empty-headed secretary-turned-reporter. Ambitious gold-digger.* How *dare* she? Madeleine was one of the most clever, insightful people Elena had ever met. She cared about people more than money.

She was kind, decent, and loved with her whole heart. "I'll kill her," Elena hissed. "How dare she say this about you? I'll sue her into the ground. Get me Felicity!"

Madeleine's hand came out to latch onto Elena's forearm. "Hey? Take a breath for a sec? Look, I know she crossed a line. But let's not do some knee-jerk thing. Let's talk first."

"She called you *empty-headed*." Rage filled Elena. "A gold-digger. My mid-life crisis fling! I'm apparently desperate?"

Perry's cheeks darkened, and he looked like he'd rather be anywhere but in the middle of this.

"Fuck it," Elena snarled, "I don't care what people say about me. God knows I collect insulting nicknames. But she attacked *you*."

"Um, I'm not sure you've focused on the big thing here," Madeleine cut in. "She also outed you."

Elena paused. *Oh.* Her brain had skated right over that. Well, hell. She and Madeleine had never addressed their relationship. It was obvious to her valued staff members, such as Perry. But they'd never discussed officially coming out. "She outed you too," Elena murmured.

"I'm just some Australian freelance reporter. But you're…*you*. Emmanuelle was obviously hoping shareholders would choke on their cornflakes and see you as a lightweight flake having some scandalous fling."

Elena glowered. "Nothing she said is true." God, why had she never properly discussed any of this with Madeleine before? It had been so easy to hide themselves away at the ends of the earth in Sydney and forget their private life was newsworthy. "You are no fling," Elena said heatedly. "I'm…a lesbian. This isn't some experiment. What she said has no truth."

Madeleine wrapped an arm around her shoulder. "I know." She glanced at Perry. "We know."

"We do," he said kindly. "Most people will see through what she wrote as the bitter, petty revenge it is. The problem is that 'most' people isn't 'all'. This could be harmful if left to fester."

"But if we sue," Madeleine said, "it looks like we're saying we think our relationship is shameful or wrong."

Elena ground her teeth. "I can't believe this. Lecoq loses the circulation wars, so she shreds me personally? Defames us as air-headed and desperate?"

"She did much worse than that." Perry said thoughtfully. "She outed you. I don't mean she outed *you,* which is bad enough. She's *outed* you. It can be seen as homophobic violence given how dangerous outing can be for some. So a woman heading a magazine about fashion—the gayest industry on earth—just committed homophobia because she was pissy she'd been beaten professionally. Now how do you think that'll play in our world?"

Madeleine gave a slow smile. "Oh…dear. That's true. Perry? Could you give Elena and me five minutes?"

"Sure." He disappeared.

"What has crossed that furtive mind of yours?" Elena asked.

"That depends. How would you feel about being outed in a big way?"

"I thought I already was." Elena folded her arms.

"Please, *The New York Daily Commute*'s readership barely gets above a hundred and fifty thousand on a good day, and only then because it's given away on street corners. Do you think even ten percent of people will read that Lecoq crap on their subway ride? They'll flick through news and sport, if that. What I'm asking is how you'd feel if you woke up tomorrow, and *everyone* knew."

"I…" Elena hesitated as she turned that over. Her conservative Polish-American parents had likely worked her out years ago but were sticking to "don't ask, don't tell". Not that she was close to them. Her most intimate friends, well, friend—Perry—already knew. So…that just left herself. Being talked about and criticised were nothing new given her job. But none of it had ever been so personal. "What of you?" Elena dodged. "Won't people wonder if you got ahead thanks to dating me? Lecoq's mud could stick."

Madeleine snorted. "You mightn't have noticed, but I made a point of never writing for any of your mastheads. As for me personally? Everyone in my life knows and is cool. Mum thinks you're adorable by the way. That's hilarious."

"Adorable? Me?" Elena stared in astonishment.

"Yup." Madeleine snickered.

"Does she know my reputation? The names I'm called? They're not unfounded."

"She knows. She still thinks you're adorable—has done so ever since you got me that birthday cupcake."

Elena sagged. "You're both as mad as each other. I never *could* intimidate you even the slightest."

"Nope." Madeleine grinned. "Don't know why you even bothered. So in answer to your question, I'd be honoured to be outed as yours." She added softly, "Now stop stalling and tell me: *Is* this a big deal for you?"

"Professionally? Once, I might have thought it was a disaster. But after today's figures? Hell, they're lucky to have me."

"Damn straight." Madeleine chuckled. "Sooo….did you just convince yourself? Or do you still have doubts?"

Elena sighed. "I always have doubts. But that's me. I always ensure I've thought of all angles. It's what makes me so successful. I live with doubts."

"And personally?"

"I've loved having you all to myself. It's been wonderful not having to share you with the world, our secret. But I'm not ashamed of us."

Madeleine nodded. "All right. So, I do have a plan. It's a subtle way to point out the error of Emmanuelle's ways and possibly spark a grovelling apology—while you stay above it all."

"Oh?" Elena liked the sound of that a great deal.

"Let's get Perry in here to run it past him too."

A moment later, the art director returned with a pensive look on his face. His gaze scraped the whole room, as though fearing there might be blood on the walls. He paused at the champagne bottle on the desk, shifted his gaze, and then squinted at something by the windows.

Elena followed his eye. *Oh.* Yes, well, he hadn't given her much time, had he? Or, rather, Madeleine hadn't.

"Is that…?" He pointed at Elena's crumpled thong.

"You'd be well advised not to finish that thought." Elena glowered at him, willing a blush not to rise on her face.

Perry snorted. "Celebrating earlier, were we?"

Elena tossed him a death glare.

Madeleine laughed hard.

And the planning began.

173

Four days later, Maddie nervously eyed the Features Editor for the esteemed *US Review* magazine she was sitting opposite. The woman was in her sixties, with a sharp face and a weary expression.

"To recap," Dorothy Follows said, "you wish to change that brilliant pitch you emailed last month and instead write something on…" she consulted her notes, "…the ethics of outing gay people?"

"More than that." Maddie leaned in. "I'll talk to people who've been outed and how that affected their life. Some celebrities, political figures, maybe a coach on a high school team, an ethicist. I'll ask where we draw the line in a nation that prides itself on free speech."

Fallows regarded her. "An interesting concept, but no."

Maddie's heart sank. "But it's so wrong."

"It is. It'd be like running a story on the ethical question of racism. Why would we, when the answer's obvious?"

"It's, um, topical?" Maddie said weakly.

"How so? Who's been outed?"

Maddie fidgeted and wondered if she should be honest or…

"You know you could have just pitched me an exclusive on you and Bartell if you wanted to tackle Emmanuelle Lecoq's outing you."

Maddie blinked, stunned.

"Glossy mags are a small world, Ms Grey." Fallows looked amused. "We're well aware, for instance, of who always goes to media events together. And then you coming in with this pitch, right after Lecoq's story, well…"

Oh. Maddie's cheeks burned.

"So I can offer a cover for you and Bartell's…" she twirled her finger "grand romance."

Maddie shifted uncomfortably. "That's not what I had in mind."

"Oh, I'm well aware. You intended to embarrass Lecoq with your evils-of-outing story, without getting any mud on you or your lover. Right?" She arched an eyebrow.

"I just think she should understand what she's done."

"So don't go soft. Own it. If you get out in front of the story, spin it your way, so that the vacuum won't get filled with someone else's lies and innuendo. Yes, you'll have to put yourselves out there, get muddy, but it's a better result: *You* set the message."

"Elena's private. She'd never—"

"Even if she says no, I'm still offering *you* the chance to tell your story."

"But I'm a no one."

"You really think the woman who turned the head of the world's most mysterious and ruthless media baron is a no one? Look, Lecoq's rumours are now out there. They'll keep swirling until they're addressed."

"Paparazzi have been staking out our home and Elena's office," Maddie conceded with a huff. "Since the day that damned story hit."

"Shocking," Fallows said dryly. "Can you do it by the thirty-first? I'll need it that soon if I'm to capitalize on Lecoq's stunning idiocy."

"I haven't agreed yet."

"So think about it and get back to me ASAP."

Maddie nodded. "I'll let you know."

Elena was in a foul mood, having dodged more intrusive reporters on her way into her office building. Damn them. It would only get worse when Madeleine's story came out. She'd dearly wanted to say no, but Elena had been helpless in the face of her lover's pleading look.

She wouldn't be involved herself, of course. The very idea of explaining herself to strangers who had no right to her life made her shudder. But Madeleine would make it work.

"Tell the truth for both of us," Elena had told her. "Just remember, if you make me sound even the slightest bit soft…" She'd pursed her lips in a veiled threat that only made Madeleine laugh.

Elena wished it were over already. Instead, each day the rumours intensified.

The word from Perry was that *CQ*'s staff were in near open revolt about Lecoq's article.

"I can see why Véronique calls the media *cafards*," Felicity Simmons hissed, as she stalked up to Elena's desk. "Your stalkers might be few, but they are persistent as scuttling roaches."

Elena glanced up at her Deputy Chief Operations Officer. While the highly strung former lawyer had lost some of her skittishness in the past year since her promotion, she still reminded Elena of a well-bred dressage horse—all tight ribbons, flounce, and attitude. "So, what calamity brings you to my floor? I thought you were working on Hudson Shard's launch next month."

"I'm multi-tasking." Felicity slapped a newspaper page down. "And you'll want to see this."

A full-page advertisement from *The New York Times* stared back.

We, the following fashion designers, photographers, advertisers, artists, and models declare a boycott against CQ Magazine while Emmanuelle Lecoq remains editor. As proud allies or members of the LGBT+ community, we feel outing a rival editor reveals a serious lack of character and judgment. Further, outing anyone who has never harmed the queer community is an act of violence and hate. It is irresponsible, dangerous, and something we cannot support. Our services to CQ are withdrawn effective immediately.
Signed...

A list of names ran down the page, some famous. At the end were social media hashtags: #FireLecoq and #boycottCQ.

"Eighty-seven names," Felicity nodded with satisfaction. "Plus dozens more boycotting unofficially."

Elena couldn't believe it. "*CQ* made half of those careers. To boycott the hand that feeds them is astonishing. I had no idea outing was this despised."

"Elena, it's not just the principle. They admire your work, respect *Style*, and are disgusted at how Lecoq treated you. They're fuming." Felicity's expression darkened. "My God, I'd happily poke her eyeballs out myself if I could reach that high."

Elena smiled at the thought of her diminutive deputy squaring off against the angular Lecoq. "Whose idea was the boycott? Yours?"

With a spectacular eye-roll, Felicity said: "It may astonish you to know I'm actually rather busy running Bartell Corporation for you. I don't have time to manage campaigns. Although I must say it's good someone's finally standing up to that ego-puffed cow. She's been untouchable for far too long."

Turning her gaze back to the ad, Elena said: "If not you, then who? Madeleine?"

"Oh, please. We both know your…Australian is far too nice."

Elena's lips twitched. "Yes, well. I'm not denying Madeleine's mystifying eternal niceness."

Felicity snickered softly. "It was your favourite designers. The Duchamps. Apparently it amused Véronique to put the 'noxious *cafard*' in her place. Natalii supplied the hashtags, including a few ruder ones not fit for print. They're trending like crazy. I hear Lecoq's sweating hard now advertisers are pulling out."

"Cockroaches do have a habit of surviving the apocalypse, though."

"Or not." Felicity called up a page on her iPad. "*US Review* just tweeted a story about the *CQ* boycott. They have nine million followers. *Vanity Fair* followed suit. Another five million."

"Oh. Dear." Elena trusted her smile was as evil as it felt.

"Right? Check out *CQ*'s share price today on the back of the boycotts, low circulation, negative publicity, and advertiser withdrawals." She held up her tablet again.

Elena stared at the plunging arrow. "Seriously?" That really was low. A daring plan suddenly hit. Her fingers tingled. "Can you get me Tom Withers? I might need to make a large outlay soon."

Felicity's eyes narrowed. "You wouldn't." Her voice was almost a whisper. "Would you?"

"Wouldn't I?" A hint of mischief laced Elena's tone. "Tell no one. Speed is of the essence."

Felicity's expression was awestruck. "Yes, Elena." Her voice came out a dry gasp.

Maddie was beside herself the day her article was out in the *US Review*. She'd barely slept the previous night, wondering if Elena would hate it. A few hours spent staring at the long, fluttering lashes and quiet intake of breath of the woman asleep beside her hadn't answered the question. Her lover had refused to read it first, saying only that she trusted Maddie.

The hardest thing had been balancing Elena's need to be seen as fierce and tough with all the ways Maddie knew she could be generous and kind.

So Maddie had written the truth: How they'd met. Late-night chats in an empty newspaper office. How they'd come to understand each other, two watchful souls connecting, despite being worlds apart. And that gut-wrenching day Elena chose business over Maddie.

Clutching the glossy magazine, Maddie stared at the cover in confusion.

Elena was pictured with the headline: *Elena Bartell on love, life, and power: 'It would be a grave error to take me on'.*

What? Maddie hadn't quoted Elena saying that. She flipped to the story and then gasped. Two first-person articles were sitting beside each other.

The Mogul.

The Journalist.

Elena had written something after all? Since when?

Elena's piece was a dry, humorous recounting of meeting a "style-deficient reporter from Sydney" and finding her manner to be "blunt to the point of interesting" and her company to be "acceptable despite her refusal to do anything I demanded".

It was funny. God, Elena so rarely showed this side to the world. The piece also made it crystal clear they'd never been involved while Maddie worked for Elena.

The article also explained how Elena had married because she was expected to. And then she'd found love where she hadn't expected to. It finished with an explanation.

"I write this piece solely to correct the record. To suggest Madeleine Grey is brainless or a fling is disgusting. Madeleine is an exceptional, award-winning journalist. She is kind, honest, amusing, and beautiful. Madeleine is a remarkable woman whom I love and wish to have in my life forever. That's all there is to say. The end."

Holy shit. Maddie grabbed her phone, dialled Elena, and croaked out one word. "Why?"

"Ah, you've seen it."

"You didn't say a word! And what happened to you not commenting?"

"I didn't tell you because you might talk me out of it. And I did it because it occurred to me that whatever you'd write would all be about making *me* sound good. It wouldn't enter your head to correct the record on you, would it? Having read your piece, I was right."

"I…oh."

"So I decided to correct the error." Elena's amusement was evident. "Meanwhile, my board issued a statement this morning backing me, condemning Lecoq's smears, and pointing out Bartell Corp's stellar success."

"How does that feel?" Maddie asked quietly. She knew this was what Elena secretly feared: Making a mistake that could see her empire ripped from her. It made sense, since it had happened before. Lecoq had stolen Elena's promised editorship when they'd both worked at *CQ*. Overnight, her career had ended.

"It feels…acceptable." Background voices murmured and then Elena spoke again. "I was in a meeting with Perry and Felicity when you rang. They're being very complimentary about your article." She sighed. "Really Madeleine, did you have to make me sound nice?"

"You *are* nice!"

"Many would dispute that."

More disjointed talking. "Felicity has asked me to convey to you that your article was accurate, nuanced, beautiful, and you should stop being smug."

"What makes her think I'm being—"

"She is quite sure you are." Elena chuckled. "I've shooed them out now. Madeleine, I want to say that Felicity wasn't wrong. What you wrote was beautiful. I'm constantly amazed you see me that way."

"Elena, it's the truth."

"To you."

"Is there any other kind? And you can talk! You told the whole world you want me in your life forever."

"I was merely being accurate." Elena sniffed for effect. "I'm a big believer in truth in publishing."

Maddie laughed. "Forever's a long time. You should probably put a ring on it."

There was a silence as they both digested Maddie's startling comment.

"Oh…" Maddie faded out. *Fuck.* "I mean…"

"*Did* you mean that?" Elena asked softly. "You'd be amenable to…you wish to be proposed to?"

Oh, hell yes. "Yeah?" Maddie groaned at herself. "Only, can we not do this over the phone? Because I've seriously just made this the worst proposal hint ever."

"Understood." Elena sounded delighted. "We will…table this discussion."

Only Elena could make a future wedding proposal sound like an agenda item.

Maddie laughed. "Sure, yep, table that sucker." Her phone pinged. "Ooh, someone's sent me a link to Lecoq's statement about our *US Review* article." She fell silent as she read. "She says she was taken out of context and didn't out anyone. That's such bull. You're the only media mogul with a round office and a helipad."

"Don't forget the only media mogul with a hot, young lesbian lover." Elena chuckled.

"You're in a weirdly good mood. I thought you'd be skittish today with everyone knowing your business. What's up?"

"Well, aside from being almost proposed to..." Elena's voice dripped with amusement.

Geez. Maddie would never live this down.

"...the *CQ* drama hasn't quite finished. Give it another, hmm, nine or so weeks. It depends on how competent Felicity and Tom are."

"Elena Bartell, what *are* you up to?"

"You'll see." Her voice was all purr.

Elena strode into *CQ*'s gleaming office as if she owned it. Of course now that that was actually true—as of an hour ago—it did make the saying all the more delicious.

Bartell Corp had snapped up the freefalling shares at *CQ*. Her management team had done some fast footwork with key *CQ* board members to smooth takeover proceedings. And, now, here she stood, with a fifty-one percent stake in *CQ Magazine*.

Heads snapped around as she passed, curiosity burning. Staff had no clue yet. The news would break within the hour.

The managing director playing escort pointed out a corner office. "That's Ms Lecoq's. As per your instructions, she has not been, er, kept in the loop about any of this. I'll gather the staff for your meeting afterwards." He strode off.

Elena entered the office filled with shiny trinkets, pop art, framed covers, and appalling yellow and blue decor.

Lecoq's head shot up, suspicion coating her features. "What the hell? You can't just barge in here."

Ignoring her, Elena strolled the room.

"Look, about the article," Lecoq said cautiously, "I may have…misspoke. It was a throwaway line. Suddenly there're boycotts and irate shareholders? Maybe you could spread the word that we've sorted this out between us?"

"Why would I do that?" Elena moved to the window and stared outside. "You want me to clean up your mess? You've just realized how offensive what you did was after staff, investors, and Twitter all pointed it out?"

"It was a flippant remark." Lecoq actually sounded flustered. "Come on, Ellie…"

"Your commentary on my life isn't why I'm here." Elena turned. "You're in my chair."

"Excuse me? This isn't—"

"Bartell Corporation is the reason *CQ*'s shares are no longer plummeting. We bought them; you're welcome. *CQ* is now my company. And that's *my* chair. You're fired."

Horror flitted across Lecoq's features. "B-but…"

Elena felt little sympathy. This woman had ridiculed Madeleine and told the world she was nothing. *How fucking dare she?* "Effective immediately. Security will pack up your things."

"All this…because I suggested you're gay?" Lecoq gaped at her.

Elena's eyes narrowed. "Don't be so asinine. I'm not ashamed of who I am. You're the one who made it seem tawdry."

"Revenge then? For…losing your job to me years ago?"

"I run a Fortune 500 company now," Bartell drawled. "I'm fine."

"So it's because I hurt the feelings of your piece of fluff?" Malice flitted into her eyes. "You're all protective because I suggested you screwed your secretary? How precious!"

Elena inhaled sharply and leaned into Lecoq's personal space. "You know, you're nothing to me," she snapped. "If you'd just kept your mouth shut, none of this would have happened. But you're not that smart."

"I'm—"

"No. You're not. Do you know the only thing more foolish than spreading lies about the woman I love? Spreading lies about who your *new publisher* loves. And since I don't allow fools in my employ, don't bother seeking a job at any Bartell company. Not that I need to blacklist you. No one in fashion will work with you now. You're toxic. And you did it to yourself." She straightened. "We're done."

With a cold, satisfied smile, Elena swept out of the room.

Elena signed off on the documents she was reviewing. It was late but she was finally done. She stretched.

A throat cleared.

She glanced up to find Madeleine leaning against her office door frame. She blinked at the sight of her, in a grunge band T-shirt, tight black jeans, and boots. "This is a familiar look. Weren't you wearing this the first time we met?"

Madeleine sauntered over. "It seemed fitting given what I heard today."

"Oh?"

"There's this insane rumour that my beautiful corporate warrior woman defended my honour. She bought out *CQ*, fired its nasty editor, and then gave the staff a speech. Something about how she's giving them all a month to prove themselves. And she's going to base herself there for that time to see what they're capable of." She laughed. "Now isn't that where we came in?"

"Except I don't recall some garage-band extra getting in the elevator with me today and insulting me." Elena smirked.

"Argh! I didn't insult you! As you *well* know." Madeleine shook her head. "So tell me, why the stay of execution? You told me this morning that if you hadn't bought out *CQ* it'd be bankrupt in a year. Shouldn't you be holding the last rites?"

"Truthfully?" Elena said. "I just wanted to edit one issue of *CQ*. Tick it off my bucket list and move on."

"And *then* you're firing them? Is it fair to give staff false hope?"

"It's not false. They're being reviewed. I've decided to merge *CQ* and *Style*. *CQ* has some excellent writers and designers. The management's the cancer. Besides, a merger will send a rocket up *Style* that they can't be complacent. I can clean house on two magazines." Her eyes glittered. "Just because I made *Style* doesn't give it a free pass."

Madeleine shook her head. "God, that's so you."

She shrugged. It was.

"So," Madeleine grinned. "You actually did it. Beat *CQ*."

"I did." Satisfaction warmed Elena.

"And all it took was Lecoq outing you."

"All it took was her coming after you. I have my limits—a fact I pointed out to that diseased raccoon. I fired her for stupidity."

"You fired her for being mean to me. You're such a romantic." Madeleine stole a kiss.

"Lies!" Elena snorted. "My God, though, Lecoq has zero taste. You should have seen her office. I might have to get a flame thrower in before I take over." There was a thought.

Madeleine slid her arms around her. "I'm really happy for you."

"I couldn't have done it without you. Or the Duchamps and their boycott. I might have to send them flowers. A whole houseful." Her lips curled up.

"That'd go down about as well as last time." Madeleine laughed.

"Honestly, I never thought I'd ever get back my first dream."

"And you did. You got the girl, too."

Elena licked her lips and darted a nervous look at Maddie. "You know, I've been thinking. About the proposal you made?" She was pleased how flippant she sounded. She swallowed. *Now or never.*

"What proposal?"

Elena gave her desk a testing rap.

"Oh!" Madeleine's eyes widened. "Are you serious? And don't you dare tease me like last time. That was so cruel promising desk sex and not delivering."

"About as cruel as you leaving me to attempt a serious conversation with Perry while my thong stared at me from across the room."

"Okay, that was a little evil of me."

"So it *was* on purpose? Distracting me from retrieving it?"

"You deserved it. Torturing me with impossible fantasies." Madeleine looked unrepentant.

"Hmm." Elena's lips twitched. "Perhaps it was a *little* cruel. I'm prepared to make amends."

Madeleine's face lit up. "Are you seriously talking desk sex after all this time?"

"Don't be ridiculous. It's something else." She knocked the desk again, above the drawer. "Open it."

Madeleine slid open the desk drawer. A velvet box sat inside.

"I promised to 'table' something last time," Elena said. "This counts as a table, does it not?" She held her breath, placed the box between them, and opened it to Madeleine.

She stared at the diamond ring for so long that Elena wondered if she'd made a terrible mistake. Elena had spent an eternity trying to find the right one, even enlisting the services of Perry, who was officially insufferable now. "Don't you like it?" she asked pensively.

"Are you kidding?" Madeleine's eyes shone. "I love it. But you know…a beautiful ring like that usually comes with a question."

"Is that so?"

Madeleine nodded. "Spoiler alert, I'm going to say yes. And then I'm going to kiss you. And then we're going to have hot fiancée desk sex."

"Well, now I'm conflicted." Elena laughed. She held the ring out, and said seriously, "Madeleine Grey, I knew the day we met that you were trouble. How right I was—and how much I needed it. Needed you. I love you. Will you…"

"Yes!" Madeleine slid the ring on and kissed her breathlessly.

"You do realize I didn't actually ask you anything," Elena pointed out. Her heart was thundering, her mouth dry, and she couldn't seem to control her grinning mouth. She'd never felt anything like this before. She was pretty sure it was a sign of true love—or a heart attack.

"Asked and answered." Madeleine laughed. "Now I'm pretty sure promises were made." She patted the desk, a gleam in her eye.

"I'm quite sure I didn't agree to that," Elena protested, although truthfully, it was the reason she'd proposed in her office: To give Madeleine her fantasy.

Maddie's T-shirt was already half off her head. "Uh-huh," came the muffled sound.

With a sigh to hide her mounting excitement, Elena sat back, unbuttoning her silk blouse. She watched appreciatively as Maddie tried to haul her skinny jeans down her legs. "You're so beautiful," Elena noted quietly.

Kicking her jeans away, Madeleine grinned. "I love it when you get mushy."

Elena slid off her blouse and gave an imperious look. "It's not mush. It's accuracy. And the truth is you *are* beautiful." She lowered her voice. "I love you more than is sane, Madeleine."

"I love you too." Madeleine smiled. "And who knew you were so romantic?"

Elena sighed at the frankly preposterous comment and kissed the lie straight off those lips.

If you enjoyed this short story, check out *The Brutal Truth* by Lee Winter, the novel in which Elena and Maddie met and fell in love.

Partners

by Jae

Austen capped the red marker, stuck it back into her cockatoo penholder, and studied the sketch with a satisfied grin. She couldn't wait to hear what Dee would think. The candy cane–shaped chew toy had been her partner's idea, and Austen had improved on it by making it a bird perch with a little bell at one end.

Even three months after establishing their company, she loved how smoothly they worked together.

She jumped up with a little too much vigor, sending her office chair halfway across the small room, and picked up the sketch to take it over to Dee.

As soon as she opened the door, a familiar booming voice reached her.

Back when they had both worked at Kudos Entertainment, shouting from Dee's office hadn't been anything out of the ordinary. Her uncle had made her the company's problem fixer, so she had stepped in whenever an employee had messed up, a supplier couldn't deliver, or something else had gone wrong.

But now her job no longer consisted of knocking heads together, and their tiny company had only two part-time employees, so what on earth was going on? Was Dee on the phone with someone?

Austen stepped closer.

Just as she contemplated knocking, the door was wrenched open, and Courtney, their administrative assistant, hurried past Austen without stopping. Her head was down and her shoulders up, like a turtle retreating into its shell.

What the…? Austen stared after her.

A loud thump against the wall drew her attention back to Dee's office. Cautiously, Austen walked through the still-open door and stopped to pick up the stapler Dee must have hurled across the room. At least it hadn't been the computer mouse she had given Dee for Christmas shortly after they had first met.

Dee was pacing back and forth in the small space behind her desk. The neat chignon she wore at work was coming undone as if she had run her hands through her hair repeatedly.

For a moment, Austen stopped, stapler in hand, completely mesmerized by Dee's tall frame, her powerful movements, and the intensity radiating off her. Then she gave herself a mental kick. *Stop ogling and find out why she's having an Attila moment.* She closed the door behind herself with an audible click to make her presence known.

Dee whirled around. When their gazes met, the fierce expression on her face softened for a moment.

"What's going on?" Austen asked.

Dee snarled. "I'll have to fire Courtney."

The vehement words hit Austen like a sharp gust of wind, making her sway back for a second. Then she braced herself and dropped into the visitor chair. "First of all, if anything, *we* have to fire her." She firmly set the stapler down on the desk. "We run this company together, don't we?"

"Yeah, of course," Dee said immediately. She eyed her desk chair and then reluctantly dropped into it so she was no longer towering over Austen. "When I tell you how badly she fucked up, you'll want to fire her too."

"What happened?"

Dee pinched the bridge of her nose as if a massive headache was forming. "She royally messed up the Kickstarter campaign for the parrot-friendly Christmas tree."

"Wait! How can she have messed that up? That's fully funded and practically done, isn't it?"

"That's what I thought too. But Courtney really has a special talent for messing things up." Dee hurled a dark glare in the direction of Courtney's tiny office. "I swear that woman can't even focus long enough to click the right button on a website. Instead of editing the campaign to add the latest updates, she canceled it. Now all pledges are voided. Poof! All our funding is gone!"

For a moment, Austen couldn't breathe, and a heavy weight seemed to squeeze all the air from her lungs. "G-gone? But…but…isn't there a way to undo it or start a new campaign or…?"

"Do you really think anyone will give us money after that snafu?" Dee shook her head. "We lost our backers' trust, and building it again or finding new backers will take too long. There's no way we would be able to get it out in time for the holiday season."

Damn. Austen slumped against the back of her chair. She had really looked forward to offering their customers a Christmas tree that was safe for their pets. It would have been a unique product that none of their competitors had thought of so far, and it would have put Feathered Friends on the map as a company that knew what bird owners wanted. She stared past Dee to the glittering band of the Willamette River right across the street. Finally, she inhaled and exhaled deeply. "Okay. So it happened. How can we move forward from here?"

"First thing we should do is fire Courtney," Dee muttered. "Or maybe pull out every single one of her brightly painted finger- and toenails with a pair of pliers first and *then* fire her."

The vivid description made Austen smile despite the seriousness of the situation. She reached across the desk and gently nudged her partner. "Come on. Everyone makes a mistake every now and then. Firing her probably isn't the best way to deal with it—and neither is shouting at her." She couldn't keep the gentle rebuke from her tone. "All that's going to do is make her even more nervous, and that's not going to help her job performance."

Dee leaned back and folded her arms across her chest. "Well, coddling her the way you've been doing isn't helping either."

"Coddling?" Austen echoed. "I'm not coddling her. I'm just being friendly."

"Yeah, but that's the thing, Austen. You're not her friend. You're her employer, and you need to start acting like it."

"And that means I can't treat her like a human being?" Austen refused to accept that. "Did you see the look on her face when she ran out of here? She's terrified of you."

Dee shrugged. "Maybe she'll take her responsibilities more seriously now."

Austen stared at her. Sometimes she couldn't believe that this tough businesswoman was the same person as her gentle, considerate lover. "Is this really how you want things to be at Feathered Friends? You're no longer at Kudos. We're a tiny company. It's like a family. There's no need for you to keep acting like the ice queen who has employees for breakfast and then picks her teeth with their bones."

Dee snatched up the squishy stress ball from her desk and started kneading it. "No."

"No, that's not how you want things to be?"

"No, we're not a family. We might be tiny, but we're still a business," Dee said, her tone firm. "Treating employees like family members doesn't work. There needs to be a hierarchy and clear expectations, or it's all going to hell in a handbasket."

"I've got nothing against clear expectations, as long as it's not the expectation that employees will be shouted at and threatened to be fired whenever they make a mistake."

Dee pressed the badly mangled stress ball against her desk with so much force that it started to resemble a pancake. "Or the expectation that employees will be coddled and defended, no matter how badly they harm the company."

They stared at each other across the desk. Austen refused to back down and look away from Dee's heated gaze.

"This good-cop-bad-cop game you're playing isn't fair." Dee pronounced every syllable clearly, as if she needed all her self-control not to shout at her.

"Game? What are you talking about?" Now Austen struggled not to raise her voice too. "I'm not pla—"

"Yeah, you are." Dee flung the stress ball into a corner. "You're letting them get away with too much, and that forces me to be the ice queen."

A knock on the door interrupted, and Eliza, their second employee, stuck her head into the office. She looked from Dee to Austen and back. "Um, sorry to interrupt. We just got the list of materials from the potential new supplier."

Austen suppressed a sigh. Eliza wasn't responsible for ordering materials. That list had been emailed to Courtney, but she had sent in Eliza because she didn't want to face Dee.

"Courtney says they look great because their paints are all nontoxic," Eliza continued. "She wants to give them the go-ahead, but I wasn't sure, so—"

"No!" Dee shot out from behind her desk. "Jesus, I told Courtney at least three times that paints, even nontoxic ones, are out. Birds can choke on the paint chips. What we need is a vegetable-based dye that will—" She took a deep breath and squeezed her eyes shut. When she opened them again, her gaze went to Austen and she visibly reined herself in. "Can this wait?" she said to Eliza but didn't look away from Austen. "We were in the middle of...um, something important."

"Oh, sure." Eliza backed away. "I'll just tell Courtney not to do anything until she talks to you."

"It's okay," Austen said to Dee. "Deal with this. We'll talk later."

Dee searched her eyes. "Are you sure? I can—"

"I'm sure." Austen stood. Arguing back and forth wasn't accomplishing anything other than hurting each other, and that was the last thing she wanted. "We'll talk once we've both calmed down, okay?"

Dee hesitated for a few moments and then nodded. "Okay."

Austen slipped past Eliza, ignoring her curious looks, and walked to the stairs without detouring to her office. She needed some air.

Austen stretched her arms out along the back of the bench, tilted her head back, and let the spring sun warm her face. A jet boat roared past on the Willamette, and the wind blew through the cherry blossoms on the tree behind her, carrying the scent of empanadas from a nearby food cart.

Her stomach grumbled. Too bad she had run out of the office without her wallet. Lunch would have to wait. She wasn't sure she could eat right now anyway, with all the snippets of their heated conversation bouncing around her head.

Coddling her the way you've been doing.

You're not her friend. You're her employer, and you need to start acting like it.

She had known she and Dee had very different business approaches, but this was the first time they had argued about it. Apparently, it wasn't the first time Dee had thought about it, though. Why hadn't she said anything before? They should have been able to talk about it instead of letting things build up.

One thing Dee had said in particular kept going through her mind: *This good-cop-bad-cop game you're playing isn't fair.*

Was there some truth to that?

It was tempting to blame it all on Dee and her inability to adjust to a new leadership style.

But deep down, she knew it wasn't that simple. Maybe she had been a little too lenient with Courtney. Admittedly, it wasn't the first—or even second or third—mistake their admin had made. She was fresh out of college, so Austen had hoped she just needed some time to settle into her first real job. Instead of taking action and confronting Courtney, she had just waited and tried to be positive and encouraging.

Apparently, Dee had felt forced to take up the slack and step in.

Austen should have seen it coming. Sitting around, waiting patiently for a problem to sort itself out, had never been Dee's strong suit. She should have—

"Is this seat taken?" a gentle voice asked from two steps away.

When Austen opened her eyes and turned her head, she wasn't surprised to see Dee standing in front of her, shuffling her feet.

Relief flooded her. Dee had searched her out. That was a good sign, right? A lump lodged in her throat, so she nodded wordlessly and slid a little to the side.

Dee sat on the bench next to her, close but not touching.

The inches between them felt like a deep rift.

Should she be the first to reach out and—?

"Um, here." Like a peace offering, Dee held out a familiar box that said, *Good things come in pink boxes.* "You left your purse with your wallet in the office, and I thought you might be getting hungry."

Dee had obviously braved the long lines at Voodoo Doughnut, three blocks away from their office.

"Thank you." Austen's voice came out a little croaky. She opened the lid. The scent of chocolate and cinnamon wafted out, making her stomach growl again. Two of the baked goods were Chuckles—donuts with chocolate frosting, dipped in chocolate powder, and topped with peanuts, caramel, and chocolate drizzle. They were her favorite. She picked one of them up, but then held it without taking a bite.

Their gazes met over the box.

"Um, that didn't go so well, did it?" Dee said quietly and pointed her thumb in the direction of the office.

"No, it didn't. Clearly, there are a few things we should have talked about much sooner. I just thought it was all going great and…"

"It was. It *is* for the most part. Everything has been amazing. I should have put this one setback into perspective and not let it get to me so much, but…" Dee drew a deep breath. "After all the shit I had to take from my uncle and the rest of the family when the Disney deal fell through, any kind of screw-up really puts me on edge."

Austen put the donut back into its box and took Dee's hand. "That wasn't your fault, and I will never do what your family did and put the blame on you if something in our company isn't going well. I hope you know that."

Dee held her hand tightly. "I know. It's just… I want us to succeed. I want Feathered Friends to have a first year that will blow everyone's socks off."

Austen had a feeling she knew why. Dee's father telling her she didn't have a head for business probably still stung. "To prove to your family that you can do it without them."

A hint of red tinged Dee's cheeks. She lowered her gaze to where she was stroking Austen's hand with her thumb, then peeked up again. "That's part of the reason. Is that so wrong?"

Austen squeezed her fingers. "No. I'm all for showing your family how wrong they were not to appreciate you more."

"But?" Dee asked.

"But don't you think there's a different way to do that? I kind of liked the thought of getting to start over together, and Feathered Friends being a place where you don't have to be Attila but can be just Dee." She studied Dee's face. "I mean, you don't really want our employees to be scared of you, do you?"

"No?" Dee made it sound like a question and lifted one corner of her mouth up into a crooked smile.

Austen suppressed a chuckle and nudged her with her elbow.

"No," Dee repeated more firmly. She looked into Austen's eyes. "I especially don't want you to be scared of me or of disagreeing with me. I'm sorry if I got a little…intense earlier. I don't want to do that with you. I guess I'm used to being in attack mode while at work because it worked for me at Kudos. Talking nicely to people," she shuddered and made a face, but there was a playful twinkle in her eyes that lightened the mood, "is a big adjustment. But I'll try to stop the shouting, okay? I just ask that you consider that sometimes, clear words are needed in business, even in a small company."

"Deal," Austen said.

Dee blinked. "Wow. That was easy."

Austen grinned at her stunned expression. "See? Sometimes, you get better results when you're not trying to intimidate people."

"Never worked with you anyway," Dee said. "Not even on the very first day, when you dropped that tree topper on me."

"Hey, stop telling it like that! I didn't drop it on you; you were rearranging the lights on the tree because you're a control freak, and it fell." The familiar teasing soothed Austen's rattled nerves.

Dee shrugged. "Tomato, tomato. So, that's settled, then." She reached for the apple fritter in the box and took a big bite, a clear signal that she was all talked out.

A goose waddled over and tried to snatch the fritter from her hand.

"Mine!" With a possessive snarl that made Austen grin, Dee shooed the goose away.

Austen picked up her donut again, but before she could enjoy it, she needed to know. "What are we going to do about the Kickstarter?"

Sighing, Dee lowered her apple fritter. "Not much we can do about it. I'll call them as soon as we get back to the office and explain that it was all an accident, but I'm not sure that'll make any difference. Worst-case scenario, we'll either have to postpone the parrot-friendly Christmas tree project or find funding for it elsewhere."

"Even if we can't launch it this year, it won't be the end of the world," Austen said, trying to sound upbeat but not sure if she managed it.

"No, guess not."

Austen slid closer on the bench, and they rested against each other in silent comfort while they finally ate their treats. They shared the second chocolate donut. When Austen reached for the last donut—one with pink frosting and colorful sprinkles on top—Dee stopped her.

"That one's for Courtney." Dee looked away under the pretense of wiping her sticky fingers on a tissue. "I guess I, um, owe her an apology."

Austen couldn't help grinning. "Aww. I knew it. Deep down, you're just this big old softie."

"Am not." Dee used her Attila glare on her, which was rendered less intimidating because a bit of chocolate marred the corner of her mouth. "I still think we should fire her. Maybe you could ask your friend Sally if she wants to come work for us."

"I don't think that's a good idea."

"Why not?" Dee asked. "You liked working with her at Kudos, didn't you?"

"Yes, very much so, but I want you to be able to start over with a clean slate, and Sally just knows your...um..."

"My charming Attila side," Dee supplied.

"Yeah. Plus your family still isn't talking to you, and stealing one of their employees won't help improve your relationship with them."

Dee waved her hand in a dismissive gesture. "I don't care."

Austen tilted her head and studied her. Someone else might have missed it and seen only the unyielding stare of her gray eyes, but Austen saw the hint of vulnerability around her mouth that Dee hid from the rest of the world. "I think you do." She tenderly wiped that bit of chocolate from Dee's face. "For now, let's give Courtney one more chance. And should it really become necessary to fire her, let me be the one to do it."

Dee arched her brows, making the thin scar from the tree topper incident rise up on her forehead. "Are you sure?"

Austen wasn't, but she still nodded. "I thought about what you said earlier..."

"Forget what I said." Dee brushed apple fritter crumbs off her lap. "I was angry with Courtney, and I took it out on you. That wasn't fair."

"No, it was me who wasn't fair. You were right about that." Austen lowered her gaze. "I haven't really shouldered my part of the responsibility for Feathered Friends so far. I guess I was just so used to you being the boss who makes all the tough decisions and me just being the sidekick."

"That's okay. I don't mind handling the tough decisions, as long as I know you have my back."

Austen put her hand on Dee's leg and rubbed it. She appreciated Dee's attempt to protect her. "Thanks, but I mind. I want us to be partners. You were right. It's not fair to put you in a position where you always have to be the bad cop. I can't expect you to change your leadership style and still keep pushing all the ugly tasks on you, like your family did. So from now on, you get to be the one who brings them donuts, while I'll be the one to take our employees to task when they mess up."

Dee put her hand on top of Austen's and looked at her with something like amazement. After a few seconds, she shook her head, smiled, and kissed her.

She tasted like chocolate and forgiveness, and Austen hummed against her lips.

When the kiss ended, Dee linked their fingers. "You know what? Let's talk to Courtney together."

"I'd like that. And then let's head over to my place. We can call Kickstarter from there." Austen stood and tugged her taller partner up with her. Hand in hand, they walked back to the office.

Austen tossed the little plastic ball once more. It bounced across her living room and rolled to a stop against a box of toy prototypes they had taken home for Toby to try out.

With an excited screech, her cockatoo rushed after the ball, picked it up with his beak by one of the small holes, and carried it back to Austen.

"Good boy." Ball in hand, Austen paused.

Dee's voice from the bedroom, where she was talking to the Kickstarter hotline, had fallen silent. Was she done with the call?

When the door opened and Dee stepped into the living room, Toby flapped one wing to say hello and imitated the *ping* of a microwave—his way of asking for a treat.

Dee gave a distracted smile and fished a peanut from her pocket.

For the last three months, Dee had been the one to feed him so he would bond with her, and slowly, their strategy was paying off.

Judging by Dee's grim expression, her call to Kickstarter had been less successful. She dropped onto the couch next to Austen with a weary sigh.

Austen reached for her hand. "What did they say?"

"They can't reinstate the campaign. The pledges were canceled automatically, so there's nothing they can do for us."

"Fuck," Toby screeched.

"My sentiment exactly," Dee muttered.

Austen let out a sigh. She had expected this kind of answer, but hearing it was still tough. "Okay, so Kickstarter is out. What about taking out another loan?"

"I'd rather not do that before we've paid off the first one. Looks like we'll have to postpone the project until next year." Dee slipped out of her shoes and kicked one of them across the room.

Toby immediately went after it and sank his beak into the expensive leather.

"Shit. Toby, no!" Dee jumped up to rescue her footwear.

Austen's gaze trailed after her. She hated seeing Dee so dejected. If only they had some other way to finance the project, but they had both put all of their savings into Feathered Friends already, and she didn't own anything of value to—

She paused midthought. Well, she did own one thing that might bring enough money to cover at least part of the project if she sold it, but she had never thought that she would ever consider parting with it. She barely even wore it out of fear of accidentally losing it.

"What's wrong?" Dee crossed the room with long strides, dropped back onto the couch next to her, and wrapped one arm around her. "The last time I saw that expression on your face was when you were debating whether you should forgive me for not telling you I was Kudos's second-in-command."

"Nothing's wrong. I just…" Austen bit her lip and leaned against Dee's strong shoulder. "What if I…sell my mom's sapphire ring? It won't cover the full sum we need, but it should be good for at least—"

"No," Dee said fiercely. Her arm around Austen tightened. "No. I appreciate what you're trying to do, but I know what that ring means to you. Even if we have to postpone the Christmas tree project indefinitely, I'm not letting you sacrifice your mother's ring."

Austen slumped against her.

Dee tenderly combed her fingers through Austen's pixie cut. "You really were willing to give up your mom's ring just so my family won't think I'm a failure?"

"Mmm," Austen mumbled against her shoulder.

"God, you're something else." Dee pressed her lips to Austen's head. "If push comes to shove, I could borrow against my 401k. That would give us enough money to get the Christmas tree project off the ground and maybe hire another employee."

"No," Austen said without having to think about it. "Thanks for offering, but you know raiding your retirement fund is not a good idea. We'll just have to accept that we won't be able to fund any big projects this year."

They looked at each other. Just as they were about to exchange a heartfelt kiss, Toby landed in Austen's lap and let out a demanding *ping*.

Laughing, Dee got up. "He's right. We need some food—non-donut food. We'll figure out what to do about the Christmas tree project on Monday. For now, we're off the clock."

"Hmm, off the clock… Does that mean I can seduce the company's co-owner without it being unethical?"

Dee gave her a slow, sexy smile. "Only if said co-owner doesn't seduce you first."

Austen dug into her second piece of chocolate birthday cake—not just because she loved anything chocolate but, more importantly, if her mouth was full, no one would expect her to make small talk with Dee's family.

Not that they were talking to her—or to Dee—anyway.

Dee's father, her uncle, her four brothers, and several cousins were busy discussing their various businesses. Austen caught words such as *cash flow*, *net profits*, and *asset turnover*.

Jesus, what is this? A business meeting or Tim's birthday party?

Dee's youngest brother didn't seem to mind. He was probably used to birthday parties like this because discussing business was all his family did at get-togethers.

Well, the male part of the family.

In a stunning example of last-century gender roles, the women were all squeezed into Janine's kitchen, discussing kids, marriages, and recipes.

All but Dee, who had been kidnapped by her eighteen-month-old niece and nephew. She lay stretched out on the living room floor and was building a castle with colorful wooden blocks. Clearly, Dee hadn't spent much time around kids in the past and had no idea how to deal with them. She tried to get the toddlers to participate in stacking up blocks, but the twins were more interested in toppling over Dee's elegant towers. When the blocks scattered all over the floor, Mason and Mila giggled and jumped up and down. Dee's scowl made them laugh even harder.

Austen hid her grin behind another forkful of cake.

Tim's wife, Janine, dropped into an empty seat next to Austen and regarded her with an amused smile. "Are you eating for two?"

"What? No! We're not… I mean, we are, but it's not like we can…um…" Austen's cheeks heated.

Janine laughed. "I meant, are you eating Dee's cake too since she's busy entertaining Mason and Mila."

"Oh." Austen shoved another forkful of cake into her mouth.

"Although you two really should think about having a baby. Dee's so adorable with the kids." Janine gestured across the room.

Dee had apparently given up her attempts to make the twins appreciate her architectural genius. She lay still as the toddlers piled blocks onto her.

Aww. Austen watched her with a smile. "Maybe one day, if Dee is up for it. But first, we have to get Feathered Friends off the ground. Plus we're not even living together."

"Dee still hasn't asked you to move in with her?" Janine widened her eyes comically. "And here I thought lesbians were supposed to be the U-Hauling kind."

Austen shook her head. "Not us. We spend the entire day together at work, so we thought it would be healthier for our relationship to keep separate places for a while."

Not that they ever spent their evenings apart. Most days, they drove to Austen's apartment after work and spent the evening there so Toby wouldn't have to be alone. Half of Dee's clothes had somehow migrated to Austen's place by now, and even though the apartment was small, Dee hadn't asked for some alone time yet.

"That sounds reasonable." Janine rubbed at a wrinkle between her brows as if trying to remember something. "I'm not sure, but I don't think Dee has ever lived with any of her girlfriends."

She hadn't, and that was part of the reason why Austen had wanted to give her space and take it slow.

They both turned to look at Dee again, but that spot on the floor was empty.

Austen's gaze veered through the living room, then froze.

Instead of still lying on the floor, covered in colorful blocks, Dee was standing with her father, Caleb. Gone was the more playful expression that she often showed when it was just her and Austen. She hid behind the poker face that Austen had seen her wear during tough business negotiations.

The twins were tugging on her pants legs, vying for her attention, but Dee was completely focused on her father.

"Oh wow," Janine whispered. "I didn't know they were talking again."

"They weren't—until now," Austen whispered back, her gaze still on Dee and her father, who stood stony-faced while he listened to whatever Dee was saying.

"I'd better go get the twins so they can talk," Janine said.

Under the pretense of helping with twin number two, Austen rushed after her. She wanted to be close in case Dee needed her support.

"I could have told you that from the start, Danielle," Dee's father said as they came closer. "You should have set up a company with a broader customer base."

Dee's shoulders stiffened almost imperceptibly. "Actually, niche companies can be just as successful nowadays. Pet bird ownership is on the rise in the US, especially in cities where people don't have enough space for a cat or a dog, and a lot of them own multiple birds. We could have easily funded that project if not for—"

Her father clucked disparagingly. "Yeah, yeah. You know what your grandfather used to say. If *ifs* and *buts* were candies and nuts, we'd all have a very merry Christmas."

Dee's lips blanched because she was pressing them together so tightly, probably in an effort to hold back what she really wanted to say.

Austen swung Mila up onto her hip, but instead of carrying her off, she took up position next to Dee in silent support.

Caleb ignored her presence, while Dee shifted her stance so their shoulders brushed.

"Um, speaking of Christmas…" Dee looked her father in the eyes. "That project I was telling you about needs to be launched in time for the holiday shopping season."

"So?"

"Um, well, as I said, we lost our funding because of a little glitch. I was wondering if you would be willing to lend me the money."

Wow. Austen couldn't believe it. Never in a million years would she have thought her proud partner would ask her father for help. Warmth spread through her chest. Dee had been trying to get a little recognition from her family for decades, so Austen knew how hard asking her father for money must have been. It meant the world to her that Dee had put the success of their company over her need to prove herself to her family.

Caleb stared at his daughter as if she had asked him to donate a vital organ. "Lend you money?"

The chatter and clinking of china ceased. Every family member stared at Dee and her father, who faced each other in the middle of the living room in a silent stand-off.

"Why would I do that?" Caleb asked.

Because she's your daughter, Austen nearly said, but she bit her lip and kept silent, not sure if Dee wanted her to get involved in this discussion.

"Because it's a good investment. I'd…" Dee glanced at Austen. "*We* would pay you back, with interest, within a reasonable time frame, of course. I don't expect any gifts."

Her father shook his head. "I wouldn't be doing you a favor in the long run. You kids need to learn to run a successful business without relying on family money, just like I did. I started with one tiny clothing store, and now look at me." He spread his arms wide as if to indicate an empire. "Sixty-two stores all over the country."

"I'm thirty-seven, Dad—hardly a kid—and I already know how to run a business. I was the COO of Kudos for fourteen years, and I was a huge part of making it a Fortune 500 company." Dee looked around for her uncle and former boss. "Wasn't I, Uncle Wade?"

Her uncle swirled around the ice in his whiskey. "Yeah, I guess so."

Austen couldn't stand it any longer. She put her free hand onto her hip and stared at her former employer. "You *guess?*" she burst out. "Dee kept Kudos running, and everyone knew it. She was the one who got you the Universal deal, and she—"

"We." Dee reached for her hand and squeezed softly. "*We* got them the Universal deal. You and I. But that doesn't matter. My accomplishments never mattered in this family. It was stupid of me to even ask. Come on. Let's go."

Austen handed Mila off to Tim, who hurried after them. "Dee, wait. Why didn't you ask me? I could lend you some money."

"Nah. You've got a family to take care of, and I know Uncle Wade doesn't pay you as much as he should." Dee gave her brother a friendly slap to the shoulder. "Don't worry about it. We'll get the money somehow."

At the door, Dee's mother caught up with them. "Danielle, wait. Take some cake." Since Dee had already grabbed her jacket and opened the door, Phyllis pressed the box into Austen's hands.

A piece of paper sat on top of the box. For a second, Austen thought it might be the bakery's phone number. Then she realized it was a personal check. A check with a lot of zeroes. She swallowed hard. "Um, Dee…"

Dee turned.

With a trembling hand, Austen held out the check to her.

Dee's gaze went from the check to Austen's face, then back to the check and finally to her mother. "Mom, what...? You heard what he said. I won't take any of his money behind his back." She took the check and tried to press it into her mother's hands, but Phyllis refused to take it.

"This isn't your father's money." Phyllis pointed at the signature on the check, which was her own. "You didn't just inherit your head for business from his side of the family." She lowered her voice to a whisper, as if it was a secret she didn't want anyone to know. "I invested the money I inherited from your grandfather wisely, and over the years, I increased it tenfold. Now I heard of this promising little company that produces toys for pet birds, and I'd like to invest in it."

Dee stared at her mother as if she had never seen her before.

Austen could empathize. She had met Dee's mother only twice before, but as far as she knew Phyllis had never contradicted her husband or shown any support for her daughter's career. Austen had always assumed that she probably didn't approve of women working outside of the home and would have preferred to see her only daughter married to a man, with a gaggle of kids.

"Mom..." Dee's voice was hoarse.

"Phyllis," Caleb called. "What's taking so long? Don't coddle the girl, or she'll never learn."

So that was where Dee got her ideas about what constituted *coddling*. Austen turned and stared at him. So supporting their daughter was seen as coddling in this family? Wow. A wave of gratefulness for her own parents overcame Austen. She couldn't wait to get out of here so she could give Dee a long, tight hug.

"Be right there," Phyllis called back. "I'm just giving them some cake to take home." She turned back toward Dee. "I hope you enjoy it."

"Um, I'm sure we will." Dee gripped the check tightly. "Thank you for the... cake. We'll pay you back for it, of course."

Phyllis smiled pleasantly, as if they were really just talking about two pieces of chocolate cake and not fifty thousand dollars.

Jesus, this family was weird. Austen stumbled after Dee as if on autopilot.

Outside, in front of their car, they stopped and stared at each other.

Dee held up the check and studied it from all sides, as if halfway expecting it to be forged. "Who was that woman and what did she do with my mother?"

"I have no idea. I didn't even know she had her own money."

"Neither did I, and I bet my father doesn't either." Dee snorted bitterly. "Can't have his wife outshine his financial success, so she just stays in the kitchen with the other women and pretends she doesn't understand a word when the men are talking about investments." Finally, she lowered the check and prepared to get in on the driver's side.

"Dee?"

When Dee turned, Austen put the cake box on the roof of the BMW and rushed into her arms.

"Oof." Dee wrapped both arms around her. Her chest lifted and fell against Austen's as she breathed in her scent. "What's that for?" she asked without letting go.

Austen buried her face against Dee's shoulder. "For not being like your family," she mumbled into the fabric of her jacket. "Even though your mother turned out not to be so bad after all. I just wish she would support you more openly and shout from the rooftops how proud of you she is. I know I am."

Dee held her even more tightly. Normally, she wasn't much for public displays of affection, but now she didn't seem to care if half of Portland was watching them. "Austen?" she asked after a while, both arms still around her.

"Hmm?"

"Now that we have the money for the Christmas tree project and probably several other product launches, we'll have to work a lot of overtime."

Austen nodded, her face still pressed to her favorite spot against Dee's shoulder. "I know. Don't worry. I'm up for it."

"I know. I'm not worried about that." Dee hesitated.

"But?" Still in Dee's arms, Austen pulled back a few inches so she could see her face. Dee looked uncharacteristically insecure, making Austen's pulse speed up. "What is it?"

"Yeah, well, with us having to work late most days, all the back and forth between my house and your apartment seems like an unnecessary waste of time, so I was wondering…"

Austen held her breath.

"Wouldn't it be more reasonable if you moved in with me?"

Austen's lips curled into an amused smile. Leave it to her partner to phrase moving in together like a smart business strategy. "Reasonable?"

"Yeah. It's slightly closer to work; there's more space than in your apartment, and the neighbors aren't as close, so they wouldn't complain whenever Toby gets a little too loud." Dee finally broke into a grin. "And I just want you there. I want us to live together, be partners in business and life and all that. So, what do you think?"

Instead of a verbal reply, Austen tightened the embrace, bridged the few inches between them, and kissed her.

"I take it that's a yes?" Dee asked when they came up for air.

Austen laughed. "What do you think?"

"Hmm, I don't know." Dee looked at her with that playful twinkle in her eyes that only Austen got to see. "Maybe you need to kiss me again so I can make sure I understood your answer."

"Well, you did say clear communication is important in business, so…" Austen threaded her fingers through Dee's hair and pulled her down for a second kiss.

If you enjoyed this short story, check out *Under a Falling Star* by Jae, the novel in which Austen and Dee met and fell in love.

Other Books from

Ylva Publishing

www.ylva-publishing.com

All the Little Moments

G Benson

ISBN: 978-3-95533-341-6

Length: 350 pages (139,000 words)

Anna is focused on her career as an anaesthetist. When a tragic accident leaves her responsible for her young niece and nephew, her life changes abruptly. Completely overwhelmed, Anna barely has time to brush her teeth in the morning let alone date a woman. But then she collides with a long-legged stranger…

Code of Conduct

Cheyenne Blue

ISBN: 978-3-96324-030-0

Length: 264 pages (91,000 words)

Top ten tennis player Viva Jones had the world at her feet. Then a lineswoman's bad call knocked her out of the US Open, and injury crushed her career. While battling to return to the game, a chance meeting with the same sexy lineswoman forces Viva to rethink the past…and the present. There's just one problem: players and officials can't date.

A lesbian romance about breaking all the rules.

Under a Falling Star

Jae

ISBN: 978-3-95533-238-9

Length: 369 pages (91,000 words)

Falling stars are supposed to be a lucky sign, but not for Austen. The first assignment in her new job—decorating the Christmas tree in the lobby—results in a trip to the ER after Dee, the company's COO, gets hit by the star-shaped tree topper. There's an instant attraction between them, but Dee is determined not to act on it, especially since Austen has no idea that Dee is her boss.

Damage Control
(The Hollywood Series – Book 2)

Jae

ISBN: 978-3-95533-372-0

Length: 347 pages (140,000)

When actress Grace Durand is photographed in a compromising situation with a woman, she fears for her career. She hires PR agent Lauren Pearce to do damage control, not knowing that she's a lesbian. As they run the gauntlet of the paparazzi together, Lauren realizes how different Grace is from her TV persona. Getting involved would ruin their careers, but the attraction between them is growing.

The Music and the Mirror

Lola Keeley

ISBN: 978-3-96324-014-0
Length: 311 pages (120,000 words)

Anna is the newest member of an elite ballet company. Her first class almost ruins her career before it begins. She must face down jealousy, sabotage, and injury to pour everything into opening night and prove she has what it takes. In the process, Anna discovers that she and the daring, beautiful Victoria have a lot more than ballet in common.

L.A. Metro
(The L.A. Metro Series – Book 1)

RJ Nolan

ISBN: 978-3-95533-041-5
Length: 349 pages (97,000 words)

Dr. Kimberly Donovan's life is in shambles. After her medical ethics are questioned, first her family, then her closeted lover, the Chief of the ER, betray her. Determined to make a fresh start, she flees to California and L.A. Metropolitan Hospital. When she meets Jess McKenna, L.A. Metro's Chief of the ER, the attraction is immediate. Can either woman overcome her past to make a future together?

The Lily and the Crown

Roslyn Sinclair

ISBN: 978-3-95533-942-5

Length: 263 pages (87,000 words)

Young botanist Ari lives an isolated life on a space station, tending a lush garden in her quarters. When an imperious woman is captured from a pirate ship and given to her as a slave, Ari's ordered life shatters. Her slave is watchful, smart, and sexy, and seems to know an awful lot about tactics, star charts, and the dread pirate queen, Mír.

A lesbian romance about daring to risk your heart.

Chasing Stars
(The Superheroine Collection)

Alex K. Thorne

ISBN: 978-3-95533-992-0

Length: 205 pages (70,000 words)

For superhero Swiftwing, crime fighting isn't her biggest battle. Nor is it having to meet the whims of Hollywood star Gwen Knight as her mild-mannered assistant, Ava. It's doing all that, while tracking a giant alien bug, being asked to fake date her famous boss, and realizing that she might be coming down with a pesky case of feelings.

A fun, sweet, sexy lesbian romance about the masks we wear.

Requiem for Immortals

Lee Winter

ISBN: 978-3-95533-710-0
Length: 263 pages (86,000 words)

Requiem is a brilliant cellist with a secret. The dispassionate assassin has made an art form out of killing Australia's underworld figures without a thought. One day she's hired to kill a sweet and unassuming innocent. Requiem can't work out why anyone would want her dead—and why she should even care.

A dark lesbian thriller with plenty of twists in its tale.

The Brutal Truth

Lee Winter

ISBN: 978-3-95533-898-5
Length: 339 pages (108,000 words)

Aussie crime reporter Maddie Grey is out of her depth in New York and secretly drawn to her twice-married, powerful media mogul boss, Elena Bartell, who eats failing newspapers for breakfast. As work takes them to Australia, Maddie is goaded into a brief bet—that they will say only the truth to each other. It backfires catastrophically.

A lesbian romance about the lies we tell ourselves.

Irregular Heartbeat

Chris Zett

ISBN: 978-3-95533-996-8

Length: 261 pages (94,000 words)

When drummer Diana Petrell leaves her rock-star life to return to ER medicine, she won't let anything stop her—not even falling for aloof mentor, Dr. Emily Barnes.

Emily isn't happy having to babysit an intriguing resident with a ten-year gap in her résumé. But then the lines blur.

What happens to their careers when Diana's secret comes out? A lesbian romance that asks how much we'd risk for love.

Heart Failure

Chris Zett

ISBN: 978-3-96324-316-5

Length: 274 pages (101,000 words)

Dr. Jess Riley's perfect life as a top cardiologist and new mom shatters when she has a heart failure. Forced to move home, she's shocked to find her mother has taken in Lena, a struggling artist with a broken heart.

They slowly form a friendship which turns physical. But is it too soon? Should two barely mended souls risk more?

An enemies-to-lovers lesbian romance about daring to open your heart.

About the Authors

G Benson

Benson spent her childhood wrapped up in any book she could get her hands on and—as her mother likes to tell people at parties—even found a way to read in the shower. Moving on from writing bad poetry (thankfully) she started to write stories. About anything and everything. Tearing her from her laptop is a fairly difficult feat, though if you come bearing coffee you have a good chance.

When not writing or reading, she's got her butt firmly on a train or plane to see the big wide world. Originally from Australia, she currently lives in Spain, speaking terrible Spanish and going on as many trips to new places as she can, budget permitting. This means she mostly walks around the city she lives in.

Cheyenne Blue

Cheyenne Blue has been hanging around the lesbian erotica world since 1999 writing short lesbian erotica which has appeared in over 90 anthologies. Her stories got longer and longer and more and more romantic, so she went with the flow and switched to writing romance novels. As well as her romance novels available from Ylva Publishing, she's the editor of *Forbidden Fruit: stories of unwise lesbian desire*, a 2015 finalist for both the Lambda Literary Award and Golden Crown Literary Award, and of *First: Sensual Lesbian Stories of New Beginnings*.

Cheyenne loves writing big-hearted romance often set in rural Australia because that's where she lives. She has a small house on a hill with a big deck and bigger view—perfect for morning coffee, evening wine, and anytime writing.

Jae

Jae grew up amidst the vineyards of southern Germany. She spent her childhood with her nose buried in a book, earning her the nickname "professor." The writing bug bit her at the age of eleven. Since 2006, she has been writing mostly in English.

She used to work as a psychologist but gave up her day job in December 2013 to become a full-time writer and a part-time editor. As far as she's concerned, it's the best job in the world.

When she's not writing, she likes to spend her time reading, indulging her ice cream and office supply addictions, and watching way too many crime shows.

Lola Keeley

Lola Keeley is a writer and coder. After moving to London to pursue her love of theatre, she later wound up living every five-year-old's dream of being a train driver on the London Underground. She has since emerged, blinking into the sunlight, to find herself writing books. She now lives in Edinburgh, Scotland, with her wife and four cats.

RJ Nolan

RJ Nolan lives in the United States with her spouse and their Great Dane. She makes frequent visits to the California coast near her home. The sight and sound of the surf always stir her muse. When not writing, she enjoys reading, camping, and the occasional trip to Disneyland.

Roslyn Sinclair

Roslyn Sinclair is a writer and teacher currently living in Georgia. Though a Southern girl, she's found writing inspiration everywhere from Kansas City to Beijing. First thing in the morning, before she goes off to prep lesson plans, you can find her writing her books in longhand at her kitchen table. When she's not writing or teaching, she's probably reading, taking long walks, or going for a drive on the twisty mountain roads near her home.

Alex K. Thorne

Alex K. Thorne graduated from university in Cape Town, South Africa with a healthy love of the classics and a degree in English Literature.

She assumed that this entitled her to a future of pretentious garden parties, while drinking fancy tea and debating which Brontë sister was the wackiest (Emily, obvs).

Instead, she spent the next few years teaching across the globe, from Serbia to South Korea, where she spent her days writing fanfiction and developing a kimchi addiction.

When she's not picking away at her latest writing project, she's immersing herself in geek culture, taking too many pictures of the cats and dreaming about where next to travel.

Lee Winter

Lee Winter is an award-winning veteran newspaper journalist who has lived in almost every Australian state, covering courts, crime, news, features and humour writing. She is now a full-time author and part-time editor at Ylva.

A 2015 and 2016 Lambda Literary Award finalist, Lee has also won multiple Golden Crown Literary Awards.

Her books range from lesbian mysteries and thrillers to romance, plus a superhero fantasy.

Lee's main writing love is the glorious melting-the-ice-queen theme. She argues there should be more of it in our mainstream entertainment because on-screen ice queens are usually portrayed as icy, bitchy, and evil, without any context or redemption. Lee loves to peel away the layers of women who aren't open about their feelings, and who melt for just the right woman.

She lives in Australia with her long-time girlfriend, where she spends much time ruminating on her garden, politics, and shiny new gadgets.

Chris Zett

Chris Zett lives in Berlin, Germany, with her wife. TV inspired her to study medicine, but she found out soon enough that real life in a hospital consists more of working long hours than performing heroic rescues. The part about finding a workplace romance turned out to be true, though.

She uses any opportunity to escape the routine by reading, writing, or traveling. Her favorite destinations include penguin colonies in Patagonia and stone circles in Scotland.

ISBN: 978-3-96324-328-8

Also available as e-book.

Published by Ylva Publishing, legal entity of Ylva Verlag, e.Kfr.

Ylva Verlag, e.Kfr.
Owner: Astrid Ohletz
Am Kirschgarten 2
65830 Kriftel
Germany

www.ylva-publishing.com

First edition: 2020

Credits
Edited by Alex K. Thorne, Amanda Jean, Amber Williams, Astrid Ohletz, Judy Underwood, Michelle Aguilar, and Sheri Milburn
Cover Design by Ladylit

Made in the USA
Monee, IL
12 August 2021